The Community

Joe Hakim

Wild Pressed Books

This one's for Andy Coles:

'It is what it is.'

The Community

It has no form, no shape.

There is no sense of time or space. I don't know when it is, I don't know where it is.

There are five of us here – I could be one of them, I could be all of them, I don't know – I can't tell.

I'm scared and confused.

We are scared.

But there's a voice – at least, I think there's a voice. Maybe it's a thought – it could be the last *singular* thought I'll ever have. And it keeps saying:

What have I done?

Phase One

*You want more? It's our memories you're after, right? Details. . .
you want details. The sights, the sounds, the smells. All the
sensations. Everything. You want to share it. Experience it.*

It's okay; I get it now.

Steve

The first time I saw a UFO was a Thursday - PE day - and
for years after, I often wondered if it was something I
dreamt, because no one acknowledged the event after it
happened.

We were on the field and it was my turn to use the
javelin. Wilson's ingenious javelin activities involved
putting a plastic marker on the ground and reeling off
his usual borderline-racist spiel about people in Africa
using spears to hunt food.

'That's a rabbit,' he said, pointing towards the
small, red, plastic dome. 'You miss it and your tribe
doesn't eat tonight.'

'But wun't a rabbit move around, Sir?'

'It's a fucking rabbit, just get on with it. Look at
your arms, son - they're like rubber-bands with knots at
the end, you should be able to sling it to the other side
of the field.'

3

Wilson had this way of picking out the things you were most self-conscious about, and then broadcasting it at the top of his voice so everyone else could take the piss as well. He walked away, leaving me standing there with the javelin. I prepared to sling it at the crap plastic non-rabbit while Pete Ashworth attempted to light half a fag he'd pulled out.

I noticed the sound first. But... it wasn't really a sound as such. More like some sort of low-frequency buzz. You could feel it in your ear, like you sometimes get when you're around electronics. Intense, disorientating.

'What the fuck is that noise?' I said.

The sky quickly lost colour, like someone turning the contrast down on a telly. And then the ball of vivid blue light appeared. It was high up, distant. At first, I thought it was the beginning of a storm but there was no clap of thunder or flash of lightning. The blue ball hung suspended in the air for a moment before slowly falling.

'Are you all seeing this?'

Everyone stopped what they were doing. We all turned to look at the blue light. I felt this chill run through me, this judder that made my entire body rattle. Wilson came running over.

'What's that, Sir?' I asked, pointing at the sky.

'Ashworth, gimme that fucking fag, now!' he barked.

'Sorry, Sir,' Pete handed it over.

Wilson shook his head, took the fag and stalked over to the back of the science block. He didn't seem the slightest bit interested. It was like he couldn't see the light, it didn't register with him.

'I think it might be some sort of flare,' Gaz said.

The hair on the back of my neck stood up.

I glanced at the others to see if they looked as scared as I felt. Pete stared up at the sky, shielding

4

his eyes with his hand. Gaz slowly shook his head. We all stood there, gobsmacked.

The light continued to descend before stopping, suspended in the air. It was fucking creepy - you just don't normally see this sort of shit, especially not before lunch-break. It felt like the time my shit of brother made me watch *A Nightmare on Elm Street* just before bedtime. Everything stopped, like someone had just hit the pause-button on a video.

The more I stared at the light, the more I thought I could make out some sort of shape behind it. And then it split into three parts. Three smaller balls of light rapidly changing colour, flashing.

Gemma

We were in the gym when the lads saw the UFO. We'd reached that age where the lasses and lads were split up - the lads out on the field having a kick-about and half the girls stuck doing netball. The other half, including me and Claire, had to do this cheesy workout, set to music.

The teacher played the same crappy eighties tune every time.

What was it again?

Oh yeah, that's it, Terence Trent D'Arby, *Sign Your Name Across My Heart*.

It's funny, and maybe it's just hindsight, me remembering the past all wrong, but even though we were inside the school and we didn't see it, it was like I knew something was happening. I just felt it somehow. Maybe everyone did.

Like I say, it might just be hindsight.

Pete

Yeah, when we were on the field doing PE, Wilson would usually just let us kick a ball around. Sometimes, if he was in a good mood, he'd let us nip round the back of the science block for a fag, but not today...

Not that day.

After we'd dragged all the athletics crap from the cupboard - rusty shot-putting balls, bent javelins and rickety hurdles - we split into groups and took it in turns using the equipment. The sky was claggy with clouds, huge grey things that crowded together to form a scowl, and every now and then, a few dollops of water would hit the grass.

And then we saw the light. We watched, slack-jawed as it moved and made its way down to earth, before splitting into three smaller lights.

'Maybe we should go inside,' I said. I wanted to run, get away, but my feet wouldn't budge.

'Shut up, I want to see what they do next.'

I should have smacked Steve in the gob for telling me to shut up, but I didn't. I was rooted to the spot. It seemed we all were. I didn't let on, but I was totally creeped out. I felt a vibration, a small crackle of electric current running up and down my back. I clamped my jaw shut to stop my teeth chattering. It sounds mad, but it was like something was reaching inside me, scanning me like an X-Ray machine.

Suddenly, the three balls of light moved; they darted away towards the horizon and within seconds they were gone altogether. I strained my eyes to see.

'Jesus,' I said, 'what was that?'

Gaz tugged at his ear. 'Probably just a flare,' he said.

Gaz

At first, I thought it was just Steve being weird, because he *was* a bit weird. But I heard it too. Well... I felt it. Maybe I heard it?

'Yeah, mad, innit?' I lit up my fag. 'Can you hear it, Chris?'

Chris had a blank look on his face, like he was trying to remember something. He scratched his head furiously, his big blond curls bobbing up and down on his scalp. Chris was my best mate. He was a fucking pudding, a pudgy fucking pudding, but he was always there for me. Still is.

'Chris... Blondie, are you fucking deaf or what?'

'Sorry.' He looked like he was coming around from anaesthetic. 'I had this really weird feeling, like...'

His voice trailed off.

'Like Deja vu?' I said.

'Yeah!'

Steve

We all went out that night. The tunes were on, and everyone was talking, laughing, fucking about. Then Barry Thompson turned up. Barry and Kirk had been big mates at one time, but something happened. Probably something to do with Claire. Barry had a thing for Claire, everyone knew about it.

Barry had been twagging off school, so he hadn't seen the UFO.

Although we talked a big game, the truth was even though we'd dabbled with stuff, we were still small-fry. Bit of smoke, bit of speed, rush, that kind of stuff, so we were all surprised when Barry opened his hand and it contained all these pills.

7

Jamie

We would knock about on the school field after tea-time.
The playing field was one of the few areas that we could
hang around without being shooed off by some killjoy.

Our gang included me, Steve Carter, Pete Ashworth,
Chris Morton, and we were usually joined by the *couples*
- Kirk Banks and Gaz Porter had both managed to snag
girlfriends - Kirk with Claire Taylor and Gaz with Gemma
Tock. Bringing girls along was a new development.

We'd talk about music, school and getting off our
faces. Someone would bring along a battery-powered
tape-deck and we would listen to banging tunes. Techno
mix-tapes, or *The Prodigy Experience*. We must have
played that fucking tape to death.

Gaz

Pete was the first to try one of Barry's 'pills', showing
off as usual. Didn't even ask what they were, just
grabbed one and popped it in his mouth. Soon as he
swallowed it, Barry cracked up.

'What's so fucking funny?' Jamie asked.

'Sorry,' Barry said, laughing. 'I don't know what
they are. I found them at the back of the field.'

It all kicked off then. Kirk grabbed Barry, gave him
a dig. Pete stuck his fingers down his throat, made
himself throw up. Me and Chris got hold of Barry, and
Kirk made him eat the rest of whatever they were, to
teach him a lesson.

It worked; we hardly saw him after that.

1

Steve

Something is pulsating, a non-stop throb somewhere over my head.

My throat's dry, so I get up. Hear a gurgling noise in the distance. Stumbling through the kitchen, I realise that it's the sound of the boiler, the giant mechanical heart at the centre of my flat. Hot water gushes out of the tap and straight down the drain. An arterial spurt.

Off with the hot tap, on with the cold. I fill the kettle and switch it on, distracted by the continuing grumble of the bioler. I make a cuppa and take it through to the living room. After a few loud clunks and clicks, the boiler finally gives up. It's quiet after that, and the silence feels ominous, like the flat has gone into cardiac arrest and I'm just a bystander, unable to step in and revive it.

I'm pissed off. Has the tap been running all night? Have I got a huge gas bill heading my way? Judging by the sound of the boiler, there's a good chance that it's on its way out. *Great.*

I peer out through a gap in the curtains before opening the window to let a bit of air in, expel the previous night's odours of vinegar, smoke and feet. It's quiet outside. The houses opposite, with their terraced Lego-brick uniformity, are docile and safe. No slamming doors, no shouts or whistles. I think about opening the curtains but instead head back over to the sofa to have another smoke.

I sit down and my phone starts to vibrate. I pick it up and see that it's work. I ought not to answer it, but I do.

'Now then,' I say.

'Steve?' It's Matt; he sounds out of breath.

'This is I, me... Steve,' I say, following up with a phlegm-filled cough.

'How's it going?'

'Not bad.' At this early stage of the conversation, no one wants to give anything away.

Matt crumbles first. 'I've got a favour to ask...'

'*Really?*'

'Yes, really,' he says.

'Let me guess... someone hasn't turned up.'

'That's about the size of it.'

'And you want me to come in?'

'Yeah,' he says.

'Can I ring you back in five? Just woke up, man.'

'Look, he needs to know sooner rather than later.'

'If I have to give you an answer now, it will be "no". Give me chance to drink some coffee and think about it; it may turn into a "yes".'

There's a pause. Then Matt says, 'Five minutes?'

'Make it ten. Five is just a figure of speech.'

'Speak soon,' he says, and the line goes dead.

Guzzle some coffee, finish a cig. I don't *want* to go in, and don't feel any sense of obligation or company loyalty or any of that shit, but I need the money. And it grants me a favour in return, a day in lieu, should I need it. It will also get me up off the sofa and out the house for the day. The prospect of having yet another dressing-gown-and-weed day is enticing, but the truth is I spend more than enough time

10

clad in my dressing gown, smoking dope and playing video games. Too much time, you could say. In fact, my whole life is a battle against the strong desire to do nothing except sit in my dressing gown, smoke dope and play video games all day.

Soon enough, the phone goes off again.

'So, what are you going to do?'

'I'm going to come in,' I reply.

'*Thanks,*' Matt says. For him, expressing gratitude in any form is painful.

'Just need to get my shit together. Should be there in the next half-an-hour or so.'

'See you when you get here.'

Before I leave the house, I realise that it's Wednesday. That means it will be mainly inventory and stock duties. That's why they need more staff. Ordinarily, they'd battle on short-staffed, but there are lists to be printed off and ticked, shit to be moved around on shelves. Stock rotation. All hands on deck, and they need all the hands they can get.

The shop is part of a corrugated industrial complex, which resembles an aeroplane hangar that has been split into units. As I reach the entrance, my phone rings. It's an unknown number, probably someone trying to sell me something, so I ignore it. Opening the door, I wheel my bike in. Matt is at the other side of the shop, behind the games counter, peeling orange-coloured cut-price stickers from a roll and placing them onto DVD and game cases stacked up in front of him. Behind the main counter, Georgie files discs away into drawers.

I nod at Matt and he nods back.

'Hey Georgie,' I say.

She smiles at me. 'Hey.'

The sole remaining female member of staff, Georgie's presence exerts a calming influence on the rest of us. Without her around, we'd quickly descend to the level of fart

11

jokes and conversations based around high scores and unlocked achievements.

'Where's the boss man, man?' I ask.

'He's in the back,' she says.

This week, her hair is the colour of pea and ham soup.

'ALRIGHT MATT!' I shout across the shop.

He doesn't speak, instead raises his hand. Matt's face is a deep red, and perched atop his bright green polo-shirt, it makes him look like a set of traffic lights.

There's no one in the staffroom, so I open the stockroom door and poke my head around. Paul sits on the floor, surrounded by piles of stuff. There's a clipboard and a stack of paper in front of him. He's chewing the end of his pen, zoned out.

'Hey Paul.'

It takes him a moment to acknowledge my existence. 'What are you doing here?'

'Matt asked me to come in. Said you needed an extra pair of hands.'

'That's right,' he says.

'That's why I'm here.'

'Good.'

Pause. 'So what's happening, Paul?'

'I'm taking stock.'

'Need any help?'

He shakes his head, slowly. 'No, I got this.'

'I'll leave you to it then.'

I shut the door behind me as I leave and head out the double doors that lead onto the shop floor. Straight to the fridge. Take out a tin of Monster and go over to the counter. 'Put this through for me please, Georgie,' I say, dropping some coins on the counter. 'Think I'll need a couple of these before the day is out.'

'Rough night I take it?'

'No more than usual.'

'How's Paul?'

'I think there's a real chance that today might be the day,' I say, cracking open the tin.

'Really?'

I take a big gulp. 'Yup. He's got that look in his eye. I just hope he doesn't decide he needs to take us down with him. Thank god for our country's strict gun control laws.'

Georgie giggles at this. Since the announcement of the store's upcoming closure earlier this year, Paul's mental health has become the focus of much speculation. Going into administration has crushed him. And now, almost twelve months after finding out, the end is nigh. I watched a YouTube video about *Groundhog Day*, the Bill Murray film, last week. It was a theory about how the film is structured around the Kubler-Ross model of grief. It made me think about what's happening with the store. We're stuck in the denial phase when we should be dropping toasters in the bath.

The problem is the increased stock. When the other stores shut, we received their stuff to shift. It feels as though we're trapped in a perpetual state of price-slashing – the closing-down sale to end all closing-down sales. *Everything Must Go.* Ironically, the huge amount of surplus we have to stick in the bargain bins means we're busier than ever, which prolongs the agony, as we will limp on until there's nothing left to sell.

No wonder Paul is losing the plot.

I grab a basket and go over to the drop-box, the little caddy at the front door where people can post their returns if they can't be bothered to come in and leave them on the counter. Undoing the padlock, I open the door and pile all the cases into the basket, and then take them over to the counter. I stack them up at one side, open each one and remove the discs in their plastic sleeves, then sling the empty cases into a trolley. I then take the scanner, run it over the barcodes on the discs. Each one generates a *ping* as it registers on the computer screen. Sometimes, there's a double-ping, which indicates an overdue item.

Put all the discs into a box, ready to be filed away, and take the trolley around the store, placing the empty cases back on the shelves. Done it so many times I don't need to think about it. The only problem is I've got more time to ponder other things. Like how I've been here in this job for nearly ten years. Ten fucking years. Flashback to my late twenties, out of work and out of luck, handing over the completed application form to Paul, then getting the phone-call. *It's just temporary*, I told myself. *Something else will turn up.*

Ten fucking years. If I'd robbed a bank, I'd have been out by now.

The layout of the shop floor is so familiar I could do this in my sleep. In fact, I *have* done this in my sleep. Horrible, repetitive dreams, just going through the motions of daily life – the mundanity: repetition, repetition, repetition. Indistinguishable from the waking world and far, far worse than any nightmare. Because waking up and going to work is just a continuation of the dream.

Has boredom ever killed anyone?

All manner of thoughts pass through my head: jumbled up, random nonsense. The background noise of my brain is intensified by the confused buzz of weed and caffeine.

Today's thought for the day is another regular ponder, a real favourite: *how the fuck does some of this shit get made?* It hits me every time I put some obscure independent British film or generic American action sequel back on the shelf. Scanning the backs of the cases as I take them out of the trolley, I don't recognise a single name in the credits. The four-star ratings and quotes on the front cover are attributed to publications and websites that I've never heard of. Where does the money come from to finance these films?

Finishing my rounds, I go and say hello to Matt at the game counter. He's about half-way through the trade pile. His face seems baggy, suffering the physical after-effects of trying to maintain a false smile for hours on end. 'Thanks for coming in,' he says. 'I owe you one.'

'It's no problem, no problem at all.' I try not to sound too smug.

'What's Paul up to in the back?'

'Trying to do the stock count, I think.'

'He's been in there all fucking morning,' Matt spits the words out. 'I mean, why does he even bother turning up?'

'Habit, I guess.'

Sauntering around the counter, I pick up a stack of DVD cases. Take a roll of stickers, and start peeling the old stickers off the cases, so I can place new ones on. Each new Sale brings its own "point of sale". We put up posters,reassemble the cardboard bins and stands in different configurations, and plaster stickers all over everything. The following week, a New Sale is brought in to replace the old one, so all the posters and bins and stands and stickers have to be removed and replaced. This has gone on week after week, for nearly a year.

'He needs to pull himself together. I mean, he's still getting a decent salary. He's gonna get a big fucking redundancy. And me: fucking muggins, is stood here running the fucking show.'

I can understand Matt's bitterness, but I don't feel any sympathy. About three years ago, I walked out on the job after splitting up with my ex. Went mental. When I came crawling back, they only gave me a ten-hour-a-week contract, on the understanding that my walk-out would be seen as a break in employment. So officially, I've only worked here for the last three years for ten hours a week, despite the fact that I've never worked only ten hours. When the doors finally do shut, I'll be lucky to leave here with a month's wages in redundancy.

I take a break. Grab another tin of Monster from the fridge and head out to the car-park.

'Just going for a smoke,' I shout to Matt as I open the door. No response. I'd have never have got away with this before, but no one gives a fuck anymore.

I crack open the tin and take a gulp, take the baccy from my pocket and roll one. I spot Graham, the security guard at the Pound Shop next door, give him a wave. He waves back, puts his fingers to his head and pretends to blow his brains out. I give him a thumbs up, but I don't know why. Chances are I'll be slinging an application into the Pound Shop once this place shuts for good. The thought of working there fills me with dread, but I can't see any other options.

Anlaby Road is busy. About to flick my cig into the gutter, I spot someone shuffling along the pavement on the other side of the road. He looks like an extra in a zombie film. Even at this distance, his movements suggest that he is completely off his tits, smacked up or something. Suddenly, he stumbles onto the road, and begins walking across it. Horns blare as cars swerve to avoid him. One of them misses him by inches. I tense up, sensing that something awful is about to happen. He continues walking, narrowly avoids being hit by a bus. It's like a real-life version of *Frogger*.

But his luck doesn't hold out.

With mounting horror at the inevitability of what's about to unfold, I can only watch as a car coming in off the Boothferry Road roundabout ploughs straight into him. He's flipped into the air, limbs flailing. He lands on the bonnet, a dull metallic thud of flesh and bones hitting metal, followed by the sharp crack of glass as he smashes into the windscreen. There is a scream of rubber against asphalt as the car swerves into the path of oncoming traffic. As the driver of a lorry slams his brakes on, tyres screech. Another car comes off the roundabout, but the driver clocks what's going on and brakes in time.

A chorus of skidding and screeching.

Everything goes quiet. It's like everything has been suspended. A shiver rattles my body, and the hair on the back of my neck stands up. It reminds of that time on the school field when I saw a blue light in the sky. I feel the same sense of dread, of anticipation, like the world has stopped. I find myself walking towards the accident – on auto-pilot. I feel numb, like it's not real, it hasn't really happened – it must be some elaborate piece of street-theatre. I half-expect someone to yell: "CUT".

I reach the road. Car doors swing open. Close up, someone opens his door and stumbles out of his car, shaking and confused, he vomits before collapsing. The guy who wandered into the road lies on the tarmac now, a broken, bloody mess, his arms and legs arranged into new and unnatural angles. Drawing closer, I realise that his eyes are open.

The lorry driver; a stocky, bald, middle-aged bloke with a tattoo of a spider on the side of his head, jumps down from the cab.

'What the fuck just happened?' His voice is shrill with panic.

A taxi-driver emerges from his car and runs over. 'I've called an ambulance,' he says, holding his phone up.

People filter out of shops and houses. Some of them go to the aid of the driver, while most – including me – gather around the guy on the pavement. Blood pours from his mouth; he's still conscious. Fucking hell. His mouth begins to move. I hear a gurgling noise coming from his throat – it sounds like my boiler. He tries to speak. He looks at me, tries to make some sort of gesture with his hand but it flops loosely on his wrist.

Crouching down beside him, looking at him more closely, I recognise him. Somewhere beneath the blood and mucus, there's a familiar face.

'It's going to be all right, mate,' I tell him, knowing full well it won't be. 'Stop trying to move, they'll be here soon.'

I want to hold his hand, but it feels like a bunch of broken twigs, so I place it on his chest.

He tries to speak again, makes a guh-guh-guh sound.

'What's he trying to say?' a woman asks.

I can hear the sirens. 'Don't try to speak,' I say.

17

Somehow, he lifts his broken hand. He tugs at my trousers, so I get onto my knees and tilt my head, place my ear near his mouth.

'They're going to fill the void within us all,' he says.

Taking his other hand, I notice something in his palm when he opens his fingers. They appear to be tablets. Little white ones. I move my hand over his and scoop them up. Poor fucker doesn't need to get caught with a load of pills on him, after going through something like this.

And then it hits me.

It's Pete fucking Ashworth. Pesky Pete. *Shit.*

I stand up, shouting. 'Where's the ambulance, for fuck's sake?'

The crowd surges forward. People have their phones out, ready to take photos and record videos so they can post them on social media. The police arrive and start moving people back, so I take advantage of the confusion, step away from the crowd and stash the pills in my pocket.

2

Gemma

Hate waking up, I do. Sounds horrible and I shouldn't think it, shouldn't even let it enter my mind, but it does.

And I do.

Don't mean it in a suicidal sense. God no, don't want to kill myself. Don't want to die in my sleep or anything like that – couldn't abandon my bairns. Couldn't do it. Just love sleeping, that's all. I'm not lazy or bone idle – although some people might disagree with that. I just enjoy sleeping. *Crave it.* Look forward to it. It's nice. I like to make it into an event.

Have you ever fallen asleep on fresh, clean sheets just after jumping out of the shower?

When I'm asleep, I'm alone. Not in a miserable *whoa, poor me*, sense. More like in a *this is my time*, sense. There's nothing wrong with that.

Lee wakes me up most mornings. Big tough Lee, my boy. He's full of it. Full of everything – attitude; hormones, ambition, all of it. Crammed in.

I've been dreaming again, but I snap out of it when the door creaks open. Lee creeps in.

'Mam, I need some money,' my son says, filling up the room.

'Where's my purse?' I mumble.

'It's in here somewhere,' he says. 'Must be.'

It's early. So early that Laura must still be asleep. 'I'll be through in a minute, just gimme a minute,' I say.

'You told me to wake you up,' he says, bottom lip beginning to emerge.

Don't respond immediately, that would just lead to trouble. Casually saying something along the lines of, 'I didn't ask to be woken up *this* early,' would only piss him off. Things would escalate from there. Instead, I say, 'Thanks, would you mind sticking the kettle on?'

I get out of bed, slowly.

Lee's pacing around the kitchen by the time I get downstairs. A mug of tea has been planted on the table.

'There you go, Mam,' he says, clearly chuffed with himself.

'Thanks, son.'

Lighting up a cig, I glug some tea. To be fair, it *is* a sunny morning, so I decide to make some breakfast. Eggs, a drop of milk, plenty of salt and pepper. Scrambled. Buttery toast. A bit of grated cheese.

'Better wake your sister up,' I say.

He smiles. 'Will do.' He gets up and goes upstairs.

He's becoming the image of his Dad, Gary.

Fucking Gaz.

Lee's around the age his Dad was when we first started seeing each other. Teenagers. I find myself thinking back to being back at school, on the field with everyone, messing around, listening to tunes, smoking fags and taking the piss out of each other. It feels like something strange is happening, like some great cosmic trick is being played out. The longer Gaz is absent from his life, the more Lee is starting to resemble him. The more I try to move on towards some sort of future without Gaz, the more I'm reminded of him.

Lee's a good lad, he really is. My son. My bairn. But he's stuck in that awkward gap between being a boy and being a man. He can't help it, he's getting to that age, but something's going to give eventually. It has to, so it will. He never hears from Gary, and there's no one else around for him to look up to, so he's becoming the alpha male, occupying the role in the absence of anyone else, but without taking on any of the responsibility. He wants his independence, yet he's not prepared to go out and work for it. He just expects it.

My Dad always used to say, 'Never wish your childhood away,' and he was right. He was right about a lot of things. I miss Dad so much. It would be nice to have him around right now – he'd sort Lee out. He had his own way of seeing things, talking about things. He could make you look at everything from a totally different perspective.

There's a big stack of worries and concerns, they're all over the place. In the cupboards, on the table. Pinned to the fridge door. I feel them leaning against me already, but it's too early to let them crush me. Today is the day for getting stuff sorted, but first thing on the list is breakfast.

I roll the eggs around the pan until they fluff up. I spoon up three portions, put the slices of toast on the table.

'Morning, Mam,' Laura says, striding into the kitchen. 'That smells really good.'

'Here,' I hand her a plate. 'Get a fork and go and sit in the living room. You can put your programmes on.'

She takes the plate and walks through to the living room, plonks herself on the sofa.

'Lee,' I shout. 'Come and get it.'

'Down in a sec,' he shouts back, his voice booming down the stairs.

Take my scrambled egg and toast into the living room. Laura is watching a programme about a poor American teenage girl who lives in a hotel with some wealthy relatives. Can't really tell what's going, lots of shouting and shrieking. The general story seems to revolve around how the girl

21

adjusts to her new life. Laura stares at the screen intently as she spoons the egg into her mouth. She hardly blinks.

'What the fuck is this shit?' Lee says, announcing his arrival.

'Mam, Lee's swearing,' Laura says.

'Watch your language, Lee.'

'But it *is* shit,' he retorts.

'Mam, tell him,' Laura says. 'You said I could watch it.'

'Why don't you tell me?' he says, voice beginning to rise. 'Or can't you be bothered to speak to me yourself?'

'Shuddup,' she snaps.

'*You* shuddup,' comes the reply.

'Enough,' I say.

'Yer little geek,' Lee says.

'I'm not a geek. You're a geek.'

'*Enough!*' I shout. 'For once, it would be nice to start the day without you two at each other's throats.'

'She always gets to watch what she wants,' Lee whines.

'Have you heard yourself? Grow up.'

The peace and relative calm of ten minutes ago has gone, shattered. Lee glares at me, sets about his eggs, scooping them up and finishing them off in a couple of gulps. He demolishes the toast and gets up. His plate clatters as it lands in the sink.

Laura sighs. 'What's his beef? Why does he have to be like that? Jeeez.'

She draws out the last word in the same the way the American girls on the telly do. It manages to be both cute and annoying simultaneously.

'He's a bloke,' I offer.

While Laura's getting ready for school, I look through some of the bills. Gas, water, and electric are all due soon. And then there are the other bills. The mobile phone bills, the internet. The telly license that I still haven't paid. The red letters from

22

the catalogue and the credit card. The furniture and electrical items on hire-purchase. The overdue letters from the loans I've taken out to plug the gaps, keep things ticking over. And then there are the contracts for the things (some of which I'm still paying for) that I've put on buy-back at the dosh shop.

It's a huge tangled web of debt and worry. How did this happen? How did it get like this?

After my third coffee my head clears, and I focus. I spread all the sheets of paper out over the table, and lean back. I try and arrange them in some sort of priority. I start with the essentials – gas, water and electric – and then follow those up with items according to date on the bill, or value. I pick up a notepad and make notes of the dates and amounts of money I'll be receiving over the next few months. The idea is to create some sort of system. Of course, that means leaving some things until the very last minute. But then I realise I haven't taken all the things on buy-back into consideration, and there's the money that I've got to pay *Perfect Home* for the new washing machine.

The system that I'm trying to create starts to disintegrate. The numbers and words in my notebook quickly become unintelligible squiggles that don't mean anything. An alien language.

I've always been shit at maths.

It begins in my stomach. Works its way up my throat and into my mouth. I feel sick, dizzy. Mad scenarios play out in my mind. Bailiffs at the door again. Losing the house, all of our stuff. Me, Lee and Laura out on the street, having to live in sheltered accommodation. Everything is falling to bits. It started when Gary moved out last year and now I'm waiting to see how far it goes. I feel powerless, and I resent feeling like I was somehow dependent on Gary, when the truth is that I'd been surviving without him long before he left.

I hear Laura moving about on the landing, so I push all the bits of paper into a pile, scoop them up and dump them back in the drawer.

My thoughts are thick and black. My hands judder and shake. I go over to the fridge and open the door, get out the cheese and marge. I take a knife from the drawer and bread from the cupboard, set about making Laura's sandwiches. It's a simple, menial task, and I relish it. Right down to neatly wrapping them in cling-film once I've finished making them. Snap open the lunchbox, gently place the sandwiches alongside an apple, a drink and a yogurt. For some reason, an image of a coffin being lowered into the ground pops into my head, so I banish it by ensuring that the contents of the lunchbox are placed in the perfect position; make sure that nothing is squashed while at the same packing everything in snug so it doesn't rattle around inside.

'Hey, Mam,' Laura says.

'Hi. Are you ready?'

'Nearly,' she says, brandishing a brush. Sometime last year, Laura decided that she was old enough to start getting herself ready for school, but she still likes me to brush her hair.

'Come on then,' I take the brush from her hand.

'Are you okay, Mam?'

'I'm fine,' I say. 'What made you ask that?'

'You're really quiet. Like, all the time. Like you're daydreaming.'

'I'm just tired, sweetie. Things on my mind. Nothing for you to worry about.'

Laura turns around, looks me in the eye, and says, 'And that's all it is, Mam?'

'It is,' I say. I put my hands on the sides of her face, plant a big kiss on her cheek, and gently turn her head to face the other way. I begin again, brushing the thickness of her dark, dense hair – Gary's hair – and try and think of nothing except this moment we're in together, mother and daughter.

'You can always talk to me, Mam.'

'I know,' I say.

24

We walk to school. The sun's out and it feels good to be walking alongside Laura. As time speeds up – years blurring into weeks, into days – I know that it won't be long until Laura insists on walking to school by herself, leaving me at home, the embarrassing parent.

Why does time seem to speed up as you get older? Why can't it slow down?

We approach the gate. Laura spots a couple of her friends and runs off to join them. I will hang around the playground until all the kids get called in. I always feel incredibly self-conscious around the other parents.

Looking around, I see them with their well-manicured nails, well-manicured lives. I feel scruffy and unexceptional, a prematurely greying freak with nothing to offer. Sometimes, I can almost feel them dismissing me, hear the sneers within their heads: *Would you look at the state of her?*

I thrust my hands into the pockets of my trackie-bottoms. I should get over it, get over myself, but I can't. Self-pity is a drug.

The bell goes off, and all the kids assemble into lines. The teachers come out to the playground, and Laura turns around and gives me one last cheeky wave before she goes in.

I stop off at the corner shop on my way home to pick up some bits and bobs that I don't really need. I dread going home, being in the house by myself, so I do anything to delay it.

My first action when I get in is to light up a cig. Exhaling, I try and plan out my day. I've got to go to the dosh shop to try and get an extension on my loan, and I've also got to go to the council centre to discuss the ongoing situation with Lee. He's leaving school soon, and I don't know whether he'll be able to go to sixth-form, so I need to find out what happens with our council tax benefit.

After the cig, I go upstairs to speak to him. I know what will happen; that it will take mere seconds for our conversation to descend into a screaming match, but I have to keep trying to get through to him somehow.

I knock on his door. Wait a few seconds. There's no reply, so I knock again, louder.

'What is it?' comes the reply – eventually.

'We should have a talk.'

'About what?'

'About *things*,' I try to not sound as though I'm pleading.

I hear a muttered *for fuck's sake*, and then, 'I'm in the middle of a game.'

'Well, pause it then.'

'It's online. I can't pause it.'

'I'm coming in,' I push open the door.

The room smells of feet, weed and sweaty boys. The curtains are shut, blocking out the sun. I can hear gunfire and explosions; all I can see is the light of the screen illuminating Lee's feet. The room is an utter state. Clothes slung everywhere. It's like it's never been cleaned. To my absolute disgust, I notice a stack of plates that appear to have things growing on them. I shake my head.

'What the fuck are you doing?' he screams. 'This is my fucking room, no one comes in here without my permission.'

'And this is *my* fucking house,' I scream back – it's started.

I pick his clothes up, scoop up the socks and pants and sling them into a pile in the corner so I can take them downstairs later.

'Get off my stuff,' he snarls. He throws his controller on the floor, wrenches his headphones off and throws them at me.

I hold my ground and try not to tremble.

'Look at the fucking state of this place, Lee.'

'It's my place, my state, doesn't have anything to do with you,' he says, and he tries dragging the clothes out of my hands, leading to a short tug-of-war that he wins easily.

'We can't carry on like this,' I say.

26

I can't help but shrink. He's a big lad and he's intimidating when he starts throwing his weight around. My arms are shaking. I know he won't hit me – I hope he won't hit me – but my adrenalin is flowing. I can't let him see me flinch.

Changing tactics, I leave the clothes and collect the plates and cutlery instead. My stomach is churning from fear, and it's made worse when I discover a big patch of gunk and mould accumulating in the bottom of a mug.

'All you do is sit here surrounded by filth, playing video games all day.'

I hear the faint sound of sniggering coming from his headphones. It sounds distorted – somehow inhuman.

'What else am I supposed to do? There's no fucking jobs.'

'Go to college then.'

'And do what?'

'I don't know, learn a trade. Maybe just something you enjoy doing. Something other than playing video games or hanging out with your mates.'

He pauses. 'I've got plans,' he says.

'What kind of plans?'

He clams up. He switches the console off, gets his coat.

'What are you doing? Where are you going?'

'*Enough* with the questions and the constant digging,' he says. 'You complain when I'm sat in, you complain when I go out. What am I supposed to do?' He glares at me. 'And what is it that *you* do all day, Mam? Aside from watching telly and getting old.'

My hand is up and at his face before I realise what's happening. The slap makes me jump.

'I sit on my arse,' I say, my voice cracking. 'And I try to work out how I'm going to pay for my son's food and fucking video games now that he's left school and I don't get any money for him.'

He reaches up and touches the red mark blossoming across his cheek. He's a hard-man, wants to be a hard-man,

27

so he doesn't react or cry. I can hear the little gasps in his throat tightens, as he tries to strangle his tears.

'I'm off out,' he whispers.

I wait until the front door slams, before I walk over to the window and throw open the curtains. Then I take the plates downstairs, carry the wash basket up and throw all the dirty clothes in it. Strip the sheets from the bed, fetch the vac upstairs and have a go around the room.

Wiping the crud and dust away from the desk that houses his console and telly, I notice a small brown box. I know I shouldn't open it – I'd rather not know what's in it – but can't help myself. Peering inside, my curiosity is undercut by nerves. It's full of little plastic baggies. The first and biggest bag is full of weed, and I breathe a sigh of relief, but then I see something else. A couple of the bags are full of small white chunks. My heart jumps into my throat.

'Oh god,' I say.

My son's a drug-dealer. Crack or something.

Tears roll down my face. I take one of the little bags over to the window, hold it up to the light. Looking closer, I see that the small white objects aren't blocks, or chunks or anything like that. They look like grains, or seeds. They're hard, white and bony. There's something familiar about them, like I've seen them before. Going back over to the box and looking through it again, I realise the bags aren't full of drugs. They're all full of these things. I place the bag back into the box, click it shut, and replace it on the desk.

I feel numb, worn out with everything. It's like it's not even real anymore, like all this is happening to someone else and I'm just observing it. Or remembering, somehow.

———

I'm smoking a cigarette in the kitchen downstairs. My phone rings. 'Hello?' I say as I pick up.

'Um, hi. It's Craig from the cash-shop,' the voice at the other end of the line says. 'Can I speak to Gemma?'

'Speaking.'

'Before I go on, can you just confirm your birthdate? For security reasons.'

'Two-ten-seventy-eight.'

'Okay Gemma, sorry to bother you. It's just a reminder call that your item is about to expire.'

'Shit.'

'Excuse me?'

'What is it? Which item?'

'It's the Galaxy Tab.'

'Right, okay.' My mind races. 'Would it be okay to come in next Tuesday?'

'Will you be redeeming or renewing?'

'Renewing.'

'Just a reminder that if you renew next week, you won't get the full twenty-eight days.'

'That's fine, I'll get it out before then,' I say, quickly, just wanting the conversation to end.

'Okay, not a problem, see you then.'

Yet another thing to panic about. It's Laura's tablet. One of her Christmas presents from last year. When I told her that I might have to "put it aside" for a couple of weeks, she understood. She knew if I'd have asked Lee about putting his console in, well, it would have kicked off.

I take that worry, that guilt, put it in a box and stick it in a pawnshop/stockroom in the back of my mind. Go back to worrying about Lee. I need to find out what's going on – I mean, I don't know what those things in the bags are. I have to find out what Lee's got into. Can't put my finger on it but there's something not right about this whole situation.

I feel as if there's something huge in the background, lurking. It's everywhere, but it's just out of sight. I can't explain what I mean but somewhere, deep inside me, is the knowledge that "it" surrounds everything. Every*one*.

And with that, the adrenalin is back, and my hands become sweaty and rigid. I want to grab hold of something and squeeze it. Break it. I feel like I'm going mad.

I've lived like this for too long. Lurching from one micro-crisis to another. I've been left with this heightened sense of anticipation – this constant, horrible feeling that something bad is just around the corner. Anxiety rushes through me, leaving me empty. My stomach gurgles and I gulp in air, as it paralyses me. There's so much I need to do, so much to confront.

I used to take Lee and Laura out to Hessle Foreshore when they were little. Lee would pelt rocks at the Humber, hoping they would skip. Me and Laura would lay on our backs and look straight up at the sky. With nothing to interrupt it, the sky would go on and on forever.

And now everything is as vast as that sky. It presses down on me, all the time.

My breath quickens. I move my hand up to my chest. Close my eyes and try and focus on other things, but I can't. Disconnected thoughts flicker through my brain like sparks, forming and dissolving, forming and dissolving.

Blue balls of light, suspended in the sky.

Stumbling into the living room, I put the television on. Need to drown out the noise in my head with mid-morning, celebrity cookery programmes. With bargain basement reality shows and bland American sit-coms.

The panic fades.

I have about an hour before I need to get ready for work, and instead of doing something constructive, like putting a wash on, I continue to sit there, zoning out.

My eyelids droop. I slip into a half-sleep on the sofa.

Sinking deeper, I find myself lying on the kitchen floor of a partially submerged house. The house lilts and tips, and water begins to emerge from the gap at the bottom of the back door. The water slowly spreads out across the floor and immerses me. I stare straight up at the ceiling, feel the water as it runs through my hair and trickles into my ears. It's cold and my spine rattles as I lift my right arm up, stretch it out as though I'm reaching towards the ceiling. Hear the splish-splash of feet from somewhere around me but can't pinpoint exactly where. Someone is walking towards me, the footsteps approaching my head, but I can't turn my head to see who it is. Can't move anything other than my arm, so I keep reaching towards the ceiling, focusing on the dangling bulb.

He leans over to look at me, his upside-down face slowly entering my field of vision from the top. First his forehead, and then his eyes, his nose, his mouth and chin.

I don't recognise him, even though there's something familiar about him. It's like he's smudged, blurred. He opens his mouth. And all these little white seeds, the same ones I found in Lee's room, pour out of his mouth and all over my face, into *my* mouth.

Waking up, I'm confused and scared. On the telly, a panel of women have a loud discussion about the merits of waxing as opposed to shaving. It's gone eleven. Need to get ready for work.

With the telly off, the shrill voices from the programme continue ringing in my ears, heralding the onset of a headache. In the kitchen, I get the iron from the cupboard. Plug it in, open out the board, go and fetch my work gear from upstairs.

Five hours – eleven until four – I can do it, no problem. No problem. I'll even have a couple of hours before I pick Laura up from the after-school club at six. Bring her home and get the tea on. Have an early night. Hopefully Lee will turn up at some point. I'm not going to force speaking to him tonight if it's late. We'll see how it goes.

3

Gaz (and Chris)

I'm watching the ball go around the wheel. Actually, it's not a real ball. And it's not a real wheel. It's graphics on a screen, arranged to look like a ball and a wheel. Stood next to me, Chris has his hand clenched into a fist, bunched up near his mouth. He wears a strained expression, like he's desperately trying to squeeze a shite out.

'C'mon, c'mon,' he mutters into his knuckles.

My hands are placed either side of the screen. This is the best bit, really. This is what it's about – the anticipation. This is the purest part of the whole dreadful enterprise. That moment before the ball drops. Before the cards are dealt. Before the horses reach the finish line.

The brief moment of possibility, when it's all up for grabs, there for the taking. For me, it's the ultimate buzz. Fuck booze and dope – fuck *fucking* – this is where it's at.

The non-existent ball bounces before dropping into the non-existent wheel. Lands in number 9. Red. Odd. First twelve.

Fuck, fuck, *fucking* fuck.

'Shit,' I snarl, giving the machine a sly kick. The cashier glares at me from behind the counter.

'That's too bad, man,' Chris says. 'Too fucking *bad*.'

Against all common sense, I go for it again. It's all about the zero section. I hammer my lucky numbers, 18, 29, 28, 3, 32, 31; and place a single chip on zero itself, just in case. Bang the button and go through it all again. This time it's 30. Different number, equally as shit. It slowly sinks in that I've done my brains in again and nearly spent my wages for the week. Again.

Big Gaz the fucking liability. I can't be trusted to look after myself, never mind a family. They're better off without me, and days like today prove exactly why.

I feel sick.

I stumble outside onto Anlaby Road. Everything's fucked. I'm fucked. Even though I've only been in the bookies for half an hour, the sun seems extra bright and punishing, like I've been trapped in a cave for a month, and now I've been thrown back out into the world.

'Fucking rigged, them machines, I tell ya,' Chris says.

I twat Chris in the mouth. Not really hard, because he is my mate after all, but hard enough to work off some frustration. I feel a little bit better.

'What the fuck did yer do that for, Gaz?' he whines. 'Cun't you have smacked someone in there instead of me?'

'They're probably all carrying knives in there,' I say. 'What d'yer think I am? A fucking idiot?'

'I was going to take us for a pint as well,' says Chris, obviously upset.

'I'm sorry Chris, I din't mean it, bud.'

'Well you can fuck off now.'

'C'mon, don't be like that,' I get the little bald pudgy fucker in a headlock.

'What are you doing? Get the fuck off me.'

Poor little Chris. A good kid, a good mate since school, but forever destined to be one of life's punch bags.

34

'Take me for a pint, Chris. I'm your best mate, and yer business partner.' I swing him around before letting him go.

'Wanker,' he says. I take his cap off, ruffle his thinning tuft of hair, and plonk the hat back on his head.

We both light up before taking a walk down to the Carlton Hotel. It's early, but it's getting busy already. There's a bunch of people sat out the front, drinking lager and talking shite. I know a lot of them, know that they've never done a decent day's work in their life, but here they are. Tops off and roasting themselves red. Dicko, Dave, Frank and a bunch of others. They cheer as we walk up.

'Alright fuckos,' I say, as we approach.

'Here they are, Hull's very own dynamic duo,' Dicko's laughing.

'How's tricks, you work-shy cunt?' I say.

He's sat with this lass. She's got black hair, pulled back into a ponytail. I give her a quick scan, up and down. She has a few tattoos on her arms. There's a big one of a dolphin with "Damien" written underneath it. She's wearing a cut-off top that shows her belly.

'And who's this?' I say to Dicko. I don't recognise her, but I'm intrigued.

'Gaz, meet Lizzie, our lass,' Dicko says.

'Pleased to meet you,' I say, holding my hand out.

'Likewise,' she says, softly. She takes my hand and loosely shakes it. The tips of her fingers stroke my palm as she pulls her hand away.

I wink at her and she smiles, and I notice she's got one of those wayward-snot stud piercings on her lip. Everything about her cries out *filth machine*.

'Gerrus a pint in Chris,' I say, and Chris trots off inside.

'How's business?' Dave asks.

'Not bad. Got a load of copper last week, made a fucking fortune.'

Dicko laughs. 'And how long did that last?' He turns to Lizzie and says, 'Gambling mad, this cunt.'

'Like to take risks?' she asks, smiling.

'Summat like that,' I reply. Chris appears with the pints.

'Where's ours?' Dicko asks.

'Fuck off and get your own,' Chris says.

It feels good to be sitting out drinking. Under the blaze of the sun, I even manage to block out the burn of the big loss. As the day creeps into night, everyone gets more and more pissed. Conversations become louder and louder. There's a bus stop right outside the Carlton. These two lasses walk up, can't be much older than thirteen, fourteen, but they're proper tarted up. Short skirts, cut-off tops, bright red lipstick, the lot.

Dave, who is completely munted by this point, stands up and shouts at them. 'Come and sit with Uncle Dave.' He slurs his words. 'Tell me what you want for Christmas.'

They look at Dave with complete disgust. 'Drop dead, yer bald cunt,' one of them says. Everyone in the beer garden erupts with laughter.

Dave looks pissed off. He stands up and starts unzipping his flies. 'Wanna know what a real man's cock looks like?' he shouts.

There's a chorus of 'whoas' and 'calm downs'. Dicko grabs his shoulder and sits him down. 'Fucking behave yersen,' he says. 'Or you'll end up on the register. Fucking D-Wing, yer dirty old bastard.'

I think about Laura, think about her when she's older, imagine some dirty old fucker like Dave saying shit like that to her. My temper rises. I squeeze Dave's other shoulder and pull him up out of his seat towards me.

'Seriously, give it a fucking rest now, Dave. We're having a good night, don't ruin it.'

Dave shrugs, goes to open his mouth like he wants to say something, so I square up to him, let him know I'm not fucking about with him.

'Fucking try it, I dare you.'

36

Dave knows he wouldn't stand a chance, so he sneers, says, 'I'm out of here, you fuckers an't got a sense of humour.' He marches out of the beer garden.

I catch a glimpse of Lizzie. She's looking back at me.

Chris suddenly stands up, swaying.

'I need to get off.' He looks like he's about to throw up.

'C'mon Chris, don't be a killjoy,' I say.

'No seriously, I need to go.'

I take him to one side. 'Do us a favour Chris. Do us a twenty,' I say.

'I can't, I'm nearly broke as well. I've been buying your beer all fucking night.'

I give him a playful slap on the face. 'C'mon, you know I'm good for it. Besides, tomorrow is gonna be a good day. I can feel it. It'll be a casino night.'

It doesn't take him long to cave in. Never does. 'Here you go,' he hands it over. 'I'm serious, I need it back, soon as.'

'Have I ever let you down?'

He doesn't answer, just slinks off.

'Bye, Chris,' Dicko shouts.

Everyone joins in. 'Bye, Chris.'

Chris doesn't turn around, only sticks his hand in the air, waves and carries on walking.

———

Dicko, Lizzie, Dave – who's come crawling back – me and some of the others end up back at Dicko's flat. We have a carry-out from the offie, and Dicko gets his weed out. Someone sticks some tunes on, and a quiet drink turns into a little party.

I'm watching Lizzie as she dances around.

'She's alright, in't she?' Dicko asks me.

'Yeah Dicko, she's alright,' I say. 'How did you meet?'

'She lives a bit further down the road, friend of a friend.'

'Nice one. Kids?'

'Unfortunately yeah, but they spend a lot of time at her mam's, so it's not too much of a hassle.'

37

'What else you been up to?'

'Nowt really,' he says, sighing. 'I'm on sick now because of my leg, so I'm not getting as much hassle from dole.'

'Your leg? What's up?'

'I broke it two years ago, remember?'

'I do.'

'And it's still not right. Can you believe it?' he says, chuckling.

'*Get well soon*, brother. Really like this flat by the way.'

'It's great, innit? Got set up in here after I was in Willie Booth House.'

'I like it.'

'Yeah, it's good. Gorra bit of a pest problem, but other than that it's sorted.'

'Pest problem? What d'yer mean – East European neighbours or summat?' I know how his mind works.

Dicko gives out a belly laugh. I don't join in.

'No, not neighbours,' he says. 'Keep finding these little white spiders everywhere. Ugly little fuckers they are. Need to get in touch with the landlord about it.'

'Weird.'

Our conversation is interrupted by a crash from the kitchen.

'What the fuck was that?' Dicko says, rising from his chair.

We go into the kitchen. Dave, totally off his face, has become the first casualty of the evening, passed out on the kitchen floor. It's too much of a good opportunity to resist. Dicko finds a marker, and we give Dave a fine old moustache and specs, take some photos and stick them on Facebook.

Eventually, everyone either passes out or leaves. Dicko gets up, stumbles into the bedroom and collapses, leaving me alone with Lizzie. It's a bad move on Dicko's part.

She goes to the bedroom to check on him.

'Snoring his fucking head off,' she says as she comes back into the living room.

38

She sits on the sofa next to me. I hand her a spliff. 'So how long have you known Dicko then?' she asks.

'Years,' I say. 'He was in the year above me at school. Anyway, are you and Dicko a hot item then?'

She laughs. 'I wun't go that far. He's a nice guy, good to hang around with, but he's always pissed.'

'True, Dicko loves a drink.'

'It's all the fucking Valium he takes as well,' she picks at her fingernails. 'Always fucking nodding off.'

'That's Dicko for yer,' I say, laughing.

She's looking at me, so I decide to chance it. I gently rest my hand on her thigh. She doesn't move it away, so I take that as a green light. I move in closer.

'So he's not doing it for you then?' I ask quietly.

'Not nearly enough,' she whispers.

I move in for a kiss and she lets me. I reach under her top and grab one of her tits. I start kissing her neck. She reaches down and unzips my fly, takes my cock out and begins stroking it. I'm a bit fucked up myself, and feel a slight panic that I won't be up to the job, but thankfully I get hard. She leans down and puts it in her mouth

'Are you getting off on knowing he's in the next room?' I hiss into her ear.

'Maybe,' she says. I turn her around and slide her knickers and jeans down.

It's over quickly. After we're done I fall off her, and back onto the sofa. She places her hand over her fanny and crawls off the sofa, awkwardly.

'You fucking idiot,' she says, pissed off.

'What?'

'You fucking came inside me,' she says. 'What the fuck did you do that for?'

'Sorry.'

She jogs into the bathroom and shuts the door. I pull my pants back on, pluck the roach from the ashtray and move over to the window. Lighting it up, I stand there and have a look at what's going on outside. It's late – dark and quiet, save for the occasional taxi that swooshes past. Dicko's flat is on the top floor of an old converted house. It's got a good view of the Carlton, practically opposite.

I notice someone standing at the bus stop outside the Carlton. A tall bloke, bald head. As I'm looking at him, I realise he's looking up at the window, like he's watching me. There's something *off* about him. He's gangly, thin. Like a bad drawing that's come alive somehow. And then I notice he's got a little girl with him. What's she doing out there, this late?

She's familiar. I know her.

It's Laura. *My* Laura.

He slowly raises his hand, opens it, and he drops something. In the streetlight it looks like rice, or confetti.

What the actual fuck?

I'm trying to shout, but I can't. I want to smash the window, scream at them, but he just stands there, motionless, head tilted up. What's he doing? Why has he got my daughter?

———

I come to, like I've been asleep on my feet. There's no one out there. No creepy stickman. No Laura.

I move away from the window. Maybe it's just the weed, but I feel the prickly sensation of paranoia running up and down my spine. My head swims and I stagger, almost fall over. I give it a minute, and then I get up and look out the window again but he's gone, and when I check the time on my phone, I realise that a couple of hours have flown by.

What the fuck just happened? What the fuck was all that about?

I start to think about Laura, and Lee and Gemma.

Guilt. Guilt swims up my chest and into my throat, my eyes. It's been so long since I've seen them. I need to see them, but I can't. Can't see a way back, can't even think about how

I'd go about starting to mend things. And the longer I leave it, the worse it gets.

I'm no good for them, I'm a fuck-up, a disgrace. Maybe soon, when I've sorted myself out a bit, when things are back on track.

Excuses. Always excuses. I'm the lowest of the low, just like my Dad. I'm toxic, and I don't want to infect my kids. They'll understand one day, when they're older.

Everyone's still asleep, so I make my way out of the flat. It's real early, like milkman-early – even though you never see milkmen around anymore.

I think back to when I was a teenager, when I used to knock around with people like Barry Thompson and Kirk Banks. Intense nights, walking home in the early hours after a mad one, which was most weekends. Drifting down Spring Bank, the night being nudged to one side by the day, the moon tagging the sun into the ring. Still fucked up, high; sweat-soaked shirts stuck to our backs, the smell of baking bread from Jackson's wafting its way into our nostrils, the first angry growls of an empty stomach. The slow whir of the milk float as it passed by.

Magic. Magic times.

There's still magic around, of course. I'm not ready to give up just yet, but increasingly, the magic times are buried beneath a hangover, beneath regret and age. Things are more difficult now. It takes effort to make it look effortless.

Why do I feel like this? A blue sky shouldn't make me feel blue. Thankfully, the café across the road is open. It has bacon. Sausages. Stuff like that.

More figures have appeared at the bus stop. Not the stranger from last night, but a bunch of lads. They've got their backpacks on. Off to do a shift in a greenhouse somewhere, picking and packing cucumbers for peanuts. A hard day's work for a shit day's pay. They're welcome to it. I did that shit myself for a couple of years. Agency work. It's a mug's game. I'm all for grafting, but I want to graft for

41

myself, and no cunt else.

It's time for a fag. Light one up, inhale. I'm the master of my own fucking destiny, me. I'm not having some entitled prick docking me an hour's pay just because I roll up fifteen minutes late. No way.

I clock in for no fucker.

The lads with the backpacks climb onto the bus, and I cross the road and sidle up to the bus stop, stand where the weird bloke was. When I look down, there's a pile of something. I bend down, pretending to tie my shoelaces, and have a closer look. Somehow, the pile is perfect, like someone has arranged it into a structure. I pick one of the objects off the top and have a closer look. It's like a seed or something: hard, white and smooth. Strange as fuck. I place it back on the pile and stand up.

In the café, blokes in Hi-Viz vests sup tea and rapidly demolish full-English breakfasts. I stroll up to the counter. Three women run around, cooking and serving and shouting orders back and forth. The air is thick with the smell of sizzling meat and the sound of eggs hissing as they hit the pan. A small radio crackles away in the corner. I'm starving.

One of the women comes over. She's got long, curly hair, dyed bramble-red. Thick peach-colour lipstick that looks as though I could reach over and peel it off.

'Alright, love,' she says. 'What can I do for yer?'

I go through this whole ritual of pretending to decide. I scan the menu, stroke my chin, all that. I don't know why. I know what I want. 'Er, I'll have a sausage sandwich please.'

'Anything else?'

'No.'

'Okay, coming up.'

4

Claire

I'm absolutely knackered. Done in. Can't wait to get home and have a nice glass of wine. I'd like to drink a full bottle but I can't, not really. Got to pick Natasha up from Mam's in the morning.

I like most of my customers. Really, I do. But no matter how nice they are, you have to be careful, because if they think you're too friendly, think that they are actually your friends, then they start to take the piss.

Like tonight for example.

I don't mind people taking their time to sup up, there's nothing worse than being hounded out of a pub or bar once time's been called. That's one of the ways in which we are different to your typical Hull boozer. But we're still located in Hull and that means from time to time we have to deal with the god-awful sense of entitlement that runs right through the new young elite.

When I was at school, back at Amy Johnson, I used to get the same comments in all my reports: 'Claire is a very capable young lady, but unfortunately, she is a big fish in a little pond and sometimes she uses this as her excuse to coast along.'

Sometimes the words were different, but they always conveyed the same message.

There's a table of them. One of them is a new signing for City. His "darn sarf" accent sticks out. I think one of them is a DJ on a local radio station. There's a couple of others with them, and there are three girls, all shrieking and shouting because they think that they're one blowjob away from joining Hull's A-list. Pathetic really.

Dan sees me staring at them from the end of the bar, decides to go over to them. Dan's got a good head on his shoulders. Out of all the bar staff who work for me, he's the one who seems to be the most switched on. He doesn't need telling twice, he gets on shift and gets on with it. There's also the small matter of him being over six feet tall in his socks and being blessed with a face that wouldn't seem out of place in a Gucci advert as well.

'Hey guys, have you all had good night?' Dan says as he approaches the table.

'Night's not over yet,' one of the girls says, looking him up and down.

'We always have a good night,' the DJ says, leaning back on his chair and spreading his arms out wide.

'Any chance of another drink?' the football player asks.

'I'm sorry, we rang the bell,' Dan says. 'It's locking up time.'

'What? I didn't hear the bell,' the football player says. 'Anyone else hear a bell?'

The girls giggle. The DJ puts his arm around one of the other lads, says, 'Just a little one? We'll be out of your hair in no time.'

Another one of the girls, a petite, sour-faced redhead, says, 'Get one for yourself. Pull up a chair.'

Dan smiles. 'I'd love to, but I'm still working. Night's over, time to move on.'

The football player stands up. 'I'm Anthony Longcroft, and I came to Hull to tear it up.' His companions cheer. 'Now get me a fucking drink before I tear *you* up.'

44

The laughter subsides. Things have taken a turn. It's time to step in. I move over there. 'Everything okay?' I ask.

'Who the fuck are you?' Longcroft says.

'Come on now,' the DJ says, possibly sensing a situation developing. He stands up. 'Let's get going.'

'What difference does one more drink make? What's the fucking problem?' Longcroft says, chest puffed out. His entourage shrug, collectively.

'There's no problem,' I say. 'I'm the manager. Just wanted to see what the commotion was about.'

'There's no commotion,' Longcroft says. 'Just a thirsty customer who wants to know what the hold-up is.'

I place a hand on his shoulder, and with the other I gesture towards the bar.

'Anthony, is it?'

'Anthony Longcroft.'

'Well, Anthony, my name is Claire Fletcher. I'm the manager of this place, let's go over to the bar and see if we can sort this out.'

Longcroft shuffles past his friends. 'I'll get this sorted,' he says, giving them the thumbs up as he squeezes out from behind the table.

The other members of staff are already putting the stools on the tables, so I go behind the bar and pour a shot of Sambuca. I hand it to Longcroft.

'Cheers' he says, and knocks it back.

'As I was saying Anthony, I'm the manager of this place, and I'm also a member of the Princes Ave Bar and Restaurant Association. I've worked here for a long time. And in that time I've encountered many, many, jumped up premiership fuckwits like yourself who have drifted to Hull, and upon arrival have convinced themselves that they are the Ronaldo-shaped superstar that the Tigers so desperately need. And judging by that big dollop of white powder on the end of your nose, I can see that you've already acquainted yourself with some our local wildlife – I'm going to go out on a

45

limb here and say someone like Mark Toft, or one of his cronies – so your already massive ego is well on its way to becoming planet-sized.'

Longcroft shrinks a little as the bluster evaporates.

'Go on,' he says.

'One of the things that particularly pisses me off is the thought that my fucking toilets are being used for illegal activities, which is one of the reasons why we set up the Association around here. It means that you fuck up, and not only are you barred in here, but barred from every bar and pub right along the Avenues. I'd also have to let my good friends in the Humberside Police know about your activities. And then there's the Hull City chairman who spends quite a lot of time in here and is something of a close personal friend. Because believe it or not, he's always very interested to know how new players are settling in.'

He looks at me, wipes the end of his nose.

'It's okay, I get it.'

'I don't give two fucks what you get up to. Just don't fucking do it in here,' I say.

He nods, and I come from behind the bar and accompany him back to his table.

'Let's go,' he says.

Everyone stands up to leave. 'Thanks guys,' Dan says as he starts to collect the glasses.

As the group walks past, I look at Longcroft and smile.

'Welcome to Hull!'

The house is empty when I get in. I kick off my shoes and head into the kitchen.

There's an unwashed empty coffee cup on the draining board, and some coffee granules around the machine. So he's been back here at some point today then.

I look at Natasha's picture, pinned to the fridge door. It's a big yellow sheet of paper. There's a house in the background.

46

I'm in the middle, with messy hair and overlong legs, Natasha has rendered herself wearing her favourite red top, and she's complete with a huge grin that in her enthusiasm has slightly broken loose from her face. She sits on the ground to my right. In the distance, just outside the house, a scruffy-looking Max waves at us with two outstretched arms. I peer at it closer, and for the first time I realise that the severe black lines to the left of Max aren't a tree, a tower, or a structure. It's a person. A tall, dark, skinny figure standing perfectly straight, including arms and legs and everything. I look at the depiction of Max in a different way now. Is he waving at us, or surrendering to the figure?

Taking a bottle of white out of the fridge, I pour myself a glass. I quit smoking two years ago, so I have to keep my cigarettes in a little case at the back of one of the cupboards. I open the patio doors and step outside. The stone feels cool under my feet. The sensor light activates, illuminating the garden. A plant-pot or something tips over. Next-door's cat dashes past me and dives into one of the bushes.

'Little shit!'

On the way back through the kitchen, I hover near the picture again. I get a momentary flash of paranoia, hope that everything's all right with Natasha. She's a handful, always has been, but Natasha's like me. Strong-willed. Aloof.

She's fine. Everything's fine. I don't know what it is with me at the moment. It sounds stupid, but it feels as though the whole fucking house is cursed, like something big and dark is hanging over it, like a hex. Maybe I should do a ritual, burn some sage and beckon in the light or something.

I take a big sip of wine, lay back on the sofa. The cold liquid in my throat is refreshing. Everything is quiet. The night ebbs away, trickling down from my brain to my feet. The only noise is the buzz of the fridge and the tiny creaks of leather as I wriggle into the sofa. I reach down and pick up the glass. Lift it to my mouth in a steady motion, trying not to move anything other than my arm, lips and tongue.

I set it back on the floor with the tiniest of clinks.

I'm not quite asleep, but I'm close. Thoughts and recent memories start to clump together in my head, clog into a half-dream that hovers over my eyes. I'm in the bar and it's empty except for one table. From where I'm standing, it seems like miles away. I walk over to the table. The black line from Natasha's picture is sitting next to Max. A girl I used to go to school with – Gemma – sits on the other side. It's then I notice Pete Ashworth standing by the bar. Black blood pours from his eyes, from his nostrils and ears, and dribbles from the corner of his mouth. Dan approaches the table. He's naked. 'Is anyone thirsty?' he asks.

Max lifts his glass. Dan takes it from him and raises it. Pete's arms flap as he stumbles over. He starts gasping, choking. His mouth opens and loads of tiny white objects, like seeds or pills, pour out of his mouth and into the glass. Dan hands the glass back to Max, who takes it and begins pouring the white things into his mouth.

———

The sound of the front door being unlocked jolts me awake. It takes me a second to pull myself together and realise that I'm still on the sofa. I pick up my phone to check the time. Five a.m. I swing my legs around and sit up; reach down, pick up the glass of wine, swallow the last of its contents.

I hear the fridge door opening, the *psst-pop* of a bottle being opened. It's Max. After composing myself, I get up and go into the kitchen. He's sitting at the breakfast bar, beer in one hand and fag in the other.

'Thought we'd agreed to do that outside,' I say.

'Well shit, you caught me,' he says, shrugging. 'Time for that divorce now, eh?'

I decide not to respond. Instead, I open the fridge, retrieve the bottle of white and pour another glass. I walk over to Max, take one of his cigarettes from the packet, and move over to the sink. I take a big swig of wine, pull the lighter from my pocket and light up.

'How come you've got a lighter?' he asks. 'Thought you didn't smoke.'

'I don't. I like to keep one handy. Never know when you might have to start a fire,' I say, as I put the lighter back in my pocket.

Max nods but doesn't look at me. He stubs out his cigarette on the sink, flicks it in the bin, finishes his beer and then goes to the cupboard and pulls out a bottle of scotch and a glass. Glenlivet, his favourite. No doubt taken from the bar. He fills the glass, gulps it down, and fills it again.

'Where have you been?' I try not to sound too aggressive.

'With the lads,' he says, sharply.

'Right.' I take a deep drag. He goes back to the breakfast bar, lights another cig. 'Do anything good?' I ask.

'Couple of pints. Went back to Grant's for a few games of cards. Not much, really.'

'You're dressed very smart for a lad's night,' I counter, unable to help myself.

He looks at me, laughs, picks a spot on his shirt and tugs it. 'This old thing?'

I don't say anything.

'What the fuck is this?' he yells, making me jump. 'Do I need to get your approval on what I wear now, *mam*?'

'What's your fucking problem?' I shout.

'What's my fucking problem? You're the one with the fucking problem. Just because you work all weekend, don't take it out on me,' he spits, like a fucking child.

'Well, one of us needs to work,' I say.

'And there we go,' he says. 'That's what we were waiting for.'

'It's true. We'd be fucked if it wasn't for me.'

'And don't we all know it? You're such a fucking martyr,' he shakes his head in apparent disgust.

'If you helped out with Natasha more, it wouldn't be so bad.'

'Been talking to your mam again?' He stubs his cigarette out, takes a sip of his drink. 'Tell you what, I'll go then. I'll pack my stuff and move out. It'll be for the best.'

'I'm not saying that, Max.' I'm tired. Tired of the same petty arguments.

'No, because when we get down to it, you don't want me to leave, right? You want me to stay and "make it work for Natasha." So we'll do this merry dance every week until one of us cracks up.'

'I don't know, Max. I really don't know.'

Max finishes his drink, puts the glass on the table and stands up. He steadies himself, tries to feign sobriety by making himself rigid, which only highlights how much he's swaying. I see this night after night, his drunken attempts at dignity. It's so painfully obvious.

He shuffles into the hall.

'I'm going to stay with Grant,' he shouts, and after stumbling about trying to get his shoes on, he slams the door on his way out.

I'm not upset. Or angry. Or anything for that matter, other than tired. I turn off the lights and head upstairs. Crashing onto the bed, I can't even be bothered to get undressed. Within minutes I'm falling into blissful, dreamless sleep.

5

Pete

Everything is better in the summer.

Waking up confused, aching and thirsty, the light seeping through the sheet that hangs over the window feels like a blessing. Even the ever-present blare of the traffic on Freetown Way seems to have had its volume turned down – slightly. Maybe it's because of the birds tweeting in the trees.

I'm feeling soft and sentimental as I peel off the sheets. But as I sit up, I begin hacking and coughing, and a hefty chunk of something hits the back of my teeth. It tastes bitter and metallic and I have to rush towards the sink to spit it out before I retch.

It splats against the enamel of the sink. I stare at it for a while, before I turn on the tap, trying to work out whether it's green or yellow. I drink some water directly from the tap's flow. It's cold and refreshing, makes my teeth hurt, and I flush the phlegm down the plughole.

It was definitely green. I'm relieved.

I put the radio on before rolling a cig. We're not supposed to smoke in our rooms, on account of those dozy cunts who nod off and burn holes in the blankets, but they rarely, if ever, inspect your rooms. It's not like being inside. Besides, this is my third time in here. They know I can look after myself.

I hate seeing my own reflection. Try to avoid it as much as possible. But there's a big fuck-off mirror above the sink that's situated opposite my bed, so sometimes it can't be avoided. I look thin and tanned. My face has a covering of greying stubble, and the hair on my head sticks out all over the place. I'm wearing a white vest and my white and red toothpaste-stripe pyjama bottoms. I look like a homeless Stan Laurel. This realisation makes me laugh out loud. I sit back down on the bed to finish my cig. The fabric feels slimy and moist against my legs. Must have sweat like a bastard during the night.

The news comes on the radio and they're talking about people blowing each other up in a hot country somewhere. Leave them to it, that's what I say.

I yank the sheets from the bed, stick them in a pile in the corner. I get my towel and roll it up and open my door, stick my head out to see if any of the showers are free. It must be early because there aren't many people about. I spot Jonno from Gypsyville, the skinny punk with the skinhead. Hanging about outside one of the new kid's rooms. He's in his boxer shorts, covered from head to toe in daft little tattoos: band logos, grim reapers and aliens. He's tapping on the door.

'Got any baccy, babes?'

Fucking "babes"? What's wrong with these people? He's on the tab, and I can't be doing with getting tapped up for smokes this early, so I swiftly walk across the hall without stopping, enter one of the shower rooms and lock the door. The water isn't very hot, but I stand under the stream anyway. The jets of water feel like tiny needles, and I shrink away from them, but as I get used to it I step fully into the flow of water. Close my eyes and let it hit my head and neck. It feels good.

As I towel myself off, the headache begins to kick in. My hangovers are sneaky, lying bastards. Every time I wake up and think I'm going to miss the worst of it, but they're just delayed. They're like coppers; they always turn up eventually.

I make it back to my room without bumping into anyone else, and stick some clothes on, then head downstairs for some breakfast. I'm not particularly hungry, but I've got the feeling it's going to be a long day, so best to get something in my belly while I can.

I hate the canteen, especially when it's crowded. It's the one bit of this whole experience that actually reminds me of prison. Full of tossers and drop-outs – eyeing each other up, talking shit – trying to be big men. The young ones are the worst. They make too much of an effort, they wouldn't last five minutes inside a proper nick. Wearing baseball caps and flaunting "gangster" attitudes, speaking like Americans. Luckily, there're only two of them in the canteen this morning, so I won't have to deal with too much bullshit.

As I walk in one of them smiles. 'Alright, granddad?' There's a part of me that wants to twat him in the mouth. But I don't.

Angela's on today. I like her. She's round and comforting, like a big cushion. The way you would imagine the ideal aunt. Some of the others who work here – that cunt Harvey in particular – look at you with barely disguised disgust. Like if they could have you removed from the human race, they would. Like the cunts in the Job Centre, or the dosh shop. I sometimes feel like reminding them, 'If wasn't for people like me, you cunts wun't have a fucking job, and then every fucker would be looking down their noses at you, too.'

Angela comes over. 'Scrambled egg today love. Beans as well, if you want it.'

'That's grand,' I say.

I don't even have to get up. She dishes some onto a plate, fetches two slices of toast, and brings them over. 'Here you go, love. Want a cuppa tea?'

'That would be magic,' I flash her my best smile.

I feel nostalgic for something, but I don't know what. When I was kid, I used to find my mam passed-out-pissed

53

when I got out of bed. Me and our kid would grab ourselves a slice of bread and butter before heading off to school. But this, being served tea and toast and eggs and beans, it feels as though this is how it should have been when I was little. Doesn't mean I'm feeling fucking sorry for myself though. Lots of people had it worse than me, I understand that.

I'm still not that hungry if truth be told, but I hammer it down anyway. While I'm eating, I look at the name on my forearm. It says, 'Charlotte' in Old English lettering. I briefly think about her, where she is, what she's doing, but I turn the tap off before it starts leaking. After breakfast, I head back up to my room. It's a couple of days until pay-day and I'm broke, so I have a look to see if I've got anything worth sticking in the dosh shop. I've got fuck all, as per, so I'll have to stick my phone in for a twenty, just to get me through, like.

When I leave the hostel, the two cunts from the canteen are stretched out on the lawn like cats. They've got their tops off. I notice the gobby one has a tattoo of a panther on his stomach. Sloppy work – looks like a kitten holding onto his belly for dear life. He lifts his head up, says, 'Get us a tinny while you're out and about.'

I should tell him to fuck off and stamp on his leg or something, but I don't.

Dosh shop's packed today. The sun beams through the big windows, making everyone sweaty and irritable. In front of me two Polish lads are trying to get a loan. They can barely speak a word of English. One of them keeps saying, 'This man is good man, has good credit,' over and over again.

It infuriates me. I feel like grabbing them by the collar and leading them outside for a good kicking, but I don't.

When it's my turn, I approach the counter. I'm pouring with sweat by this point. I get served by the bloke, unfortunately. He's not been here that long. There's something familiar about him, like I know him from

54

somewhere, but I can't place it, and I can't be bothered to ask, so I don't.

'What can I do for you today?' he asks.

'I want to put my phone in for a couple of days,' I say, holding it up.

'Okay. What network is it on?'

'Orange.'

'How much are you looking for?' he turns to look at his monitor screen.

'Twenty, same as usual.'

'Right,' he says. 'Will you pop it in there for me, please?'

I put it in the drawer, take out the charger and put that in there too. He pulls the drawer through to his side, picks up the phone, stares at it, turns it around and looks at it from all different angles.

'Is there something wrong?' I ask.

He doesn't reply at first. Clicks the buttons on his mouse, scrolls through some pages, says, 'I don't think we'll be able to give you twenty today.'

'Why not?'

'Price guide. This particular model has gone down in price since the new version came out.' He smiles.

I can't tell if he's genuinely sorry, or whether he's taking the piss or not. 'Come on, I'm always good for it. Can't you see on the system how many times I've had it in?'

'I appreciate that,' he taps the monitor screen with his finger. 'And I can see you usually come back for stuff, but I have to think of the worst case scenario.'

'Which is?'

'You don't come back and I'm stuck with a phone that I can't sell on.' He shrugs.

'What are you suggesting then?'

'I'll do you a tenner,' he says. 'Best I can do.'

'A tenner? Piss off.'

'Well, I can't help you then.'

I take a moment to assess the situation. I can hear someone in the queue behind tut and mutter.

'Come on, do me fifteen. Please, I'm a good customer.' I try to sound as though I'm not pleading.

He gives me that look again. I want to spit at the glass between us, threaten to wait for him after work and smash his face in, but I don't.

He pauses. 'Go on then, but next time it will be a tenner, okay?'

'Thank you brother,' I say.

When I leave the shop, I'm overcome with a strange feeling I can't quite put my finger on. It's like I'm being watched. I can almost sense a presence, like there's someone or something lurking, just out of sight. It rattles me, a sharp chill of paranoia in my veins and in my gut, so I get a litre bottle of White Lightning and some fag papers and head for the little park near William Booth House. The park is almost-exclusively used by daytime drinkers – well known for it – so I tend to get left alone, and providing no-one starts scrapping or making a scene, the coppers will keep their distance as well. I plant myself on the little hill in the centre of the park and crack open the bottle. This cider has never seen an apple; it's all chemicals and additives, but the drink is cold and wet and feels good as it hits my parched throat. I roll a fag and try and thrash out some sort of plan for the rest of the day. Today would be as good a time as any to visit my cousin, our Terry. Never know, might have a bit of work for me.

As I'm sitting here, Mad Rosie and Skinny Bob approach. Rosie looks like she's out of it already. She swings her arms around, conducting an out-of-control, invisible orchestra and sings what sounds like a mangled version of *Tragedy* by the Bee Gees. Skinny Bob stumbles alongside her, grinning like an idiot – the drunken security for a deranged celebrity. And

Rosie *is* a celebrity in a way. She's always in the local paper for something – usually for breaking the conditions of her latest ASBO, or dropping her knickers and taking a piss in Queen Victoria Square. Or getting caught trying to pinch deodorant from Superdrug. Shit like that. She's routinely held up as an example of everything that's wrong with modern society. And to be fair, she *is* a fucking menace.

'Alright love,' she says, cackling. When she laughs it sounds like the flaps being ripped from the top of a cardboard box.

'Now then, kidda,' Skinny Bob says.

Skinny Bob is a human crash-test dummy. Every time you see him he's picked up some new injury. Today, he sports a huge bruise running from his jaw to his cheek – a big purple blossom.

'What happened to you?' I ask.

'Fuck knows,' he replies.

Rosie takes some tinnies out of a bag. She's also got an empty Lucozade bottle. 'Shall we have a mix?' she says, unscrewing the cap. 'Bit of the old snake-bite?'

I should say no, but I don't.

'Sure, why not?' I hand over the cider.

6

Jamie

No fucker talks anymore. People can't even be bothered to pick up the phone to tell you things. It's all texts, emails; messages on fucking *facefuck*. We're all connected, but there's never any real attempts at contact. Everything is shortened, reduced to acronyms and emoticons.

LOL. PMSL. YOLO.

I'm saying all this to Carrie as she stares down at her new tablet.

'You sound like me dad,' she says.

'Fuck off,' I say, all in good fun.

I'm a bit older than Carrie. Not that much older, but enough that she can wind me up by bringing it up. The other day, I was on about this programme that was on telly when I was younger. It used to really freak me out, it was about this kid who thought aliens were trying to talk to him through a painting or something. I couldn't remember the title, so I asked Carrie if she knew which programme I was talking about. She gave me this look, like I'd gone mad.

'When was it on?'

'Dunno when exactly, it would have been the early eighties though,' I said.

She laughed and rolled her eyes. 'I wasn't even born then.'

I pick up the remote and flick through the channels. It's all shite; repeats of gameshows, soaps and a limitless supply of cooking programmes. I eventually settle on a programme that follows the exploits of an overweight bloke with bleached-blond hair as he travels around the States, stuffing his face at every available opportunity. Because it's filmed in America, all the portions are massive. He gets to eat stuff like mad barbecued meat – ribs, brisket, pulled pork – plus grits and mac 'n' cheese. He grunts and makes sex noises as he shovels all the various things into his gob. It's pornography for hungry people.

'Look at that!' I say. 'Just look at that. Yer just don't get fodder like that in this country.'

Carrie glances up just in time to see a black guy pulling half a cow out of a wood-burning oven.

'Wow,' she says. 'No wonder they have an obesity problem in America.'

The black guy carves a big strip of meat from the carcass of the cow and hands it over to the presenter, who takes it and wolfs it down. He looks as though he's about to cry tears of joy as he licks the grease and barbecue sauce from his fingers. I sigh and yank open my bag of crisps.

'Shall we get a takeaway, love?'

Carrie does this face, places her hands on her cheeks and lets her mouth drop open, her "mock shock" expression. I love it when she does it, but I always tell her that she looks like the killer's mask in *Scream*.

'But we only ate our tea a couple of hours ago,' she says. 'You don't want to be old *and* fat, do you?'

'Fuck off.'

She laughs. 'I'm only joking. I don't mind if you're tubby, baby. All the folds will keep me warm in winter.'

'Fuck off,' I repeat.

I continue eating my crisps. They're good, but it's like they don't touch the sides.

Carrie glances at me again.

'Hey, do you know Lorraine Banks?'

'Yeah. . . well if it's the same one I'm thinking of. She's me mate Kirk's younger sister.' I pause. 'Well, we *were* mates.'

'What happened?'

I sigh, take a sip of lager. 'It was daft, really. . . we had a bit of a falling-out a couple of years ago. It was over nowt really, but there you go. Why, what's up anyway?'

'She just sent me a message over Facebook.'

'Oh yeah?'

'She's asking if you've got any old photos of Kirk.'

'What? That's a strange thing to ask.'

'That's what I thought,' Carrie says. 'What shall I tell her?'

'Fuck knows. Just tell her I haven't got any.'

'Okay, okay, cool yer boots man,' she says, in her "mockney" accent.

I don't say anything else for a while. I'm curious about Lorraine's message, but I let it go. I haven't seen Kirk in ages, and I feel guilty about it. When I eventually do speak, it's to say, 'Sorry, love, din't mean to snap at you.'

Carrie sighs. 'It's okay. Forget about it.'

After a while she gets up. 'I'm going to run a bath. Do you want it after me?'

'Yeah, go on then.' I'm laid on the floor on my back, now, looking up at the ceiling. To my left, the fat Yank on the telly is going off on one again. 'This is *outrageous* pizza,' he yells. 'Off the *hook*.' My stomach rumbles, and I resume thinking about takeaway. I look down at the furry mound that is my belly.

Carrie goes upstairs, and I haul up myself up off the floor. My shoulder clunks as I get up. I think about doing some press-ups, but then I plant myself in my armchair, pick up my tinnie, and go back to watching the pizza antics unfolding

61

on the telly. The *whoosh* of the pilot light ignites the boiler as the taps are turned on upstairs.

I'm always joking about getting older, mainly to hide the fact that lately I'm always *worrying* about getting older. I hope it's a phase, because, I mean, I'm not *that* old. Trying to focus on what I'm going to order from the takeaway, nagging thoughts keep creeping in.

You're nearly forty and you've done fuck all. Or, *you're nearly forty and you're never going to do fuck all.*

Carrie jogs down the stairs, sticks her head around the door and says, 'I'm going to light some candles and then I'm going to jump in. I'll try not to be too long.'

She's wrapped in a towel. Her hair is scraped back from her face and she hasn't got any make-up on. I'm completely in love with her, but the feelings are wrapped in massive insecurities.

'Carrie,' I wail, 'I'm nearly forty.'

She hesitates at the foot of the stairs. 'What are you talking about? You've got a few years to go yet.'

'I know, but I'm nearer to forty than I am to thirty.'

'Get a grip. Do some press-ups or summat,' she says.

I look at her and smile, happy, but still feeling worried. She returns my smile, heads back upstairs. I finish my tinnie, crush it, and sling it in the general direction of the bin. Rising from my chair, I head to the kitchen to get another from the fridge. On the way back through to the living room, I take a couple of takeaway menus out of the drawer where we dump all the crap that comes through the letterbox.

When I hear her get out of the bath, I go upstairs. Through the open door I see her in the bedroom, towelling her hair before she puts the dryer on.

'By the way, I remembered,' I shout through as I peel off my clothes.

'Remembered what?' she shouts back.

'That programme, when I was a kid. It was called *Chocky's Children.*'

Waking the following morning after a disturbed night, I'm filled with regret. I have a pain in my guts and need to make a dash for the toilet. Still half asleep, I trip over the step into the bathroom and crash out on the floor. For a second, I think I might shit myself while lying face down, but I wrestle my pants off and manage to plant myself on the seat in the nick of time.

I'm hit by another bout of cramp, and I cross my arms over my belly, gently rock back and forth on the rim of the seat as I'm wracked with further explosive bursts of diarrhoea.

'Fuck, fuck, fuck!'

There's a knock on the bathroom door.

'Don't come in!' I scream.

'Everything okay?' Carrie asks. I can hear her yawning.

'I'm fine, just don't come in.'

'Okay, don't take too long, I need a wee,' she says, and then louder: 'Is everything okay in there? Are you all right?'

I try not to groan, because I don't want her to hear what's going on.

'How are *you* feeling? I think that takeaway might have been a bit dodgy,' I shout, keeping the strain out of my voice with effort. 'The meat. It's always the meat.'

'I feel okay,' she says. 'Fine. But then again, I didn't eat as much as you. Try not to be too much longer.'

'Yeah. . .'

I can hear the creak of the floorboards as she goes downstairs. I stay on the toilet a while longer. It stings when I wipe. I open the window to let some air in and run the cold water to splash my face. My guts still hurt, but the burning urge subsides. I close the bathroom door behind me.

The kettle's boiling in the kitchen.

'Tea or coffee?' Carrie asks.

'Coffee.'

63

I gently lower myself into my armchair, reaching for the remote. I flick through the telly channels, all the while entertaining the serious notion of ringing in sick to work. The news is on.

Carrie brings me my drink and sets it on the carpet by my feet.

'I'm going upstairs to get ready,' she says.

'I'm seriously entertaining the notion of ringing in sick today,' I reply.

She looks at me. 'Seriously?'

'Seriously.'

She rolls her eyes, tuts, and disappears upstairs.

I reach down for my coffee. The newsreader wears a bright blue dress that I find difficult to look at. She reels off the latest figures about something or other. It cuts to the Prime Minister, who is giving a speech about something else or other. It might be about immigration, might be about employment; might be about something else. She looks pale, tired, and uncomfortable, like she doesn't want to be on camera. I find myself wondering if she's also having to deal with a bad case of the shits. The news then switches to a story about a virus that's spreading around Africa. It makes people's innards dissolve, and there's concern it might spread further. The camera pans around the inside of a medical centre. People everywhere are dying.

I flick through the channels again. An early morning cookery show invites celebrities to make breakfast in the studio and talk about whatever product they're currently flogging. I watch it while I finish my coffee.

Carrie's banging about above me, which means she must have got out of the shower, so I go upstairs again. Carrie is in the bedroom getting changed. In the bathroom I turn the shower on. Undressed, I sit on the toilet while the room fills with steam. After I finish, I step into the shower, letting the hot water run down my back and into the crack of my arse. Feels soothing.

The bathroom door opens and Carrie walks in. I can see her shadow through the shower curtain. The blurry shape of her turns around, pulls her knickers down and plants herself on the toilet.

'Are you going to work or not?' she asks.

I sigh. 'Yeah. I can't be arsed, but there's no excuse really. Can't afford to take a day off.'

'Yeah.'

'What time are you finishing?'

'Six. Do you want me to pick something up for tea?'

'Can do.'

She stands up. I see the shadow of her hand reaching for the toilet roll. She wipes, flushes and goes over to the sink to wash her hands before leaving the bathroom.

I stand for a moment longer under the water, before getting out and drying myself. After brushing my teeth, I shave and go through to the bedroom to put my clothes on.

My belly jiggles as my feet hit the stairs, and I think about doing some press-ups again. In the living room, Carrie's turned the cookery programme off and has a music channel on instead. There's the low thud of bass and beats, accompanying footage of a woman with a massive behind, writhing about on the screen. The air is thick with the smell of Carrie's perfume, the flowery stuff she only wears for work.

'Do you think her arse is real?'

'I don't know,' I say. 'It might be computer generated. A cyber arse. A virtual arse.'

'It doesn't look real, does it?'

Carrie tugs and pulls at her uniform, clearly uncomfortable in it. She fiddles with her sleeves, her belt, and her crotch in a repeating cycle. According to her, she is forced to wear one of the most unflattering uniforms ever created. It consists of a white, short-sleeved shirt with pale-blue vertical stripes; formless navy-blue trousers made of synthetic material, and a blue neckerchief. She also has a big rectangular badge with

65

"HARRY SHILTON'S" and "CARRIE" stencilled on it, but she refuses to put that on until she's actually at work.

I don't have to wear a specific uniform for work: just shirt, tie and trousers. Not too bad, I suppose, but it rankles me that I've had to get ready in the first place.

'Fucking work,' I say.

'What's the matter?'

'Nowt. Just the whole getting up and going to work thing. Shite, innit?'

'Yeah,' she sighs. 'What's the alternative though?'

'Dunno, just dole. Or winning the lottery.'

We have this same conversation, or a variation of it, most mornings. It's all part of our routine.

Carrie slides over to me. As she does, her hips sway in time to the beat of music on the telly. She does a little dance. Places her arms around me and smiles, giving me a kiss.

'You never know, today might the day,' she says.

'What day?'

'The day when something happens.'

Phase Two

We'd been out of school for over a year, but nothing felt that different, partly due to the fact that we'd hardly bothered to turn up for lessons towards the end of term anyway. We continued to meet up and get smashed and cause chaos at every available opportunity, just because we could.

We were young. And although a couple of us had jobs or were on courses – or whatever – most of the time we were round at Gaz's.

Claire

Everything changed after leaving school. I knew that Kirk and I wouldn't last as a couple, it was just a matter of time really. Within a month of leaving, I found myself looking at him and thinking *Is that it?*

He seemed content to hang around with the lads, get smashed, and fuck about. Nothing else. I was in a totally different place, I wanted to do stuff - earn money. Create a life for myself.

It was difficult to finish with him - he was really upset, and he didn't know what to do with himself. But I looked at Gemma, saw what was going on with her and Gaz, and there was absolutely no fucking chance I was going down that road.

Jamie

Gaz had a really tough upbringing. None of us were what
you'd call well-off, but it was worse for Gaz. His mum
was a recovering heroin addict, and he spent most of his
childhood being dragged from one shitty situation to
another. He was the kind of kid all the mams felt sorry
for, but he had a reputation for being a troublemaker, so
they didn't like having him round.

When school finished, the first thing Gaz's mam did
was kick him out. She'd done the same to his brother.
The day after his sixteenth birthday, he got home and all
his bags were packed and in the hallway. All that was
missing was a hand-written note saying *Fuck Off*.

Gaz

I tried living off my wits for a bit, but I was only a
kid. I couldn't carry on turning up at people's houses
hoping for a camp-bed or sofa for the night. I ended up
having to sleep rough a few times, but it was no biggie -
at least it didn't feel that way at the time. One of my
favourite places was in the sand pit under the slide, on
that little park on St George's Road. I'd wait until the
bag-heads had fucked off, then roll out a couple of
towels and put my sleeping bag on them.

Eventually I managed to get a place in a hostel. I
was in there with some proper shady cunts, but I was a
big lad; I'd seen enough shit growing up, so I could look
after myself.

Still can.

Jamie

After about eight months in the hostel, Gaz was given a
bedsit in a shared house down Melrose Street. There were
four rooms, each containing a bed, a desk and some

cupboards. He had to share the kitchen and bathroom but after living in the hostel it felt like a luxury pad.

A warden popped around every now and then to make sure there weren't any wild parties going on. Of course, more often than not, something *was* going on. If we heard a van pulling up or keys in front door, we'd rush to turn the music down and hide ourselves around the room in case someone knocked on the door. Sometimes, they'd smell the dope fumes and hear the giggling, and we'd all be marched out of the bedsit. All we'd do was wait around the corner for half-an-hour until the warden had fucked off.

Gemma

We got really close around that time, me and Gaz. Claire got shot of Kirk not long after leaving school, so Gaz was dead paranoid - kept thinking I'd do the same to him. He put a front on, but I could tell he was desperate. In a way, I suppose, I became his surrogate mam. He talked about kids and starting a family with me and it freaked me out. I mean, I was only like sixteen or seventeen. He wanted it both ways. He wanted to hang about with his mates but also have me at his beck and call. My mam wasn't happy. She said I'd get knocked up and become a teenage mam. Of a mixed-race child. She worried Gaz would lose interest and leave me holding the baby.

It took a few years, but she ended up being right about that.

Steve

Nearly everyone who went around to Gaz's: me, Jamie, Chris, Barry and the rest - lived at home with their parents, so his bedsit became a sanctuary. You could go round there at three in the morning if you were smashed out of your box, so you didn't have to sneak in at home and risk being caught. We were all earning a bit of coin

from tatting, and Gaz's front room was the place that
played host to the bucket and cut-off bottle.

As Gaz settled into his new pad, he got more and more
cocky and took more risks. Back then, acid was the big
thing. We got into a routine whereby we'd go tatting in
the factory-yards on a Friday and take in whatever we got
to the scrapyard first thing Saturday. After that, we'd
all head our separate ways. Go back home and get washed
and changed. Shit, shower and shave. Head into the town
centre and meet up again. Although most of us were still
technically underage, we would always be in The Cheese or
in Sargent Peppers. You have to understand, Hull's town
centre wasn't the wasteland it is now.

Gaz

Maybe it's just a consequence of getting older, but I
can't help being nostalgic. Back then we had mad times.
Mad, mad times. The rave scene hit Hull in a major way.
And some genius at Hull Fair realised that playing fast,
up-tempo, hard-core plinky-plink techno on the Waltzers
would be a sure-fire way to bring in a big crowd. For
curious school-age West Hull shit-kickers, the Future had
arrived. A giant smiley-faced spaceship had landed on
Walton Street, and it stank of poppers and sweaty
armpits. Our adolescent minds gobbled up the white
gloves and glow-sticks, the Billy and the Trips, the
klaxons and whistles, and set the tone for the best part
of a decade. And not long after, Brit-Pop turned up to
the party - drunk, stoned and with vomit all down the
front of its Ben Sherman shirt.

Jamie

Hull's town centre was the place to *be* at that point.
The problem was, we hardly had any money between us. It
was that difficult time when you're still getting on the

70

bus for half fare, even though you're off to the pub. At
best, we could manage a couple of cut price drinks each,
and after that we had to improvise by mine-sweeping -
picking up other people's drinks when they're not
looking. You could only get away with that for so long
before being clocked by a bouncer, who either slung you
out or gave you a dig.

We'd spend Saturday out and about during the day, then
spend the evening tripping - freaking out and generally
causing chaos. We got our acid from a guy called Irish
Mick, an out-and-out space cadet who hailed from
Greatfield.

When it came to getting good shit, Irish Mick was
hands-down the best purveyor of LSD throughout Hull and
East Riding. Strawbs, Purple Ohms, Super Marios... he
really was the man. Not only that, but he didn't take
the piss when it came to cost. By far the maddest shit
that Irish Mick got hold of were these things called
Blanks. They didn't have any pictures or logos on them.
Nothing. Just a tiny plain white square and
brain-meltingly strong. Steve said they were
quadruple-dipped, to make them so powerful. If you asked
Irish Mick what the fuck they were or where he got them
from, he told you he'd been visited by skinny white
aliens with big black eyes. He said they gave him them
so he could distribute them among the humans, in order to
prepare us for what was about to happen.

What can I say? The X-Files had just come on telly.
Everyone was banging on about aliens. Within a couple of
years, just about every stoner's flat would have one of
those TAKE ME TO YOUR DEALER posters on the wall.

Claire

When Kirk joined the army, I felt guilty, like I'd broken
his heart so much that the only way he could cope was to

71

leave Hull: leave the country. But it was actually a
good move for him, I'm not making excuses for myself - we
were only kids - but getting out of Hull and extracting
himself from that circle of friends was a good move.
It's a shame the way it all turned out.

Steve

One night, we got hold of some Blanks and we decided we
were going to hole up in Gaz's bedsit and go mental for
the night. Originally, the plan was to head in the
general direction of Hedon, where we'd been informed
there was a house party, but the volatile nature of acid
put some of us off. A couple of weeks earlier, we'd been
involved in a kick-off outside Ice Arena, and relations
between East and West Hull had become a bit strained - to
say the least. One of the biggest problems with tripping
is the fact that you're completely unable to engage with
violence in any meaningful way. The idea of careening
around some bird's front room on the wrong side of town
while some twat is trying to land a dig didn't really
appeal to any of us, so we figured we'd drop the acid and
have a smoke and see what happened. Stick some mad tunes
on. Go out for a late-night-buzz walk.

Jamie

We were on the bus, heading home from town. It was
around teatime, and we were already a bit merry, so we
got off at the offie for some little bottles of beer and
a big bottle of cider, before making our way to Gaz's.
We had a nice big block of Black, and a pocket full of
Blanks, so it was game on. Walking around the corner, we
saw something none of us expected to see; at least, not
for a while. Kirk stood there, near the front of Gaz's
place. He leaned against a car, fag hanging out of his
mouth.

72

'Alright fuckwits,' he said. 'I've been stood here like a fucking plank for nearly half-an-hour.'

Kirk had joined the army straight after leaving school. He was as much a wreck-head as the rest of us, but he'd always had this thing for joining the forces - used to bang on about it at school. No one thought he had a cat's chance of getting in, seeing as he had a fondness for smoking resin to the point of passing out. But against all expectations he managed to stay off the resin long enough to pass the physical, and he was accepted onto basic training. Before he went away, his last night in Hull was a mad one. The more pissed we got, the more bouncers turned us away from bars. I think Kirk was still cut up about Claire. It had been over a year, but he was still banging on about her: where she was, and with whom, all that.

We ended up in a takeaway and became embroiled in a brawl that spilled out onto the street. Unfortunately, Kirk got a right pasting. His face was messed up. Could have ended his career in the army before it even started.

Gemma

Gaz didn't like me to see him when he was off his head with the lads. That's what he told me. We started drifting apart. I wasn't going to be the token girl who hangs about cleaning up everyone else's mess. Fuck that. Me mam could barely contain how happy she was about it.

I enrolled on a food hygiene course at Hull College, along with Claire. Figured I might as well do something. Let Gaz hang about with the lads, let them all pretend things were still the same as they'd been for the last couple of years at school.

They get to be kids for a lot longer, don't they? Blokes, I mean.

Steve

Kirk's standing there, and we're all like, 'What the
fuck? It's Kirk for fuck's sake,' and he's grinning like
he's just dropped a bandit or something. All dressed up.
Good shirt, smart trousers. Big fucking chunky watch
dangling from his wrist. Kirk had never been what you'd
call the trendiest of kids. He came from a big family,
so he was the hand-me-down kid. His nickname for the
first year of school had been Gola. But here he was, all
decked out, and filled-out as well. It was obvious the
army life had been good for him, because he'd really put
on weight - in good way - on his shoulders and arms.

We walked over to him, still gobsmacked, and that was
when he delivered the killing blow.

'Check out the wheels,' he said, patting the roof of
the car he was leaning on.

It was one of those old Montegos, which confused us
all at first. It was hardly a boy-racer's car. Turned
out that he'd gone halves on it with his old man. His
dad would drive it while he was away, and Kirk would
drive it when he was home. It seemed like an odd
arrangement, but it was car: a car big enough to cram
most of us in. The night had taken a new and interesting
turn - a whole new realm of possibility opened up before
us.

We went into Gaz's, headed up to his room. There were
five of us: Kirk, Me, Gaz, Chris, and Jamie. We got in
there and shut the curtains and opened the windows.
Jamie put his Cypress Hill tape on the stereo, Gaz
skinned up, and Chris filled a bucket in the kitchen -
brought it through and placed it on a tea-towel on the
floor. I passed the beers around.

It was going to be a good night, you could feel it in
the air, like a static charge.

Kirk explained that he had passed out of basic

74

training, and one of the many perks he got was driving
lessons and a test, courtesy of the armed forces.

'I'm thinking about driving one of them tanks,' he
said, just before bobbing down with the bottle and
disappearing in a cloud of smoke.

Over by the stereo, Jamie started doing press-ups, for
some reason.

'Are you okay smoking that shit?' he said, the tip of
his nose an inch from the ground.

Kirk looked about to burst into tears, unable to hold
the smoke in for more than a few seconds. He collapsed
on the floor, coughing. Everyone else collapsed about
laughing.

'It's fine,' he said once he'd regained his composure.
'I've got a couple of weeks before I have to go back,
I'll flush it out by then.'

Gaz paced up and down, pensively smoking. 'Guys, I've
got a great idea,' he said. 'Let's drop some of the acid
and go out for a drive.'

'What kind of shit?' Chris (the Robin to Gaz's
Batman) asked.

'This kind of shit.' Gaz took the tabs out of his
pocket.

Gaz

Kirk was reluctant at first, but the offer of top drawer
grade-A-brain-rape-acid was too hard to resist. I would
be fine, of course. One of the advantages of being tall
is that I've always had the constitution of an ox, so I
could tolerate all kinds of stuff going through my
system. We decided to wait until it started getting
dark. Our plan was to drive to Withernsea, on the coast.
I didn't mind having everyone round at mine, but it was a
pain hiding from the warden every couple of hours,
especially when you were totally off yer box.

We'd drop the acid just before we set off, so we'd be coming up as we arrived. We could head for the beach and then, I don't fucking know, do stuff. Maybe pop along to the arcades and take in the lights; have a few goes on the penny shuffle.

Soon it was time, so I handed out the trips. We each placed one on the back of our tongue and then we packed ourselves into the car. The fucking Anthill Mob, guffawing and chatting and falling about. Whenever there's a bunch of young lads in a car, there's always the chance of being pulled, especially when there's five of you crammed in. Kirk hadn't drunk much, and aside from a tiny crumb of resin to make a spliff when we got there, we weren't carrying anything. We were just a bunch of lads going out for a drive and a laugh.

We reached Withernsea quickly and without incident, buzzing with the impending trip; in that strange limbo time between taking something and then coming up on it. Kirk stuck a compilation tape in the car stereo. It had stuff like *Don't You Want Me?* by Felix, and that fucking N-Trance tune on it. We were all bobbing our heads and chucking out shapes, like our lives depended on it.

Steve

We were all goofing off, like hyperactive bairns. Jamie and Chris clowned about doing the running-man and arm-dancing. Gaz gave me a shotgun blow-back and I almost passed out. Lads, letting off steam and having fun. Good old days. Hah, there it is again, nostalgia. Listen to me, going on...

It was dusk when we got to *With*. We parked near the sea front and tumbled down to the beach. We'd timed it just right, arrived as the last of the sun's light was draining from the sky. We all stood there, mouths open,

76

staring up at the beautiful, vast sky. A huge, panoramic
mess of colour and light. Amazing.

---

*'Fuck me,' says a voice, coming from somewhere off to the
left. 'I'm coming up. I'm like... I'm like, I'm...
I'm there, dyerknowwhadda mean?'*

'I know what you mean,' I say.

'So do I,' someone else says, and...

*Wait. What's happening? Who's saying that? Are we
there, back on the beach? Am I remembering someone
saying that, or is someone saying that?*

*I don't know where I am. Is this a place? Everything
is blue. And white. And I can hear... feel everyone's
memories. It's like I'm plugged into something, or
something is plugged into me.*

In Withernsea.

Where's Barry? Is he here? Is he with us?

1995. Withernsea.

*Am I talking? Somebody, please listen to me. Say
something. I don't know where I am, I don't where I
am...*

I don't know who I am.

Am I Gaz? Steve? Claire? Jamie? Gemma?

*Someone touch me. Hit me. Where are my arms? My
body?*

I feel sick. Get me out of here.

Help.

7

Steve

I'm drunk. My bloodstained work shirt is draped over the back of the chair in front of me. I look at the dark, red pattern spread across it, and raise the glass to my mouth again, take another sip of whisky. Follow it with a deep drag of the joint. The burn on the back of my throat feels good. The way my head is beginning to swim feels good. Being alive feels good.

They let me leave work early, of course. There was no way I could carry on with the stickers and stocktake after experiencing something like that. Plus, my work shirt and trousers are covered with Pete's blood.

The whole fucking thing was terrible. Still can't get my head around it.

Pete. Poor, fucking Pete. Hadn't seen him for years. Pete was one of the 'causalities', as we referred to them. Pete Ashworth and Barry Thompson.

Pete's thing was booze. I mean, we all liked a drink when we were younger, but he fucking went for it, always had to do more than everyone else. Booze and fucking Temazepam. He was a walking disaster zone. Always used to show up with a black eye and absolutely no idea how he got it, shit like that.

And Barry. Barry just lost it. Started hearing voices. It was quite scary at the time. Not long after he turned eighteen, he attacked some poor old fucker on the street. Screaming about aliens and the government. He got banged up soon after and spent the rest of his life going in and out of various hospitals and institutions.

But poor fucking Pete. He kept waffling on about mad shit right until the ambulance arrived. On about fucking aliens. I don't know whether he recognised me or not. I hope he did – hope it was some sort of comfort to him.

I'm blubbing again, like a fucking bairn. He was talking about people with jet-black eyes. Said one of the aliens was inside him, slowing burrowing its way into his mind. Turning him into something. He was obviously out of his head. Good job really; he must have been in total agony.

Fucking aliens.

When I went through to the back to explain to Paul what had happened, I found him in exactly the same position as when I first got to work. Sitting on the floor, surrounded by stuff, clipboard by his side.

'I need to go home, Paul,' I said.

'Okay,' he replied, before asking, 'What's that on your shirt?'

'It's blood, Paul.'

'Oh.'

'There was an accident outside. Someone got knocked down. I had to go and see to them.'

'Right. . .'

'So I was thinking I should go home. I'm feeling pretty freaked out by it.'

'I imagine you are,' he said. 'I think we'll be okay without you.'

And with that, I was out the door and gone.

The police were hanging about outside. I was hoping to duck past them, get home, but a young copper took me to one side as I stepped out the door.

He was young in the way that gets you depressed – too baby-faced for how you expect a copper to look. Although he was quite tall and broad, he had a pebble-dash of acne on his cheek and the kind of chin that looked as though it had never seen a razor.

'Would it be okay to have a word? I've just been talking to the security guard next door. You were the first on the scene, right?'

'Yeah, that's right.'

'What happened?'

I sigh, because I just want to go home, but I know I've got to play ball.

'I was here, having a smoke and then I spotted him staggering about.'

The young copper started scribbling notes in his little black book.

'Go on.'

'I just thought to myself: "Spice Zombie," y'know? And then I saw him stumble into the road and it all happened really fast.'

He made more notes, then reached up, tapped his teeth with the end of his pencil.

'Someone said they saw you approach him and crouch down next to him. Was he conscious? Did he say anything?'

He stared at me for a moment and started scribbling again, as if he'd forgotten something. My face burned. For a second, I thought I might have been seen taking something off Pete.

'This is really fucking weird,' I blurted out. 'But I think I know him... knew him.'

The young copper looked up from his notebook, tipped his head back and narrowed his eyes, like he's was trying to suss me out.

'Really? How did you know him?'

'I used to go to school with him,' I said as I bowed my head. 'He's called Pete. I haven't seen him for years, but I'd heard about him.'

81

'Heard what?'

'That he was in a bad way. Drugs, alcohol, all that.'

The young cop tutted quietly and shook his head, like he'd seen it all. It really irritated me for some reason.

'We're going to need a statement at some point. Are we okay to contact you here, at work?'

'Sure.'

The young copper reached up and grabbed my shoulder. Probably a gesture of reassurance, but it made me feel uncomfortable. And then something strange happened. I looked at him, at his puppy-fat face, and what appeared to be a white mist flashed over his eyes, completely obscuring his pupils.

He opened his mouth and spoke with a different voice, that didn't seem to belong to him:

'We will fill the void within you.'

I thought back to the mad shit Pete was babbling.

'What? What are you saying?'

'I said look after yourself, we'll be in touch. Are you okay? You've gone pale.'

He stared at me again, with clear eyes this time. I sensed concern in them.

'I'm not sure.'

'It's the shock kicking in. The adrenalin will be wearing off now. I suggest you go home and have a stiff drink.'

On the way home I stopped at the newsagents. I bought four cans of Monster and a small bottle of vodka. Seemed like the only rational thing to do. Now I'm sitting here in my living room, curtains drawn against the world, trying to make some sort of sense out of what's just occurred. I'm tempted to have a blast on *Fate of Mankind*, but I'm not really in the mood.

I close my eyes. Try to empty my head, but I can't. It's all the fucking Monster I've drunk this morning. I open my eyes, look at the bloodied shirt again. Poor fucking Pete. I feel like I should go online, let people know what's happened, but what would I say?

– *Hey, remember Pete Ashworth? That kid from school we used to knock about with? Well, he's dead. Smashed to bits in front of me. Still got his blood all over my work uniform. YOLO.*

Fucking *Facebook*.

I get up, agitated, and pace up and down for a while. Then I remember the pills, the things I took from Pete. I reach into my pocket and gather them up. Move over to the table by the wall and drop them onto it, a nice handful. Strangely, there seem to be more than there were, like they've been multiplying in my pocket. I pick one up, reach over to the light switch and flick it on, holding the small, smooth object up in front of my eyes to get a closer look. I realise these things aren't pills; they're seeds. *Seeds.* I've seen something similar before. My thoughts flicker back to twenty years ago. I'm on the field at the back of school with my mates, the day we saw the blue light in the sky.

Barry turned up with a handful of the things.

Holy shit. How mad is that?

Something in my brain pings like the timer on a microwave, and I know what I have to do. It feels obvious, like I've done this before. Avoiding the ones with blood on, I pick one out.

I take it over to the sink and turn on the tap, hold the pearly seed under the running water. I'm buzzing with anticipation, excitement. It reminds of when we used to meet up with Irish Mick to pick up our trips. What were we in store for? Visuals? Body-buzz? Strong ones?

I pop it into my mouth. My tongue tingles. It's like licking the tip of a 9-volt battery. I wait for a moment, expecting the tingling to fade, but it doesn't. It starts to feel intense – unpleasant – not like I remember from that day on the playing field.

What the fuck have I just done?

I stumble back over to the table and pick up the vodka, take a long swig, trying to burn the sensation from my throat, but it doesn't work. I'm gagging as I feel this thing pulsating its way down my gullet. I stick my fingers down my throat, try to spew it back up. A big jet of vodka and Monster swirls down the sink, but the seed is still in me, I can feel it. My heart races and my lungs gulp for air as panic sets in.

All the cells in my body start vibrating at the same frequency as the seed. It buzzes somewhere deeper inside me now. I tremble uncontrollably.

I'm having a seizure. *I'm going to die.*

I can't speak, can't scream. Gasp for air. *Panic.* No oxygen. *Panic.* My ears ring – a long, low-frequency sound that chimes throughout my body, my brain –.

I'm going to die.

Light seeps in from everywhere. Everything around me shatters, pierced by brilliant shards of blue light. I unravel. I fall to pieces. I have no sense of time and no concept of space. I explode into fragments.

There is nothing. Oblivion. Brilliant blue light.

But somehow, I am still aware.

Somehow, my consciousness – my identity – still exists.

I have no senses, but I exist.

I'm dying.

I'm. Dead.

I. Am. Nothing.

I am a compressed dot in the distance, lost in a black void.

Slowly, over countless millennia, I expand. I stretch out into a line, which multiplies into a tangled web of white tendrils, which shatter the empty darkness. I coalesce into shapes: squares, triangles, circles, hexagons, which combine to form structures. Pyramids, cubes, spheres, dodecahedrons.

Somehow, I know I'm in a place. Or on a plain. It sits alongside my own reality, woven into its very fabric, but is imperceptible.

There is no matter here, only energy. There is consciousness, awareness, but it is different from mine.

I don't know how I know this, but I do know it.

And I'm scared, because I'm aware that all of who I am, everything that makes me *me*, are my memories and experiences, which are rapidly drifting away from me.

I think of triangles. I think of pyramids. I think of polygons. I have no hands, but I grip my memories tightly. Squeeze them until they become solid.

Think back.

Back.

The day of the lights. After school, on the field. Listening to the...

...tunes. Everyone fucking about. The smell of cigarettes and deodorant. A sight chill in the air as the sun goes down.

Barry Thompson turns up. Opens his hand and shows us the pills.

Pete's showing off. Doesn't even ask what they are. Quickly grabs one and pops it in his mouth. Soon as he swallows it, Barry cracks up.

'What's so fucking funny?' Jamie asks.

'Sorry,' Barry laughs. 'I don't know what they are. I found them at the back of the field.'

It all kicks off. Kirk grabs Barry, gives him a dig. Pete sticks his fingers down his throat, makes himself throw up. Gaz and Chris get hold of Barry, and Kirk makes him eat the rest of whatever they are, to teach him a lesson.

We hardly see Barry after that.

'Wait a minute,' I say. 'What's happening? This all seems real.'

'What?' Pete sounds confused. 'What are you on about, Steve? Are you okay?'

I don't know. This feels like a memory, but it also feels real. I am here – 1993, on the school field, and Pete's alive. I'm alive. I close my eyes tightly, trying to block everything out...

... Nothing again, except the colour blue. I'm scared. I'm scared that if I don't concentrate hard enough, my mind will dissipate, blink out of existence. I want this to be over.

I want to go home.

I start thinking about that time Kirk drove us to With – and we were all tripping off our heads and ...

...Everything sparkles. Shimmers with meaning and significance. We run around the beach, shouting and screaming. One of us tosses a pebble in the air and it disappears into the darkness, and everyone hits the deck like a grenade has been tossed. Making our way along the beach, we stumble upon a campfire, already lit and burning. We're all confused by its sudden appearance.

'Who put this here?' A worried look flashes across Chris's face.

'This is totally fucked up,' I say. 'It's like they knew we were coming, whoever it was.'

Gaz sits down and puts a spliff together. 'That's the thing with acid. It's like the whole fucking world takes a trip with you. We've become magnets for mad shit, fellas.'

Jamie and Chris spread out on the sand near the fire, and it's all so real. I'm there, but I'm not just me. I'm Gaz, and Chris, and Jamie and Kirk. I move between them, see through their eyes, hear through their ears. I'm in their heads. All their thoughts and feelings are mine too and...

...And then I'm Gemma, and I'm at home. Trying not to think about Gaz but I am thinking about Gaz, and now I'm Gaz and I'm on the beach again. I look across at Kirk. Kirk's staring into the fire. He's still thinking about Claire and then I'm Claire, and I've just finished college. I'm not thinking about Kirk at all. I'm thinking about the future, my future – her future – our future...

... And then, a voice. I can't tell where it's coming from. I have no ears, so I'm not hearing it, but I perceive it somehow.

Try and stifle the panic, focus on the voice; use it as a beacon. *Focus.*

It's telling me to relax, to think of home, of my flat. I visualise my living room, try to see it in as much detail as possible. The big broken boiler in the kitchen. Myself, stooped over the sink, heaving. And my thoughts narrow into details: the smell of something burning in the ashtray, the various stains on my sofa cushions; the low rumble of the traffic outside. I picture the angles of the walls and doors and I begin to see again. I can hear again.

I feel my heart thumping in my chest, feel the burn of the vodka in my throat. I feel the air as it fills my lungs: the oxygen – precious oxygen – and I'm back

---

I've never been religious. Never had any spiritual leanings at all but I find myself falling to my knees and thanking God for sparing me. I pick myself up and take another swig of vodka to calm the shaking that grips me. I vomit again almost immediately, but feel glad for it, because it confirms that I'm alive. I've survived whatever it is I've just been through. *It's over.*

Just as I'm breathing, enjoying the sensation of the air filling my lungs, I feel the hair on the back of my neck stand up. A crackle of static, inside me, in my stomach. Is it the seed?

Fear. Primal fear. It's in my guts. Everything clenches. Fight or flight. It's like I'm alone in a forest in the dark, being watched.

There's something in the flat with me. I can't see it, can't hear it, but I know...

'The initiation never ends,' the presence says. But there are no words spoken. I understand only that we're communicating, but I don't know how.

'The initiation never ends, because it has no beginning.'

'What's happening to me? What do you want?'

87

I'm shaking, all of my limbs juddering. My head is swimming from all the adrenalin. I sway as I try to keep myself from passing out. I prop myself against the sink, grip it with my hands.

'You are becoming more like us, and we are becoming more like you.'

Getting my bearings straight, I begin to feel the tingling again. The vibrations start subtly and gain in intensity.

I shout, 'I don't know what you are, just make it stop.'

I squint and pick out a spot on the sink, what appears to be a small tea-stain, and I concentrate on it. But around me, the Presence begins to solidify, like a wisp of smoke gaining mass. Swirling around and gathering into the outline of a form, which fades into something more solid.

Tall, and dark. I can't quite get a grip on it. I feel as though I can only see it from the corner of my eye. There's a gut-churning sense of recognition, way beyond my lived memories and sensory experience. A deep, primal, shudder runs through me. I straighten my racked body.

'I know you,' I breathe. 'I *know* you.'

'We will fill the void within you all.'

I struggle to make out what I'm communicating with. A loose collection of particles, a cloud of mist. But soon I begin to pick out the vague outline of limbs; a torso, a head. Its wordless communications reverberate around my brain before bleeding down into my ears. Not noise, but the *memory* of noise. The sense of having heard someone speak. The more I understand, the harder it becomes to comprehend. It's too big to grasp.

I'm reduced to plain, dumb questions.

'Are you real? What are you doing?'

'I'm attempting to utilise spare particles to achieve corporeal form. We understand that your kind find it easier to communicate with a form that is familiar. It lessens the psychological impact of our appearance.'

'I'm not going mad then? Can you tell me that at least?'

'Our incursions into this reality can cause irreparable damage to the human psyche. Throughout your history there are countless examples of your kind being driven insane by our presence. These incidents are sometimes recorded as religious: as contact with Divine Beings. You seem to be coping remarkably well, however.'

The vibrations and sensations rattling through me begin to subside. *Reach back, think of it as some crazy trip.* Encourage my mind to go blank. Let the intrusion of the alien voice flow. *Just got to ride it out, that's all.*

I sit down on the sofa, let the swirling mass in front of me order itself into something approaching solid. Allow my eyes to close, focus on my breathing. Encourage the whole mad, mad, *mad* world to slip away. I feel something inside me come loose, and suddenly I'm travelling upward. A force gently pulls my soul from my body and carries it up, up, up. . .

. . . And I'm moving back in time. Everything is blue. It's 1995 and we're in With, but I'm not in the car, I'm above the car looking down. And then it's 1993 and we're back at school. I see the blue light, and I want to look away and stop this from beginning, but I can't. I keep moving back, beyond myself and into someone else. I'm a woman, living in Bransholme. I think it's the 1980s and I'm with my neighbour and we look and see the lights, and all the people are coming out into the street to see what it is. Then it's the 1960s. I'm on a field again, I'm young again but I'm a different lad knocking about with my mates. We see the blue light, see it sweep over the park and see that smaller lights are splitting off from it, and I move again. I'm shifting, turning, and I'm near the Humber. It's dark: there are no streetlights, only lanterns. It's so dark, and my thoughts are different – THIS ISN'T REAL – and then the sky lights up. A brilliant blue covers the whole town, throwing light into all the alleyways and crannies. . .

. . . I feel a vibration, something inside me – the seed –

spark. I feel a jolt, a shock, and I crash-land back into my body. It's like waking up from a dream.

'How long was I asleep?'

'You weren't asleep. You were projecting.'

'What?'

I'm hunched over the sink. I feel like vomiting, but I can only manage a few dry heaves. I feel adrift, unstuck from everything. I can't tell if I'm here, in my kitchen, or if I'm only remembering being here, in my kitchen.

I could be dreaming.

I could be someone else, watching this happen.

The *something* stands in front of me. It has the rough form of a person now, but it's not *quite* right. The limbs are too long and thin. Its reedy body is wrapped in a featureless grey two-piece suit and shirt. The features on the front of the bald head are eerie in their absence of definition, and expressionless. There's no depth or texture; it's like the details have merely been mapped onto a shape. Yet despite this, it manages to be inconspicuous. The more I stare at it, the harder it is to notice the form at all. But I know it's there, in front of me.

'How do you do that?' I can feel beads of cold sweat trickle down my forehead.

'We violate all the physical laws that govern this universe. Our very presence here is unnatural – we only exist as localised distortions of reality. Through the seed, and in turn through you, we project a representation of what we are, so that we can be comprehended by your sensory input.'

I nod, blankly, and reach for the bottle.

'It has taken us millennia to create a means of communication with you. Your various languages and cultures; the multitudes of human perceptions and beliefs, which are constantly evolving. The fluidity of your consciousness has proven to be... difficult to grasp.'

I struggle to get the lid off with my sweaty, shaking hands. I'm nearly out of vodka.

'Let me get this straight,' I pour the last dribble into a glass. '*We're* difficult to grasp. Shit the bed, talk about pot calling the kettle black.'

I'm surprised by my apparent acceptance of the current situation. I know there's a possibility I've gone off the deep end. Maybe I've had a psychotic episode – like Barry fucking Thompson did all those years ago – but the way I figure it, I've got no choice but to go along with it. This is my reality now. Expanded consciousness and conversations with an alien presence. There's no point struggling against it. It's happening and there's nothing I can do about it. Somehow it feels pre-ordained, like this all happened a long time ago, and I'm recalling it.

'I/we/us don't understand.'

It flickers, as if there's a glitch in its manifestation. I crack open a tin of Monster and top up my glass while it composes itself.

'What now?' I ask.

'There is much for us to do.'

I take a long gulp.

'In that case, take me to your dealer.'

8

Claire

'Where is he?' Mam says, face like a stone.

'He's at his mate's place. Just for the weekend.'

'Right.'

I look at Natasha, sitting on the rug by the TV; paper, crayons, glitter and glue spread out on the floor in front of her. Although I've only spent one night away from her, I feel guilty. Because of the hours I work, I often miss taking her to bed. She's at the stage where she's growing so fast that when I see her in a morning, I'm convinced she's a little taller, or her shiny blonde hair is longer. I feel like I'm creating gaps in my memories of her childhood; big enough to stick a fist through.

'Look Mam, don't start,' I say.

'Start? What are you talking about?' she says. 'I never get involved. It's your life.'

'Where's Dad?'

'He's upstairs listening to Black Sabbath.' She follows this with a sharp intake of breath – a good indication she's about to say something I'm not going to like. 'I said when you got married that there might be problems down the line.'

'No you didn't.'

'I did, it's the age-gap. I'm telling yer.'

'Come off it,' I say. 'I'm six years older than him. You make it sound like I'm a fucking cradle-snatcher or something.'

I love Mam – and I'd be lost without her – but sometimes, when she talks like this, I feel like a teenager. I want to scream and storm out of the room. When I was growing up, Mam was so determined that I wouldn't *make the same mistakes* she did that she never let up. She was on at me all the time to work, to study, to tidy; whatever. She was keen that I carve out my own life on my own terms and that I could fend for myself and didn't have to rely on a bloke to *look after me.* But since leaving home nearly twenty years ago, at no point has a single *well done* or anything approaching that fallen from her permanently drawn-tight lips. Sometimes, I could even swear that she gets a kick out of being around when things go wrong. It's like the ambition and determination she had for me all those years ago calcified into something more toxic; like envy, perhaps. Or maybe it's just me, reading too much into things.

She's about to say something else, so I give her a look that says not to. She can't help herself though. 'Like I said, it's your life. And don't bloody swear at me.'

'Are you sure you don't mind keeping her an extra couple of nights?' I'm desperate to change the subject.

'Course not. She's no bother. Off in her own world most of the time. No bother,' Mam repeats, and her eyes dart up like she's trying to keep a lid on saying something else.

It's me who keeps a lid on my urge to shout *What's your fucking problem?* I grit my teeth instead. There's a tension in the air so thick it's liquid. We're both boiling away, waiting to see who will bubble over first. I need to move, do something, so I go over and sit with Natasha on the carpet.

'Hi Mummy,' she says, as I plonk myself down.

'Hi darling. What are you up to?'

'I've just drawn this.' Natasha holds up a green piece of paper. I take it off her and examine it. There's a series of spirals and patterns, all interlocking as they disappear off into the background. A swirling, multi-colour cyclone.

'It's lovely,' I say, my heart beating a little bit faster. 'What is it?'

'It's a singularity.'

'A *what?*'

She giggles. 'A singularity. It's where our world merges into another one.'

Something about what she says, and the way she says it, rattles me. I examine her face, put my hand up to stroke her hair, and that feeling about missing her, about her being different every time I see her, intensifies. For a second, it's like I don't know her – like she isn't mine.

It terrifies me.

'I don't understand. . .'

'It's like a door,' she says. She pauses for a moment, like she's letting me take it in. Then she continues, 'It's for you.'

'Thank you, Natasha.'

Pins and needles prickle my feet, my legs and my arms.

'It's okay,' she says. 'Put it on the fridge, near the other one.'

'I wanted to ask you about the other one,' I say, finding my voice again.

'What about it?'

'I noticed that there was a creepy man next to Daddy.'

'Oh yeah, him,' she says, sighing.

'Who is he?'

'That's easy – he's an Unseelie.'

'What's an Unseelie?'

'Like a spaceman.' She thinks for a moment, her head tilted. 'Like a fairy.'

'A made-up thing,' I say. 'Like the Gruffalo?'

'No, he's real,' she says, smiling. Her grin doesn't sit right on her cherubic face. It looks forced, mechanical.

'Right, that's told me then.' I take a breath and reach into my bag for my purse, open it and pull out a twenty. 'This money is for you and Nana and Grandad. Thought you could get Domino's or something.'

'Thank you, Claire,' Natasha says.

I don't know how to respond at first. Is this down to Mam? Is she just picking up on her calling me by my name? I decide not to say anything. I don't want to create a scene. I just want to leave.

'I better get going. I'll see you Sunday.'

I kiss her, pull her close and hug her, and then I get up, giddy. I steady myself and go over to Mam. She's sitting at the dining table, idly flicking through one of those tacky celebrity gossip magazines.

'I'll be back Sunday afternoon,' I say. 'See you then.'

She doesn't even bother to look up.

'You will.'

In the car outside, I start to cry. It comes over me, this horrible feeling of dread. I feel like I'm being watched. I peer out of the windscreen, and then I check the rear-view mirrors, do a quick scan around the street, but I can't see anyone. I get myself together, and then I drive home.

———

It's Friday night, and by the look of the avenue, it's going to be another busy one.

Princes Avenue and Newland Avenue have, over the last decade or so, become the *places to be* in Hull. It's funny how things happen. I remember when George Street in the town centre used to be packed every weekend, and Princes Avenue used to be comprised of laundrettes, second-hand shops and student accommodation.

It was Pave that started it. It was a long shot to say the least. Who'd have thought a European-style café bar would succeed in Hull of all places? And not only was it a success, but it kick-started a café-bar gold rush that continues to this day, completely transforming The Avenues, and nights out in Hull.

I was lucky. Right place at the right time. I had loads of experience, and I was hungry, a little bit desperate. My Great Adventure in Spain was over, and I was back in Hull. Determined to make something of myself. Now here I am, over ten years later, managing the place and running the show.

Dan's on the bar when I get in. I say hello, remember the strange dream I had and find myself blushing.

'Alright boss?' he says.

'Fine,' I say, as I look away.

I get everything sorted for the night. There's six staff on. That's two of the newbies on the floor collecting glasses and tidying up and four more experienced staff on the bar, serving. One of the guys on the bar will stock up when there's a lull, and another will fetch the glasses from the wash and put them away behind the bar as and when is needed. Dan's in charge; he'll be keeping track of the tills – cash-drops and change – and will also be telling the rest of the staff what to do.

'Swap them around from time to time,' I tell him. 'Stops them from pissing about and moaning they're getting all the shit jobs, plus it trains up the newer staff.'

Dan's only been Bar Supervisor for a couple weeks, but I can tell already that he's up to the task.

'Thanks again for this opportunity Claire,' he says.

'It's fine Dan,' I say. 'You've been here long enough already to know how it works. If there's anything you need, gimme a shout.'

'Will do, boss.'

I can't help but admire his arse as he leaves the office. It's the tight black trousers, they do wonders for him. I settle down to get on with some paperwork. There's the stock order to do, plus the rotas for the next couple of weeks. It feels good to get my head into something, push everything else out of my mind for a bit. When it gets to about ten, I step outside the office and go into the bar. It's heaving – Friday night in

97

full swing. I stand at the end of the bar, have a look around. The young and beautiful are in, along with the slightly older who still think they're young and beautiful. Lots of fake tan and whitened teeth flashing about. I watch Dan at the bar. He seems confident and a little cocksure, something that's essential if you're hoping to run things. He sees me watching him and he smiles, tips his head in acknowledgment.

It's locking up time, so I take the opportunity to show Dan how to cash up the safe so it's ready to bank in the morning. After the bar has been stocked and the chairs have been put on the tables, I let the rest of the staff go and lock the front door after them. Dan and I move into the office in the back.

As we're counting the money, his hand brushes against my leg.

'I'm sorry,' he says.

'It's okay,' I try not to allow myself to get flustered.

He takes my calm as sign, places his hand on my thigh. He leans in for a kiss. As his lips are about to touch mine, I push him away.

'What's wrong?' he asks. He frowns in a way that suggests he doesn't get turned down very often.

'Nothing,' I say.

With what must be a practised effort at "smouldering", he tilts his face forward and looks up at me.

'I've seen the way you look at me.'

For the first time in a while, I feel warm down there. He's fit, a good-looking lad, but there's something more than that. It's a daft thing, but he reminds of me of Kirk, my high-school boyfriend. He's got the same jawline, the same bushy, caveman eyebrows hovering above baby-blue eyes.

Poor Kirk. Mam always said he was a loser, always said I could do better.

I broke his heart.

'I can't do this Dan.'

'Why not?'

'Because I'm married.'

'No one needs to know,' he says, a hint of desperation creeping in.

'That's not the point,' I say.

'So what is the point?'

I sigh and sit down at the desk. 'The point is that I'm nearly old enough to be your mother.'

'Bollocks, you're not old. You're what, thirty-five?'

I laugh. 'This is all very flattering Dan, but let me tell you a bit about myself,' I say.

He sits down. 'Go on then.'

'I started working here about ten years ago. When I was your age – probably a bit younger actually – I went over to Spain to work as a holiday rep. I'd had enough of Hull, thought it was a shithole. I looked at all my surroundings, my mates, and I thought *Fuck that*.'

'I can understand that.'

'I got a job in a bar. Worked my way up and made a good life for myself. But I ended up coming back here. Made a few bad choices, had to start from the beginning, back to square one. Worked my arse off until I made my way up to where I am now. And then I met Max. He was a bit younger than me, but that didn't matter. On a whim, we got married and then I got pregnant. Things were great for a while, but it's all started to turn to shit.'

'What's this got to do with us?'

I laugh again. 'Because as tempting as it is, there *is* no *us*, Dan. Don't get me wrong, I'm very flattered, but I'm not going to become one of those Prinny-Ave cougars who fuck all the young barmen because they're bored and have problems at home. I've got too much respect for myself. I guess what I'm trying to say is thanks, but no thanks.'

Dan shifts in his seat, embarrassed. 'I'm sorry, I didn't mean to insult you or anything, I just thought. . . '

I hold up my hand, cutting him off. 'I know, Dan. Don't worry about it. And don't take it personally,' I say. 'You're cute, but please... don't ever make another pass at me, or you'll be out the door.'

He stands up. He looks uneasy. 'Thanks for showing me the safe stuff, I better get going.' His face flushes red. 'I'll see you next week, boss.'

'See you later, Dan,' I say, as he practically runs out the door. I expect he'll be handing in his notice in the next week or so, and I'll be looking for another bar supervisor. Shame.

———

I stop off for some more wine before I start for home. I feel tired but strangely elated. I'm going over various scenarios in my mind involving Dan, most of them sexual. As I pull into the drive I notice that the kitchen light is on, but there's no sign of Max's car. After I get out of my car, I walk up the path and check the front door. It's unlocked. I open it, slowly, and stick my head in.

'Max?'

There's no response. I creep into the living room. There's a silhouette in the chair. 'Max?'

'Yeah,' the shape in the corner responds.

'You scared me. What's going on? Where's the car?'

I click on a lamp and see Max slumped in the chair, glass in hand, a bottle of scotch by his feet. He looks terrible, like he hasn't slept in days. I take the opportunity to go and fetch a wine glass and a bottle-opener. There's a loud *plunk* as I pull the cork, followed by the satisfying *glug-glug* of wine filling the glass. I pour a large one, knowing I'll need it.

I reach into the cupboard for my secret cig stash, take one out of the packet. I go back into the living room to try again.

'Come on, Max. After last night's dramatics you made it perfectly clear that you needed some space, so why are you here?'

100

'Do I have to justify being in my own fucking house now?' he snaps.

'As a matter of fact, yes, you do,' I say, calmly.

'There's no let up with you, is there?' he sneers.

'Get over yourself. Don't treat me like a mug. What do you want, Max?'

He lets out a long sigh, put his hands over his face and sits forward on the chair. 'Everything's fucked up, Claire.'

'Tell me something I don't know.'

'Just give it a rest, will you?' his voice is becoming strained.

'Just tell me what's going on, Max.'

He sits back, rubs his forehead. 'It's the gambling, Claire,' he says bluntly.

It's my turn to sigh. I light up a cigarette. 'Well, there's no point pretending I've quit smoking anymore, I suppose.'

He looks at me, gives me the puppy dog eyes. I stare at him impassively. Rage is beginning to boil deep within my stomach. It's everything I can do to not fly off the handle at him.

'What about the gambling, Max?'

'I'm in trouble, Claire. Serious trouble.' He sounds weak, pathetic.

'How serious?' I ask.

'Very.' He's mumbling, now.

'How fucking serious Max?' I shout.

He starts crying. It's a shock. It isn't like Max, at all. He's never been one for emotions. Even when things are bad he still has that fucking *front*, that fucking attitude.

'Six-figures,' he says.

I feel sick, dizzy.

'Jesus. Fucking. Christ.'

I finish my glass and pour more wine. My mind is all over the place. I don't know what to think. All I can do is mutter, 'Fuck,' over and over again.

'I know, I know,' he keeps saying.

101

'Well. We'll get it sorted. We'll have to.' I'm still trying to get my head around it.

'You don't understand,' Max says. 'These are serious fucking people. A voluntary insolvency order's not going to cut it with them. I have to pay – or else.'

He continues sobbing, which winds me up. I start shivering, and I put my glass down so I can clench my fists like I'm gearing up for a fight. My palms are sweaty, and I try and control my breathing.

'In that case, you're on your own. You go ahead and ruin your life, you're not ruining mine and Natasha's,' I shout.

'That's the thing. They know about you and the bar. And these people, they. . . '

But I don't let him finish. I'm out of the chair and across the room. I don't mess around with a slap. Go straight in with a punch, which lands squarely in his face, splatting his nose. He tries grabbing my wrists, but I completely lose it and I manage to overpower him. We end up rolling around on the floor. I'm punching the fuck out of him and he just gives in, submits. He puts his arms up, tries to block some of the blows that I'm raining down on him. I stop then. Get up off him.

My knuckles are red, aching. They're beginning to swell, already. I pick up my glass with my left hand. Max lies on the ground, defeated. His face is bloodied and bruised.

'You've never given two shits about me or Natasha, have you?' I say.

He drags himself up off the carpet and back into the chair. Blood is all over the place. The carpet, the sofa; there's even some on the patio doors. It looks like a murder scene.

'How can you say that? I mean, she's my daughter,' he says, and uses his sleeve to wipe the blood off his mouth and face. Little specks of it flick onto the arm of his chair.

'Well. A big round of applause for you! I'll be sure to remind her of that after some fucker's burned down the house.'

I'm shaking, panting. Adrenalin is still running around my body. I go into the kitchen and get some paper towels. I use some to get the blood of my knuckles, and then head back into the living room.

'Stop bleeding all over my furniture!' I sling the towels at him. Sitting down, I light up another cigarette. 'So what now? Where's the car?'

He tears a couple of sheets from the roll.

'I've sold it,' he says, dabbing his nose.

'Where's the money?'

'I've given it to them, bought us a bit of time.'

'Are you sure?'

'What do you mean, *am I sure?* You don't think I'd gamble that as well, do you?'

'I'm not going to answer that,' I say. 'First things first: I want you out of here. For good.' He opens his mouth, as if he's going to object, but stops himself. 'Secondly, I want you to tell me everything you know about these people.'

He nods. 'And then?'

I take another sip of wine. 'And then... I don't know,' I say.

He looks down at the floor, and then he stands up, reaches around and takes something out of his pocket. 'I think they sent this,' he says, handing me the paper.

I open it up. My heart sinks when I realise it's a photo of our house. In black and white, and there's a strange symbol on it. I can make out the silhouette of something in the front window.

'What the fuck is this?'

'I don't know,' he says. 'It came through the post the other day.'

For some reason, the picture reminds of the one on the fridge. 'Has Natasha seen this?'

'What do you mean?' he replies, angry. 'Do you really think I'd show her some fucked up shit like this?'

I don't answer for a while. Then I say, 'I want you to pack your stuff and leave.'

'Claire?'

'Tonight,' I say. 'Now.'

He looks at me, lost for a moment. I don't meet his gaze. I look down at the floor, and then I pick up my glass and have another drink.

He gets up and trudges upstairs. I can hear him banging about, opening and shutting drawers and cabinets.

I finish my cigarette, sit down on the sofa, kick my shoes off and light up another. What a day.

I hate drama, don't have time for it. Some people I know thrive on it, get off on it. A cursory glance at Facebook is enough to demonstrate that. That's why I hardly use it. Status update: My life is fucked but look at me.

Look at me.

I think of Natasha, Mam, and the situation with Dan at work, and now this shit. I take another sip of wine, close my eyes, and I imagine that I'm back in Spain. I've just finished a shift, and even though it's late, it's still warm and I can smell the sea, hear the rush of the waves as they break against the beach, and I don't have to be up early, so I can just sit here, take it all in.

The front door slams and I jump. I'm dragged back to this house, this present.

And I'm on my own again.

9

Gaz (and Chris)

My phone going off wakes me. I'm crashed out on my sofa with my shirt on, but my trousers have gone missing.

I answer the phone. 'Who is it?'

Pause. 'It's Chris.'

'Alright Chris. What time is it?'

'Eleven-ish,' he says.

'What's going on? What's happening?'

'That's why I'm ringing you.'

I rub my eyes, let out a big fart.

'What do you mean?'

'I'm ringing you to find out what's going on,' he says. 'Y'know... have we got any work on today?'

I take a moment. I take two. I can hear Chris breathing down the line. Donna must be on at him, little fucker, bet he's climbing the walls.

'Course we have,' I say. 'I'll be around in the next hour or so.'

I drag myself up and head to the toilet. Take my phone with me. Sitting down to curl one off, I notice a text message on my phone.

– HI GAZ THIS IS LIZZIE. REMBR ME? U NEED TO FUCKIN RING ME. NOW. IT'S SERIOUS.

I've only met her the once and that was – what – a month or so ago?

I didn't even know she'd got my number.

Fuck. What does she want?

Tatting.

I used to go tatting with the lads years ago. Back when we were at Amy Johnson. Me, Chris, Pete Ashworth, Barry Thompson; a couple of others.

You leave school and you don't have any qualifications. You don't have a job. You get offered some bullshit apprenticeship in a butcher's shop. You last six weeks. And at the same time, you want to be out and about getting fucked up and fucking birds, but you don't have any money. You're skint. So you go tatting.

Scrap metal, that's what it's all about. Copper. Lead. Tin. Aluminium. Find it and then go and weigh it in at the yard. If you do enough graft, a fucking barrowful, that's the weekend sorted.

You hang around some of the factories on Hessle Road. Get the offcuts from the bins, only takes three of you. One in the bins going through it all; one on the fence passing the stuff over; one outside on look-out, filling the barrow. After a good haul you stash the full barrow, fetch it in the morning, then take it to the yard and weigh it in. If it's good enough, you receive enough for a tenner deal of rez, some trips and a bit of Billy. *Weekend sorted.*

And here I am twenty years later, stood in front of the bathroom mirror, scrubbing my face with a flannel, getting my sorry arse ready to go out and do pretty much the same kind of work.

I rub my chin, wondering whether I should bother shaving.

106

Twenty years later. At least I'm well-preserved. Fairly. There are more lines on my face, sure, and the bags under my eyes are a lot bigger and hold more regrets, but I'm still tall, dark, and handsome.

I've still got my hair, so there's that.

———

It's after eleven when I pick Chris up from his house on De La Pole Ave. He looks like shit, worse than I do. Donna comes out with him to the van, like she's his mam, seeing him off to work. She stands there with her arms folded, glaring at me as Chris gets into the van.

'How's it going, Donna?' I ask.

'I want a word with you,' she says.

'Oh yeah?'

Chris shuffles in his seat. 'Donna, please go inside.'

She reaches up, stops him from shutting the door. She looks at me, the *bad influence*, gives me the daggers.

'Whatever he earns today, he brings home.'

Donna's quite a bit older than Chris, and they give off a strange mother-and-son type of vibe. I don't know what he sees in her, but she must do something for him, because they've bred. Twice.

I laugh.

'What *is* this? I don't have any influence over Chris. He's a grown man, he does what he wants.'

'Fuck off. When's he's out with you he wants to get pissed and go gambling, when what he *needs* to do is come home. We've got mouths to feed.'

'And some big ones at that,' I say under my breath.

'What was that?'

'Nothing,' I say, and I start rummaging around the dashboard, like I'm searching for a lighter or something.

Chris sits there, the naughty kid.

'We have to get going now, Donna,' he says weakly.

She turns her cheek towards him. He leans over and kisses it.

'Love you, baby,' she says.

'Love you, baby,' he replies.

After she slams the door shut, I watch her waddle back into the house. Staring at Chris, I say, 'Fuck me. . . '

'Don't you fucking start,' he says. 'I had a drink last night and I don't remember anything after a certain time. I wake up this morning and I don't know where I am, and there's this swooshing sound, and something hits me right in the face.'

I grab the wheel and press my foot down on the accelerator. As we move away from the house, Chris continues.

'I try moving but my arms are trapped. Then something hits me in the face again. I realise I'm in the bath, fully clothed, and Donna is at the door, slinging her shoes at me. Fucking nightmare.'

'That's fucking priceless,' I say, unable to contain my laugher. 'Really is.'

I was given a tip-off yesterday about another house clearance down Airlie Street, so I drive in that direction. It's hard to believe how much the area's changed.

Driving down Hawthorn Avenue from Anlaby Road, I remember how I used to walk that way to school just about every day for nearly five years, me and some of the lads. Past the terraced houses of Greek Street and Argyle Street. Although the streets are still there in name, most of the houses have gone. Of the blocks that remain, most of them are boarded up, with big signs that say ALL GAS AND WATER PIPES HAVE BEEN REMOVED stuck to the walls. A few years back, there was a small fortune to be made by breaking into the abandoned houses and stripping them of copper, but people started taking the piss and eventually the council wised up to it and started bricking up the doors and windows.

New-build houses are clumped together on one side of Hawthorn Avenue, overlooking the remaining two-up, two-downs. Amy Johnson is long gone of course, the only thing of her that remains is the name, now attached to the seed of a new estate that's been planted and is growing outwards to envelop the whole area.

Further down, Woodcock Street – which links Hawthorn Ave with St George's Road – serves as the prototype for this regeneration. Once a total no-go zone, it's completely unremarkable now, a haven of identical modern houses aimed at young families and first-time buyers. Its smack-addled past reputation all scrubbed off and resigned to the dustbin of memory.

'What did you get up to last night then?' Chris asks.

I'm waiting for him to bring up the twenty that I still owe him from last month, but he doesn't, so I decide not to mention it until he does.

'Had a drink. A smoke. Then I passed out.'

'Right,' he says, vacantly.

Chris looks tired and haggard. To look at him you'd think he'd been up all night, smoking, drinking and shagging. It's a shame really. Chris is one of those people who got to twenty and stopped aging. Always been fresh-faced, like a young kid. But a couple of years ago, his hairline receded, rapidly. His curly blond hair started falling out at an alarming rate. He looked odd, with his baby face and increasing baldness, like a cartoon character. He's dead sensitive about it, which is understandable. I'd fucking kill myself if I started losing my hair.

'What's going on Chris? You look like shit.'

'Well, when I woke up the kids were already awake, and Donna was in a mood, so there was no chance of sneaking off to bed for a bit. And the kids are loud and running about, and Donna's barking at them to shut up, and... y'know.'

'Kids, eh?' I say.

'Hey, speaking of which, have you got in touch with –'

'Let's not talk about that right now,' I say, and the conversation ends there.

We pull onto Hessle Road, past Asda and the Half-Way; past St George's Road and the big Wilson shoe store before arriving at Airlie Street.

'What's the score with this then?' Chris says.

'Could be a good one,' I say, craning my neck as I look around for the right house. Number twenty-seven. I spot it and there's a space just opposite. In a demonstration of excellent accelerator and brake control, I park the van smoothly.

'Just got to give Kev a call.'

I take my phone from the dashboard and look through the contacts, settling on 'BIG KEV'.

He picks up. 'Hello?'

'Kev, it's Gaz,' I say.

'Where the fuck have you been?' He doesn't sound too happy.

'I said we would be round late morning,' I reply.

'I know but. . . '

'Listen, we're here now. Where are you?'

'I'm just on road, be there in five.'

'See ya in a bit.'

'Yeah,' he says, and hangs up.

Chris rubs his temples and stares out the window at the house.

'So this is it?'

'Yup. House clearance. Kev's one of me mate's uncles. Owns a few properties around here. He had some fucking dickheads holed up in here. All sorts of capers going on. Fucking scumbags, total menaces. The whole street was kicking off and complaining.'

'Some fucking people.'

'I know. Anyway, things were about to get ugly and they just bailed one night. Disappeared with six months' rent owing, but I think he was just glad to get rid of the cunts.'

'Damn right.'

With that, I spot Kev at the top of the street. Hard not to, really – he's a big bloke, almost as wide as he is tall. Has a huge nose with a massive 'tache, like a great, furry creature that has fallen asleep on his lip. He looks like a cross between Super Mario and Giant Haystacks.

'Jesus Christ,' Chris mutters.

'I know. Fucker's sensitive about his weight, so watch what you say. Don't be fooled by his size. He was a boxer back in the day, a right hard bastard. He might look like a walrus, but he moves like a fucking cat.'

I open the door and slide off my seat and out of the van. Chris does the same, and we wait near the front door. Ten minutes later, a sweaty, red-faced Kev approaches. He pauses a moment, places his hand on the van.

'Alright lads,' he says, puffing. 'Heat's fucking relentless today, innit? Feel like I'm in the foreign legion all over again.'

'Alright Kev,' I say, offering my hand. 'Where was you?'

He gives my hand a bone-rattling shake.

'I was in the café,' he says.

'I bet they do well when you're in, eh?' Chris says, and starts laughing. No one joins in, so he stops, abruptly.

Kev stands up straight and eyeballs him.

'*What* did you say?'

'Er, nowt mate.'

I'm tempted to say nothing, let Chris dig himself in deeper until he gets gobbed, but we've got work to do so I try to change the subject.

'Sorry we were late, Kev. But we're all revved up and ready to go.'

Kev's still staring at Chris.

'Shall we have a look then?' I say, loudly, hoping to break the tension.

Without taking his eyes off Chris, Kev reaches into his pocket and pulls out his keys. It's your standard terraced house, no front garden. Kev pops his key in the latch.

'Had to get new locks fitted and everything,' he says, opening the door. 'After you, fellas.'

Chris and I walk in. It has the typical terrace interior: a hallway leading directly to the bottom of the stairs, with the living room off to the left as you walk in. Dankness hits us, the air thick with the fusty smell of damp and fermenting rubbish. As we enter the living room we're confronted with a scene of utter devastation. The room is filled floor-to-ceiling with junk and debris. There're three huge, old TVs, a sofa that has been mortally wounded and is spilling its foamy guts all over the floor, a smashed sound-system with pock-marked speakers, and countless bags filled with god-knows-what.

Tattered scraps of wallpaper peel away from the moon-crater surface of plasterboard, which has been scribbled on over and over again. A mad scramble of indistinguishable marker-pen cave-art. Bike frames lean against one wall, a sagging bookshelf overrun with various tins and bits of bric-a-brac slouches against another.

Discoloured curtains, thick with dust, stop the sun from throwing light on this whole sorry scene.

'Fuck me, what happened?' Chris says, and the question is left hanging like the shredded lightshade that dangles from the ceiling.

Kev appears. Stands with us for a moment while we take it all in.

'Wait until you see the fucking kitchen,' he says.

On the one hand, I'm happy because this job is a lot bigger than I initially thought – so it will be a bigger earner – but on the other hand the idea of spending a couple of days in this shithole fills me with utter dread.

'Before we go any further, we need to talk about money, Kev,' I say.

He sighs. 'Fair do's.'

'I mean, what are we talking here? I was expecting this to be a couple of hours tops, but this... this is something else.'

'How long do you think it will take?'

112

I look around the room. 'I'm assuming the rest of the house is this bad.'

'You assume correctly.'

'This room, the kitchen, two bedrooms and the bathroom,' I say, counting on my fingers. 'All need doing?'

'Yeah.'

I think about it for a couple of minutes, stroke my chin like I'm making some big calculations.

'Two days, two-hundred quid.'

Chris scoffs, is about to say something, then Kev shoots him that look, so he doesn't say anything.

'Done. Plus, you get to keep whatever you scrap. I'm talking totally stripped out: radiators, boilers, everything. Back to square one.'

'Chris?'

He smiles sweetly at Kev, says, 'Sounds good to me.'

Kev gives me another overly powerful handshake to seal the deal.

'If you feel like tackling the yard, there will be a bit more cash for you. Let me know.'

'Will do.'

'I'll order a skip and get it dropped off this aft. Know someone who'll do me a good deal.'

'Sorted,' I say. 'We'll get started right away.'

Kev reaches into his pocket, pulls out some notes. Counts out a hundred in new, crisp twenties.

'Half up-front. Do a good job and I might have a bit more work for you. If you take the piss, you and the little gobshite here will be looking over your shoulders every time you're up this end of Hull. Got it?'

Chris nods his head, stares down at his feet.

'Of course, Kev, you don't need to tell us,' I say. 'We're professionals.'

Kev exits.

Chris waits until the door slams shut, says, 'What a cock.'

113

'I fucking told you,' I say. 'I specifically said, 'Don't get lippy', and what do you do? I mean, you hardly ever fucking say owt, and when you do, it's to the one guy you shouldn't say owt to.'

'I can't help it if the fat fucker hasn't got a sense of humour.'

There's no point carrying on this conversation, I can tell Chris feels as though he's the one who's been wronged somehow. Always the fucking victim. I change the subject.

'Shall we have a look around the rest of the place?'

'Yes. Let's.'

I find an old cricket bat near the fireplace and use it like an explorer would a machete in the Amazon, whacking aside boxes and rubbish to clear a path into the kitchen. It's just as bleak. Cupboard doors hang from their hinges. A bin, overflowing with empty tins and takeaway boxes, occupies the corner. A battered washing machine and dryer are huddled together by a sink stacked with filthy pots and pans – now home to a diverse range of fungus and insect life. More bags cover every work surface. We peer though the dirty window into the garden. Huge, wild weeds and nettles battle for supremacy.

'This is so fucking grim,' Chris says, booting the washing machine. 'At least we might do well for scrap out of it.'

We retrace our steps through the valley of rubbish that I cleared, back into the living room, and then on into the hallway, up the steep stairs onto the landing.

'Holy shit,' Chris says, shaking his head in disbelief.

One of the bedroom doors has evidently been hit with such force that the entire doorframe has come loose from the wall.

'Holy shit,' I repeat.

'What do you think happened?'

'Fuck knows. Looks like something massive was trying to escape.'

'Maybe one of them tried doing a rattle, got locked in here and then changed his mind at the last minute.'

'Maybe.'

The front bedroom has a mattress on the floor. More bags and junk are strewn everywhere. We also find a yellow box with a biohazard sign on it, a needle depository.

'Definitely a gloves-on job,' I say.

Chris carefully navigates his way through all the crap to have a look in the other room while I continue looking around this one. I come to a stop in front of a wall covered in more gibberish and scribbles. Highlights include: "Amend your deed" and "Too vast". A good one is "Nothing, nothing, nothing".

'Gary, you need to see this,' Chris shouts from the other room.

I step over the mattress and make my way through. It's full of the same carnage, and home an army of flies. Chris is standing in the middle of the room. He looks at me, points at the wall.

'What is that all about?'

The wall he's facing has been completely stripped of wallpaper. There's a huge, black, ink drawing of some sort of spiral, like a cross-section of a tornado or something. Surrounding it are loads of little scribbled numbers, and smaller pictures of the spiral as seen from different angles. Looking closer, I deduce that the numbers are all equations. It resembles a roulette wheel in places.

'Wow,' I say, searching for words. 'That's something else.'

'Really fucking freaky, that's what this is.' Chris takes his phone from his jeans' pocket. He holds it up and takes a few pictures. 'This is next-level fucked up.'

I notice a green blackboard, like the ones they had at school, against one of the walls. More equations – this time in chalk – cover it. Chris takes a photo of that as well.

'This is definitely going on Facebook,' he says. 'I wonder what it all means.'

I have no answer, but I try to come up with one anyway.

'Just fucking smack-rats. Out of their faces, doing mad shit. That's all this is.'

'Very *creative* smack-rats, weren't they?'

Looking around, I notice loads of jars and beakers, full of various liquids and sludge.

'It's like some sort of fucked-up laboratory,' I say.

'Could you imagine having to live like this?'

'No. Don't get me wrong, I've lived in some mad places, but this is next-level shit.'

'I suppose we better get cracking.' Chris stares at his phone.

'I suppose you're right.'

'What the fuck is this?'

Chris holds up a jam jar. It's filled to the brim with something.

'Fuck knows. Are they pills?'

'Don't think so,' he says, and then he starts unscrewing the lid.

'Are you sure that's a good idea?'

'I'm just curious,' he says, removing the lid. He puts his hand in, pulls out one of the white objects and holds it up. 'Nah, they're not pills, they're. . .'

'Seeds?' I take one from the jar and place it on my palm. I can feel it tingle in my hand.

'Yeah, they are, I think,' Chris says. He looks at me. 'We've seen these before, haven't we?'

I'm staring down at the thing in my palm, when. . .

. . . *Pete doesn't even ask what they are. Just grabs one and pops it in his mouth. Soon as he swallows it, Barry cracks up.*

'*What's so fucking funny?' Jamie asks.*

'*Sorry,' Barry says, laughing. 'I don't know what they are. I found them at the back of the field.'*

Kirk grabs Barry, gives him a dig. Pete sticks his fingers down his throat, makes himself throw up. Me and Chris get hold of Barry, and then Kirk makes him eat the rest of whatever they were, to teach him a lesson.

'What the *fuck* was that?' Chris says, swaying.

I blink a few times as though I've just woken up. Chris is looking at me, wide-eyed. 'What?'

'I was thinking back to a night, years ago. But for a moment. . . '

'Shit, *you* felt it too? It was like it was fucking real,' I say. 'That was fucking freaky.'

We look down at the jar, and then each other.

'This is fucked up,' Chris says. 'What do we do with them?'

I've been thinking a lot about the past lately. That fucking nostalgia creeping in. But this was different. It was like a bridge to better times. Simpler times. It felt good. All my worries fell away, and for a moment, it felt as though I could change things. I was back then, but I still knew what I know now. For the first time in a long time, I felt like I had the power to change things. I want to feel like that again.

I place the seed back into the jar.

'Let's get rid of them.' I say. 'I wouldn't want them getting into the hands of any kids or owt like that.'

We've still got the bathroom to inspect. I'm trembling, a buzz that pings around my body like the onset of a good pill. Out on the landing I walk up to the door, place my hand on it to push it open and Chris says, 'Don't.'

'What?'

'I've seen enough for now. Let's get on with the living room and we'll have a look tomorrow.'

'What's wrong?' I say, and I'm about to start taking the piss, but Chris cuts me off.

'Seriously, this is all a bit fucking tapped. Take the piss if you want, but I just want to get on with it and go home. I feel like shit after last night, anyway.'

He trudges down the stairs.

We go back out to the van and get our gear. Gloves, shovels, bin bags and we just go for it, starting with the living room. Kev's true to his word and it doesn't take long for the skip to show up. We separate things into two piles: shit that goes straight in the skip, and shit that might be worth something. As well as the usual bags of newspapers and magazines that you always find in shitholes like this, there are some other things that turn up, some of which you don't expect.

I put the jar of seeds into a little box, pack it with paper, and stash it in the bottom of the skip.

'Check this out,' Chris says, dragging a black bin bag into the space we've managed to clear in the middle of the room.

He opens the bag and it's full of old *Fisher Price* toys and shit like that. Proper old school shit. The telephone with the eyes and wheels, the jumbo jet airport set, the little record player with the chunky dayglow discs. All these bright lumps of plastic.

'Fuck me,' Chris says, pulling an egg-shaped figure from the sack. 'It's a Weeble.'

'They wibble and they wobble, but they don't fall down.'

'It's fucking Kev,' he says, laughing, and I laugh too.

Chris can be a funny guy sometimes. He used to be a funny guy all the time, but then he got with Donna and starting popping kids out. And now he's getting old. And bald.

Chris holds up the little egg-bloke. On closer inspection, we realise that the Weeble is a milkman. He doesn't have any limbs, but he has a moulded cap, a satchel and a determined grimace. Chris has another rummage, and he finds his milk float. He seems genuinely excited by this discovery.

'Now this is what you fucking *call* a toy. These were great. I remember playing with shit like this at nursery. Plane Street church... mental,' he says, and then he sighs. He's not taking the piss, either. He's being sincere. I can tell by the way the air escapes his nostrils that he's having a moment.

'Plane Street church, eh?'

I don't know what happened with Plane Street church. I can understand it when shops or businesses fail, die off and leave behind the corpse of an empty building. Shit goes wrong, the owners can't pay the bills, so they move out.

Either someone else takes over the space and establishes something else, or they don't, and the building stays empty. Vacant. That's how it is. But a church? I mean, aren't they paid for? Don't they get their rent and bills and that paid for?

'Do you remember that night we broke in there? Tripping out of our fucking minds.'

'I do, and it still feels wrong,' Chris says. 'In some way, y'know. Sacred ground and all that.'

'You fucking fanny,' I say. 'Get over yourself. It was just fucking metal, after all. And you don't have to worry about God, he'd fucked off along with the vicars.'

'It *was* fucking mental though, weren't it Gary?' Chris says, animated. 'Do you remember when we found all them fucking bibles?'

'Yeah, I do,' I say.

And all of a sudden, it's there again. Nostalgia. Thinking back to a time when things were simple (well, simpler). It's funny, but at the time I never would have guessed that out of all of them – Steve, Kirk, Pete, Jamie and the rest – Chris would turn out to be the most loyal, the mate who stuck with me.

Inevitably, thoughts of the past soon turn to Gemma and the kids, so I really throw myself into clearing out the room we're in. Chris picks up on my silence.

'Are you sure everything is okay with you, Gaz? You seem really down at the mo.'

'Isn't everyone?'

10

Jamie (and Kirk)

The bus is chock-full of passengers. It's also late.

The LED sign at the stop flashes up with the number and time of the next bus, and it's never accurate. I leave the house at the same time every morning, and the buses turn up whenever they get around to it. Sometimes, they pull up as I'm crossing the road. Sometimes, they take ten minutes. Sometimes, twenty. All the while the sign ticks down at random intervals. One morning it said that the bus would be arriving in three minutes. It stayed stuck on three for around eleven minutes before it turned into two. *Eleven minutes.* I timed it on my phone.

When the bus eventually arrives, I'm disheartened to find that there's standing room only. I get on and the driver sticks his head out of his cubicle and turns to the passengers.

'Move down, move down,' he shouts. 'There's more than enough room down there for a few more people. We've got more stops before town.'

Everyone looks at me as though I've walked on and got my cock out. I reach into the inside pocket of my jacket, find my buds and stuff them into my ears, put some music on.

Squeezing past a bunch of people I search for a slightly less crowded spot. I'm sweating from the body-heat and bumping into everyone. It's claustrophobic. Feels as though half of Hull is here, all crammed in together. The spaces at the front are occupied by a couple of young mams with their prams and an old woman in a wheelchair. My way is blocked by a couple of teenagers. One of them is a girl with long dark hair, a lip-piercing and goth-style make-up. She's with this tall, thin, reedy lad with angular hair and a nose that seems to point in the same direction as his fringe. I smile and nod as I barge past them, knocking into the lad, which elicits a harsh gaze from the girl. I shrug, mumble and aim to combine politeness with determination.

The bus sets off, bouncing down the road. I try to zone out, just set my eyes on a spot somewhere outside the window, on the vista of Anlaby Road as it sweeps past, its odd assortment of short, mismatched shop fronts; pubs, streets and side-roads.

We reach the stop at West Park, just before the flyover. The doors swing open, and I see the driver's left arm sticking out of the cab waving people back further. There's a huddle as everyone moves to accommodate the new passengers. I tighten my grip on the rail so as not to lose my balance. Strangers' backs press against me. I'm surrounded. Sweat trickles down my forehead. As the bus starts to climb up the flyover, I try and sway with its motion so I don't knock into anyone. The trees of West Park give way to the KC Stadium.

A lot of people get off at Hull Royal. I climb the stairs and manage to get a seat at the front of the top deck for the last few stops before the station. I can't help but look up at Thornton Estate flats as we pass them. Hull is a level city. Anything tall enough to break the skyline stands out. Big, garish, blocks decorated with a haphazard pattern of pastel-coloured rectangles. Shirts and linen pegged out on balconies flap in the wind, making the windows wink. *The building is in on the joke.*

The bus rolls past the Tiger's Lair, past the site of the old New York, past the chip shop and the Tower. It stops at the lights just before it turns onto Ferensway. I glance to the left, into the network of mirrors on the exterior of the corner building. I'm looking at the reflection of the bus I'm currently sat in. Broken into sections. I can see a gold-tinted me, sat in the other bus. Like me, he's sitting at the front of the top deck and he's looking back at me. I wave. He waves back.

The bus turns left onto Ferensway, passes the Station Hotel and the front of the station. Saint Stephen's shopping centre looms up to one side. It's tall and modern, with a glass-and-steel canopy along the top of it, ending in a curved feature that juts out and covers part of a little square, home to wooden-shed food stalls and children's rides. The angles and general design of the place evoke a ship. Quite a few buildings in Hull take architectural nods from the forms of sea-faring vessels.

A good example is Selby Street – running parallel to the train track under Anlaby Road flyover – where the end-of-terrace houses have patterns in their brickwork. The first is two blokes playing rugby, but the second, and by far the best, is a boat, as seen from the front. A single tiny bedroom window is built into the image as if it's the window on the bridge of the boat. Back when I was a kid, I often used to wonder what it would be like to live in that house, everyone did.

The bus parking bays are situated off a two-lane strip, which ends in a roundabout where the buses turn. It's really cramped and the buses jostle for space, like the passengers have to. It seems to take forever for the bus to park up. I stay in my seat until the doors open. Hopping off, I pass through the sliding door of the station and inside.

I decide to nip into Gregg's and get a sausage-bean-and-cheese melt pasty to eat on my way to work. I savour the warm, congealed, cheesy-bean juice as it oozes into my mouth. From the station, it only takes me a few minutes to reach work. The KC call centre is where I spend half my day trying to flog broadband and TV packages. The other half, I spend manning technical support, which mainly amounts to telling people to push pins into the back of their routers to reset them.

I start the day like every other, with a cup of coffee and a couple of biscuits; adjust my headset and get to work.

'Hi, my name's Jamie, I'm calling on behalf of Kingston Communications. I was just wondering if I could have five minutes of your time in order to tell you about the great new light-speed broadband and telephone package...'

The guys I work with are alright, aside from Gino. He happens to be an enormous bell-end with a planet-sized ego.

'I fucked these two *amazing* birds at the weekend,' he tells us as we have our break.

'At the same time?' Phil asks.

'At the same time, bro,' Gino says, triumphantly.

'What happened?' Mark is wide-eyed with excitement. I want to throw up.

'Yeah, and did it actually happen, or could it be you're making the whole thing up?' I snap.

Gino glowers right at me.

'What is it with you, Jamie? Have you turned into a prude or summat?'

'Oh fuck off, Gino,' I say. 'It's just boring, all your alpha-male bullshit. Maybe if you grew up a bit you wouldn't have to lie about having threesomes.'

I decide to finish my sausage roll back in the staffroom.

———————

The thought of lunch keeps me going. Between calls I run through all the possibilities. I remember that it's Wednesday, which is burrito meal-deal day at *Taco Joe's*, so my decision is settled quite quickly. The question now becomes a choice between pulled-pork, spicy beef or chicken.

The rest of the guys are off to Subway, but I'm still a bit pissed at Gino, so when they ask me, I stick with the burrito option. I get in the lift, head down to reception and step out into the Prospect Centre. Walking past *That's Entertainment*, I hear my name being called, it's a woman's voice. I stop and turn around, try and spot who it is.

'Oi, Jamie, over here!'

I see her then, stood outside *The Card Factory*. It's Sharon, another of Kirk's sisters. I go over to her and she spreads her arms wide, gives me a big hug, something I'm not expecting.

'How are you?' she asks.

We exchange a few pleasantries. Turns out she's been living down Alliance Avenue for the past couple of years, not that far away from me. Hull's strange like that: You can travel half-way across the globe and bump into someone from Hull, and yet you can live in Hull just down the street from someone and never see them about.

The conversation quickly turns to Kirk.

'How is he?' I ask.

Sharon takes a deep breath, shuffles her feet. 'You haven't heard then?'

'Heard what?'

She looks uncomfortable, can't look me in the eyes. After a pause she says, 'You should ring him.'

'Why, what's going on?'

'I don't think you should hear it from me,' she says.

I don't how to respond at first, so I just ask for his number. She reads it out and I put it into my phone.

'Make sure you call him,' she says. 'He'll be pleased to hear from you.'

There's nowhere for the conversation to go after that, so we say our farewells and part ways. I head for the escalator that leads up to the food-court.

I'm distracted for the rest of the afternoon, keep re-running the conversation with Sharon in my head over and over again. I'm not quite sure what's going on with Kirk, but from the look on her face and the tone of her voice, it's something bad. The end of the shift can't come quick enough.

———

I'm home half an hour before Carrie, and I spend the time pacing the living room, occasionally picking my phone up and staring at it.

I hear the front door opening, followed by, 'Hey, it's me,' and then the shuffle as she shrugs off her jacket and the clatter of her shoes on the floor. She senses an atmosphere as soon as she walks in.

'Everything okay?' she asks when she sees me.

'Fucking mad day actually,' I say.

'What, at work?'

'No, work was shite as usual. But when I went for lunch, I bumped into another one of Kirk's sisters, Sharon.'

'That's a coincidence,' she says as she unclips her nametag. 'What did she say?'

'Well, that's the thing. When I asked her about Kirk, she just clammed up, said I need to ring him.'

'Are you going to?'

'Yeah, she gave me his number,' I say. 'I'm just wondering what to expect. It's going to be summat bad, that much I do know.'

'Did she say anything else?'

'No, she seemed really edgy, like she was dying to tell me summat, but she can't.'

Carrie comes over and puts her arms around me. I put my arms around her, too.

'I'll go and make us a drink,' she says as she detaches herself. 'Just ring him, find out what's going on. I mean, after that message last night, and now this... I'm not going to nag you, but you know what I'm saying, right?'

'Yeah.'

She kisses me and goes through to the kitchen.

'Tea or coffee?'

'Tea please, love,' I reply.

I sit down on the sofa and find Kirk's number on my phone. My thumb hovers over the green 'Call' tab before I touch it. I hold the phone to my ear and listen to the purr of the call-tone. It doesn't take him long to pick up.

'Hello?' he says when he answers.

'Now then,' I reply.

'Who's this?'

'It's Jamie.'

'Ah,' he says. 'Now then.' There's a brief pause. 'How's it going?'

'I'm okay,' I say. 'Hanging in there.' It's my turn to pause. 'How are you?'

He laughs. 'I've been better.'

Our awkward greeting is completely understandable, but difficult. I feel self-conscious, every word I intend to utter going through a filter in my head, a *what's-the-best-thing-to-say-next?* sorting process.

'What are you doing with yersen now?' he asks, perhaps sensing my unease.

'Just working, hanging out at home, that kind of thing. Nothing exciting.'

'Where are you working?'

'Working for KC. At the call centre. It's a fucking nightmare, but what can you do?'

'Yeah,' he says, and then I hear a sharp intake of breath, like he's inhaling something.

'How about you?' Both of us are circling around the thing that needs to be said – the big revelation – engaging in a macho-bullshit conversational stand-off to try to delay the inevitable for as long as possible.

He pauses again. We're getting closer to it now. The avenues are closing, all the talk-traffic is being diverted towards the same slip-road.

'Not a lot,' he says, sighs before adding, 'I can't work at the moment.'

'Listen, Kirk... Carrie, my girlfriend, got a message from your sister last night,' I say, taking the plunge.

'Carrie Douglas? Was she in our Lorraine's class?'

'Yeah...'

'You dirty pram-stealing bastard,' he says, laughing. 'When did that happen?'

'A year or so, ago, anyway...'

He laughs again.

'Anyway, I was on my break today and I saw Sharon, and she told me to call you.'

'Right,' he says, and the laughter abruptly stops. 'What did she say?'

'Well, that's the thing Kirk, nowt. She wouldn't tell me a thing, just gave me your number. I mean, I know it's been a while since we've spoke, and the last time we spoke we fell out, and I'm sorry about that, but I just want to know.'

'Know what?'

'What the fuck is going on.'

He doesn't say anything for a while. For a minute I wonder if he's going to put the phone down. And then I hear him sigh, and he says, 'I'm ill.'

'I fucking knew it,' I say, and go quiet for a bit myself. 'What is it, how are you ill?'

'It's the big C. Cancer.'

'Fuck.'

Carrie comes out of the kitchen, places a drink down on the table next to me. She smiles at me, gestures with her thumb and silently mouths the words, *I'm going upstairs*, and then she disappears out of the room.

I'm still reeling, unable to think of anything to say.

'Are you still there?' Kirk asks.

'Yeah, I'm still here,' I say. 'Just trying to get my head around it.'

'Yeah, you and me both, mate.'

'When did you find out?' I ask. 'Whereabouts is it? In your body, I mean.'

128

'I don't really want to talk about it over the phone.'

'I'm sorry, man,' I say. 'I don't want to pry, I just... don't know what else to ask.'

'I understand, but... it's just... it's just the kinda thing that I'd rather tell you in person, if you know what I mean.'

'Yeah, I do. I do know what you mean.'

'Besides, it would be good to see you.'

'Yeah.'

He gives me his address, and I arrange to visit him the following evening after I finish work. As soon as the call ends, I immediately get up off the sofa and pace up and down the living room, trying to process the terrible news I've just heard. I feel numb. I also feel guilty. Not for his illness; I know there's nothing I can do about that, but just for not being there when he found out. I try to remember why we fell out, what the argument was about, but thinking back, it just seems daft.

Three fucking years.

Carrie comes downstairs.

'How did it go?'

'He's ill.'

'Oh, that terrible news.'

'Fucking cancer, can you believe it?'

I'm trying to keep it together. Feel like bursting into tears, so I'm scared to open my mouth.

'I'm really sorry, baby,' Carrie says, breaking the silence. 'Are you okay?'

'Yeah,' I say, and sit down on the sofa. 'It's just a bit mind-blowing, obviously. He was quite vague about the specifics. Wants me to pop and see him tomorrow after work.'

'Are you going to go?'

'Of course. I have to.' Carrie slides up near me, puts her arm around me. I rest my head on her chest and she strokes my hair. 'I've been trying to remember why we fell out, what it was all about, and I can't. I mean, I can remember the argument, I can remember that as clear as day. But I don't know what it was about, not really.'

129

'But that's not important right now, is it?'

'It's never been important. That's the point. But it happened.'

'You've just got to focus on what's happening now.'

'I know,' I say. 'But you know how people say things happen for a reason? Well, they don't. Sometimes shit happens. Shit happens and we have to deal with it as best we can.'

Kirk is living in East Hull as it turns out. It's a bit of a surprise. Kirk is West Hull born and bred. A black-and-whiter through and through. It goes some way to explaining why no one has really seen him out and about for a while.

A couple of weeks ago, I bumped into Gaz. He was doing quite well for himself. He spilt with Gemma some time ago, but he had a van and a new place, and he was doing house clearances and removals and the like. Anyway, the conversation swung around to the 'good old days', and Kirk came up in conversation. Gaz hadn't heard from him or seen him either.

'Just the way it goes, I suppose,' he said.

After my shift finishes, I make my way from Prospect Centre through town. I walk down King Edward Street towards Jameson Square. King Edward Street is squat, narrow and choked with buses. It's busy at this time, pavements crowded with last-minute shoppers and queues at bus stops. I pass the tall, granite-grey BHS building, and turn onto Brook Street. The back end of the BHS building used to be a nightclub in the eighties, but it's been empty since then, all the windows and doors bricked up and painted black. It looks like a huge, mute speaker.

I join the queue for the 32. Kirk lives just off Holderness Road, not far from Mount Pleasant. I text him to let him know I'm on my way, and he tells me to get off at the Elephant and

Castle, just past the flats, and head down the street, near the primary school. It seems simple enough.

I'm totally reliant upon public transport. Never owned a car, never learnt to drive. Whenever anyone asks me why, I have a stock reply. 'Never had the money,' I say, and it's the truth.

Kirk always used to say that not being able to drive was the single biggest thing that held me back in life. Kirk learnt to drive while he was in the army. They paid for his test and everything. He said it was the only useful thing the army taught him.

I've often thought that maybe Kirk was right, and maybe not being able to drive is the reason I've never had a decent job. Maybe not being able to drive is the reason that I've never got married or had any kids. Maybe not being able to drive is the reason that I've never left Hull; never been *anywhere* other than Hull.

The 32 appears from around the corner. An old bloke with large, hairy ears sticks his arm out and the bus stops. The doors swing open. When it's my turn I flash my ticket at the driver and he waves me on. I go upstairs and my favourite seat – the one at the front right-hand side – is free, so I go and sit on it. Because I go everywhere either by bus or on foot, I have long periods where I get to think about things. Most of the other passengers are texting, playing games and scrolling social media, but I prefer to stare unseeing out the window. I sometimes listen to music, but usually I use travelling time to think.

Maybe that's the real reason I never learnt to drive.

Last night, in bed, I tried explaining to Carrie how lately it felt as though my thoughts were being siphoned off, like an invisible vacuum cleaner had been positioned over the top of my head and was greedily sucking out the things that were turning around in my mind, leaving me blank, empty and confused. Pretty much the same way I feel now.

The bus sets off and heads down George Street. George

131

Street looks fed up and tired. *The Dram Shop* and *Brown's Books* are still there, but the rest of it is nondescript and humble. It's only the *Pozition* nightclub on its corner with Freetown Way that offers a reminder of how it used to be, way back when. I think about some of the mad nights I had down here, out with the lads. Out on the piss. Me and Gaz and Chris and Steve and Kirk and Barry. The fucking *crew*.

The bus passes *Napoleon's*, crosses Drypool Bridge over the River Hull, and I move from the West of the city to the East.

Kirk's directions are straightforward. When I get off the bus, I head down Barnsley Street, walk past the primary school and the playing field, onto the adjoining street. There are a couple of new-build bungalows, but the majority of the houses are two-up, two-down terraced houses typical of inner-city Hull. Smaller one-way streets branch off the one I'm currently walking down, and those smaller streets also have a couple of terraces off them. I stop at the top of the second street on the right and turn onto it, and as I walk to the bottom, I look out for the sign for Sullivan Villas. There's a hedge-lined entrance to the narrow path that leads off from the street. Three identical terraced houses face either side of the path, which comes to an abrupt halt at a wall which also serves as a boundary for the backyards of another set of houses forming one side of an adjoining terrace on another street.

Hull's older streets, crammed with densely-packed houses, are linked by a network of ten-foots, footpaths and narrow roads. Completely baffling to outsiders yet constructed with enough logic to be instantly familiar to anyone who has spent a good part of their life in Hull's inner city. This is the first time I've been down this street, yet it already feels as though I know it.

Kirk's house is the last house on the right at the bottom of the terrace. Each house has a rudimentary front yard, complete with a little fence and gate that sets it back from the path. A white cat jumps up onto the fence just to my left, shoots me a glance, then trots off and leaps up onto the wall at the bottom of the terrace.

Stood there at the top of the terrace, I pause for a moment. Need to get my shit together. I swallow, feel the butterflies in my stomach. I'm nervous, there's no escaping it. I briefly consider turning around, heading back onto Holderness Road to flag a bus, but there's no way I'm going to do that. I take a deep breath and walk towards Kirk's house. It's still early, still light, but everyone has their curtains drawn or their blinds pulled down. It's not surprising really. The only view from the front room of one of these houses is the window of the house opposite.

When I get to Kirk's, I lift the sneck on the gate and try to swing it open. The bottom of the gate scrapes the ground, so I have to lift it up, but it still catches and makes a loud screech as it opens. The sound sets off a dog barking. The barking is coming from Kirk's house, and by the sound of it, it's a large dog. It makes me uneasy. As I approach the front door, I hear someone shout, 'Shut the fuck up! Shut the fucking fuck up, yer little fucker!' and then I hear a barrage of coughs.

It's Kirk, no mistaking it.

I knock on the door, the noise setting the dog off again. It sounds as though it's a *really* big dog. For fuck's sake. Kirk and his fucking dogs. I hear Kirk wrestling with it.

'Who is it?' he shouts. More coughs.

'It's Jamie,' I shout back.

'Just a minute,' he says, and I hear him clattering with the dog, then a door slamming. He comes back to the front door.

'Now then,' he says as he opens it.

And there he is. Kirk. He looks painfully thin. And old. He looks *old*.

'Come on in,' he says, and I step into his house.

Like a lot of these houses, the front door opens straight onto the stairs. There's another door to the left that leads into the front room. Kirk opens it, goes through, and I follow him.

Kirk always seems to live in places that border on chaos, and this place is no exception. The sofa is pushed up against the wall that separates the stairs from the room. It's the only wall with any paper on. The other walls have been stripped down to the plaster, waiting to be decorated. On the facing wall, there are alcoves on each side of the chimney stack. There's a fireplace, with a flat-screen TV mounted to the wall above it, blaring away. The alcoves are home to shelves that are scattered with various bits and bobs; tools, newspaper, model cars, tins and boxes. In the centre of the room is a large, squat coffee table, overflowing with sheets of paper, envelopes, and assorted boxes and packets of pills and medicines.

'Make yersen at home,' Kirk says as he eases himself onto the sofa.

There are two armchairs set against the back wall, so I head over to them and sit on one. I'm sat next to the door that presumably leads to the kitchen. It's a brittle wooden door with a pane of frosted glass set into it. As I peer through, I spot the outline of something gigantic, huffing and puffing, shuffling about and rattling the door.

'Ignore him, he's a big fucking poof,' Kirk says.

'What's his name?'

'Hob-Nob.'

'I bet you don't feel daft in the slightest when you're calling out for him,' I say, and Kirk laughs.

'I struggle to take him out now. I've got someone who comes round.'

'Right,' I say, nodding.

'So how are things?' Kirk asks. He picks up his remote and turns the volume down on an old episode of *Blockbusters*. 'You look well, mate.'

'Thanks,' I say, and before I have chance to say anything else, he cuts me off.

'It's okay, you don't have to compliment me on my appearance,' he laughs. I laugh too.

I give it a moment before I ask: 'So what's going on, Kirk? What's happening?'

He doesn't reply for a moment, and then he says, 'I'd offer to make you a cuppa, but. . . '

The hint is loud and clear.

'It's fine,' I say. 'What do you want?'

'A tea please, bud,' he replies. 'Cup's on the table.'

I pick up his mug, and I stand up, face the door and place my hand on the knob.

'Hob-Nob, right?'

'Just tell him to shift, he's soft as shit,' Kirk says.

I open the door, and this huge ginger beast leaps up and begins to growl and bark. I flinch instinctively, scream, 'HOB-NOB!'

'Hob-Nob!' Kirk shouts, maximum aggression. The dog whimpers pathetically, and Kirk shouts, 'Don't make me put you outside again.'

The dog looks up at me, gives me this glare like it considers me to be the cause of all its problems. It slumps over to the corner of the kitchen and crawls onto a big, saggy, grubby bed. It's a small kitchen, with the bathroom and toilet attached via a ground-floor extension that takes up most of the garden. I'm struck by just how neat and tidy it is. The only time Kirk's surroundings are in order like this is when he's in a relationship. Based upon my initial impressions of the front room, I'd assumed he was single again.

'The mugs are in the cupboard above the kettle,' Kirk says, hearing me bumping around.

As I make the tea, it's almost as if he can hear my thoughts.

'The kitchen's alright, innit? My sisters and the nurse have a tidy when they pop round. Haven't had to wash a single pot in over a month,' he says.

I set about making the tea, trying not to get side-tracked by the weirdness of it all. When I'm finished, I step back into the front room.

'Make sure you shut the door behind you,' Kirk says, 'otherwise that ginger fucker will be in here before you know it.'

I place the mugs of tea on the table. Kirk has a plastic tray on his lap. He's putting a spliff together.

'Do you still smoke?' he asks.

'Yeah, sure. Why not?'

Tea and spliffs. For as long as I've known him, big mugs of sugary tea and large fat joints have been Kirk's staple diet. Kirk folds the skins, takes a cig from the packet and licks the seam, pulls it apart and dumps the tobacco into the centre of the skin. He breaks it up a bit, and then he picks up a lump of resin, flicks a lighter on, holds a flame to it.

'D'yer know how hard it is to get hold of this shit now?' he asks.

'What, solid?'

'Yeah.'

'It's been a while, so no.'

'Well, it's fucking difficult, let me tell you. It's all fucking weed now. Hydroponically home-grown, mind-rape shit. No wonder all the kids are going fucking mad. I remember when this was all you got, d'yer remember?'

'Yeah, I remember.'

'I mean, fucking weed was a rarity, and it was always shit, really fucking dry. But this stuff, you can't go wrong with it. Bongs, lungs, buckets, spliffs. . . All them mad fucking nights we used to have smoking this stuff, d'yer remember?'

'I remember.'

'I've been thinking about those times a lot lately.'

Kirk finishes crumbling resin into the joint. He picks it up and sets about rolling it, slowly, carefully. He tips his head and I can't help but focus on the outline of his skull, and the way his skin seems to be stretched back from his cheekbones and eye sockets over the top of his head. Deep creases appear in his brow as it furrows in concentration.

For the first time, I start to realise that unease and nervousness aren't confined solely to me. I understand that the chit-chat and tea-making and spliff-building are just stalling tactics, aimed at prolonging this brief period we are both currently experiencing, a slot of time when things between us are the same as they've always been.

After he finishes making his spliff, he puts it in his mouth, lights it and inhales deeply. Plumes of smoke billow from his nose. He shuts his eyes and sits back. He looks calm, peaceful.

Kirk's wearing baggy jeans and a hoody. He was always a stocky fucker, but now his clothes bury him. He reaches up again, puts the joint back to his lips, inhales, and then lurches forward. A hacking cough bursts out of him. It rattles his full body, and he shakes violently all over. As the coughing starts to subside, he clutches his chest. His face is bright red and tears stream down his face.

'Jesus,' he cries, grasping his top.

I'm rooted to the spot, panicking, feeling utterly helpless.

'Is there anything I can do?'

'It's fine,' Kirk splutters. 'Ahhh... just give me a second.'

He bows his head and offers me the spliff.

'Thanks,' I say as I pluck it from his fingers. I take a drag and sit back in the chair, wondering what the fuck is going to happen next.

Kirk takes a swig of tea, pain flashing across his face. Swallowing seems to give him trouble. He continues clutching at his chest. Mutters, *fuck, fuck*, and then squeezes out a belch.

'That's one of the worse parts of this,' he says.

I drink some of my tea, let him recuperate from his ordeal. It's difficult to watch.

'I got diagnosed a month back,' he says, eventually.

'A month?'

I'm dumbstruck. *A month?*

Kirk sits back, takes a breath before continuing.

'I'd been having some trouble for a while. D'yer remember that I always used to suffer with heartburn?'

'Yeah.'

'Well, back end of last year, it got really bad. Like constant. I've been on living my own for quite a while. I was seeing this lass who lives just down 'road. That's how I ended up living in East Hull. She found this place for me. She's called Kate. She's nice, but it's one of those on-and-off-and-on-again type relationships, one of *them*. She didn't want to give her place up, and I wanted my independence, so it just kinda petered out. But she still pops and sees me every now and then.

'Anyway, late last year, round Christmas, she pops down here and I'm on the sofa in total agony. It's like that scene from the film where the alien bursts out of that bloke's chest. She's really panicking and freaking, so she makes me get an appointment at the emergency clinic. I'd been suffering for a while, but I hadn't got around to getting a new doctor. So she nags and nags at me, and just to shut her up, I make an appointment at the drop-in surgery.'

'What happened then?'

'Fuck all,' Kirk says. He gestures for me to pass him the spliff back. 'I kept going back and all they did was give me fucking Gaviscon and shit like that.'

Kirk takes a drag, but not so deep as to set him off coughing, and then continues.

'I just grit my teeth and get on with it – no pain, no gain, all that. It gets to the New Year and I notice all this weight's dropping off me. I'd had to scrap my car just before Chrimbo, so I was using my push-rod to get about. I assumed it was that. For a couple of months, I was chuffed, lost a bit of my gut. But the weight kept dropping off.'

Kirk looks away for a moment. He's probably had to tell this story a hundred times or so by now.

'Eventually, last month, after a load of tests, I went to the hospital and they pushed one of those cameras inside me. That's when they told me.'

'Is it lung cancer?'

Kirk shoots a look at me. He's frowning.

'No, it's not in my lungs, it's everywhere *but* my fucking lungs. And it's got fuck all to do with smoking before you ask.'

It's clear that Kirk is on the defensive, that he's been challenged about his smoking – by the doctors, by his family – by everyone, I should imagine.

'I was just asking, Kirk. It's got fuck all to do with me what you do.'

He looks down, takes another little puff on the spliff and then hands it over to me again.

'Sorry,' he says. 'It's just that every fucker but me seems to be the expert just lately.' He picks up the tray and lays it back on his lap, sets about making another joint.

'Besides, you know what I'm like, mate. Even if they end up drilling one of those holes in my throat, so long as the fucker's big enough to stick a spliff in, I'll be happy.'

He laughs a lot at that. I try to join in as best I can, but it's an effort.

———

On the bus home, I try and get my head around what I've just experienced. It didn't take long for the conversation to get side-tracked by small talk. I told Kirk about my move into the world of call centres, Kirk detailed his plans for renovating his house. The plans had been put on hold for obvious reasons, but the way Kirk figured it, so long as he could get cracking sometime in the New Year, everything would work out okay.

When I get home, I explain to Carrie that the subject of cancer and illness had been shelved almost as quickly as it had come up. There was a sense, I say, that Kirk and I needed to establish some common foundation of familiarity – to catch up with each other – before we got to the real serious stuff.

Pacing up and down the front room, half-stoned and disorientated by the whole episode, I relay it all to Carrie, in the hope of reaching a level of understanding myself.

'This much is clear,' I tell her as I take a swig from a tinny. 'Kirk is in as much emotional pain as he is physical.'

'Blokes are so full of shit,' Carrie says. 'I don't know why you can't just have it out with each other and cut the bullshit.'

'Sometimes the bullshit is all we have,' I say.

'Have you heard yourself? You've got an answer for everything, you have. Except when you haven't.'

She places her hand on my face, and that's all it takes for the tears to start streaming. I pull her close and squeeze her, unsure what I'd do without her.

11

Pete

We spend the morning drinking, until at some point in the early afternoon, I doze off.

I wake up and Rosie and Skinny Bob have gone. I lift my head. My face feels hot and my neck feels stiff, looking up at the big, blue sky. Hull's flat and consequently the sky looks massive. It's so big I can feel it weighing down on me, pressing me into the ground. Rubbing the sleep from my eyes, I notice something crawling about on the back of my hand – a little white spider. I've never seen anything like it. Plucking it off, I chuck it to one side. My face is burning, and my head hurts as well. A wave of nausea lifts me up and propels me over to a bush. The booze shoots out in a hot jet. *Good job I ate this morning*, I think to myself, as the half-digested eggs, beans and bread hit the ground.

I wipe my mouth and straighten myself out, reach into my pocket for my baccy. It's not there. Rosie and Skinny Bob must have nicked it when I fell asleep. *Arseholes.* I'm a bit fuzzy and I'm still feeling slightly sick. I consider going back to my room and laying down but something prompts me to head to our Terry's, instead.

It's only a short walk.

'Now then, twat,' Terry says as he opens the door.

Although he's ten years younger than me, he insists on speaking to me like I'm special or something – like he's my fucking superior. Our Terry is another one of those plastic gangsters, like those cunts back at the hostel, but he does alright for himself. Knocks out a bit of weed, does a bit of this and that. Got himself a nice flat on Vicky Dock. He's gobby, but he's the only member of my family who appears to give even the slightest shit about me.

'What have you been up to today, yer fucking waste of space,' he says, grinning.

'Not a lot really. You?' I say as I take a seat.

'I'm seeing this new bird. Asian piece, fucking lovely she is,' he says.

He takes his phone out of his pocket and presses the screen before holding it out to show me. There's a photo of a young lass on a bed, on her back, legs in the air, showing off her fanny. Her face is cut off by the top of the picture.

'Nice.' I squint to get a better look, my eyes adjusting.

'Fucking filthy, she is,' he says. His grin makes him look demented.

'Where did you meet her then?' I ask.

'In town,' he says. 'Met her in Revolution Bar.'

'What's her name?'

'Natalie.'

'Doesn't sound very Asian.'

'What are you... a fucking expert on oriental names or summat?'

'Just saying,' I say.

I wish I hadn't bothered coming round. I know he's full of shit, but I'm trying to get some baccy out of him, so it's best to humour him.

'When was the last time you had a shag then?' Terry asks.

'Been a while, Terry,' I say, looking away.

142

'If you're lucky I'll let you smell my fingers sometime,' he says, the cocky bastard.

'Fuck off.' I pause for a sec before adding, 'I need to ask a favour, Terry.'

'Oh yeah? Here it comes.'

'Could you sort me out some baccy till I get paid?'

'Fucking hell,' he says. 'What would you do without me to fucking bail you out?'

'C'mon Terry, it would really help me out,' I say, looking away once again.

He tuts and looks at me like I've just shit on the carpet. He stands up and wanders off, then returns with a pouch, which he slings at me. 'Another one you owe me,' he says.

I hate being beholden to the little twat, but what can you do? Times are hard.

'Well, while yer here, you can do summat for me,' he says. 'I've got nip out, Pete. Can you hold the fort?'

'Course I can. Everything okay?' I'm excited by the possible opportunity to chill out in his flat by myself for a couple of hours.

'Everything's fine. Got to see a man about a donkey. Someone might be popping round later. If they turn up while I'm out, take the money off them and give them one of those bags out the biscuit tin in the kitchen. Or two, if that's what they're after.'

'No probs.'

'There's some weed on the tray. Roll yourself one while I'm out. Don't take the piss though,' he says, putting his cap on.

'Do I ever?'

I wait until Terry leaves, pick up the tray and roll one. The remote's down the side of the chair, so I fish it out and flick the telly on. Big flat-screen fucker it is, forty-odd inches. I put one of the food channels on and watch some yank stuffing his fat face with chili chicken wings until he nearly passes out.

It feels nice, sat here, joint in hand, staring at a big fuck-off telly. It's how I should be living. I can't work out how some fuckers like Terry always seem to land on their feet, while I end up on my arse time after time. This is the way my life *should* be. I take a big toke and puff out a milky cloud, trying not to dwell on it too much. I feel a bit sleepy, and before I know it I've dropped off again.

I wake up to the sound of someone screaming my name.

12

Barry

Things had gone from bad to worse.

Although we weren't pinning it, we were smoking the shit like it was going out of fashion. Things got seedy and filthy, quickly. Neither of us had a job. Even going and scratching-on became an effort. It quickly got to where the only thing that either of us could be bothered to do was go out and score.

Some nights, we'd have these long conversations. They'd either be about packing up and leaving Hull, or alternatively, killing ourselves in a pact.

One night, Natalie admitted that she'd had to do a few "favours" here and there to get us by. I remember her weeping, saying 'how the fuck did you think I was paying for it?' over and over again.

I thought we'd hit rock bottom, but that's when shit got really fucked up.

I started hearing voices when I was sixteen. Well, I say voices, but it was just one voice to begin with. It was during the final year of school. The voice was really quiet at first – only a whisper – but it got louder as time went on.

I was terrified, of course. Like most of my mates at the time, I had just discovered resin and speed and raves, so I assumed it was a side-effect or something. Like catching a dose, I thought if I kept it a secret and got on with it, it would somehow go away – clear up on its own.

The voice was tinny at first, metallic sounding, like a crappy speaker on a radio. I heard random phrases that didn't make any sense. It would start up of its own accord, rattle on for a bit, and then cut out.

Things went wild after school was over. Everyone I was knocking about with – Steve, Gaz, Chris, all of them – got into partying in a big way. Tripping, that kind of shit.

I probably should have guessed that doing LSD while I was hearing voices was a bad idea.

I freaked out one night and told everyone about the voice. Gave them a live broadcast of what was going on in my head. They laughed at first, thinking it was some kind of routine, but it soon began to freak them out too.

I can't remember *everything* that happened that night, but I remember waking up in hospital, my throat sore from the tube that had been stuffed down there to pump my stomach. Remember reaching up and touching the fresh stitches in my forehead. I'd head-butted a mirror, apparently.

I'd never been the most popular person at school. Always had a bit of a chip on my shoulder, and I used to get a weird kick out of winding up people like Kirk. I can't really blame them all for ditching me after that mad night. Let's face it, I was bad news, *fucked* in the head. Even *I* didn't want to be around me.

Perhaps the voice sensed my vulnerable state, because it became louder, more insistent. It was still drivel mostly, but every now and then it would say something coherent. I realised then that I needed to stay away from shit like acid and ecstasy. I didn't want to expand my mind; I wanted to block it out instead.

146

We don't really fall asleep. We just sit there, our hands laid flat on the cushion between us, palms up – close but not touching.

It's late, so late that the proper programmes on the telly – the daytime chat-show repeats, the old soaps – have stopped broadcasting. We put a casino channel on, watch the fresh-faced dealers flash immaculate smiles as they fling the ball around the wheel, the numbers scrolling down the side of the screen. After that, we flick to a shopping channel and watch the product demonstrations, the presenters and the "experts" flogging gadgets that provide solutions to non-existent problems. A band of telephone numbers and product information scrolls along the bottom of the screen. Excitable faces spew out "facts" and jargon. A price ticks down like a counter on a bomb in the corner of the brightly-lit screen. Must act now. *Must. Act. Now.* But I don't do anything and neither does Natalie.

Except sit there.

Just. Sit. There.

My head is tipped back, resting on the back of the sofa, and my eyes are fixed on the screen. I crane my neck slightly to look at Natalie. She's slumped forward slightly, her shoulders stooped, but her eyes are looking at the telly, staring, unblinking.

I notice that the milky dawn has begun to seep through the fabric of the curtains, staining them white. *How long have we been sitting here?*

I rise, slowly and deliberately, peel myself from the sofa. It's time to break the deadlock. When it comes to inactivity and indifference, Natalie is fifth-Dan master. I am in awe of her powers. I glance at her as I shuffle past. Her eyes are still open, still fixed straight ahead. I nodded off for a while, earlier, but I can tell Natalie hasn't slept a wink. For days, possibly. I don't ask her if she wants a drink. I make her one anyway.

Natalie has withdrawn – from everything. I'm finding it harder and harder to cope.

A couple of months ago, at our last place, I had a seizure. After a period of extended absence, the voice in my head returned with a scream. It was like a bolt of electricity had passed through me. Everything turned blue for a second, and it felt as though something exploded, my head being ground-zero.

When I finally woke up, I looked over and saw Natalie on the floor next to me. I remember smelling burnt hair and ozone. I was groggy and it took me a while to sit up. My arms and legs ached as though I hadn't used them for eons. Something popped in my back as I leant over to check on Natalie. I couldn't tell if she was breathing, so I started to shake her. My throat clenched, I thought she was dead, but then her eyes flicked open. She stared directly ahead but there was something weird about her eyes – her irises had been bleached almost white.

She locked herself in one of the bedrooms after that. At first, I worried that she was going to do herself in, but I could hear her moving around, scratching, scrabbling about. I banged on the door, screaming that I was going to ring an ambulance, ring the police – ring whoever. I was about to give up and fetch my phone, but the door slowly opened...

She was standing over by the wall at the far side of the bedroom. She had covered almost every surface of the room in strange markings. She'd scribbled long strands of equations onto the walls using a blue felt-tip pen, and she'd carved diagrams and charts into the doors and table, using a pair of scissors.

I didn't understand what it all meant, but I don't think I was supposed to, because she wasn't doing it for me.

In between bursts of activity, Natalie collapsed, sat mute and motionless. But her body was rigid, like a mannequin's. Her eyes were still blank. I panicked. I hugged her, stroked her hair and told her everything was going to be okay. I gently nudged her out of the room and into our bedroom. My plan was to lock her in, go and get some help. I led her into the room, sat her down on the bed, and retreated, shutting the door behind me. I wedged it in place, so she couldn't get out.

Heading for the stairs, I heard the banging start. It sounded like a wrecking ball being swung into the door, and the house juddered. I ran back upstairs. The bedroom door was being hit so violently that the door frame began to come away from the wall. As I approached, the banging stopped. Breathing hard, I waited a moment before pushing the door open, wondering what the hell I would find inside the room.

Natalie was still sitting on the bed, exactly where I had left her.

My knees gave way as I fell down next to her. I had to box off my feelings, had to put the blind panic to one side and focus on Natalie. I tightened my arm around her, squeezed her, but she didn't react to me at all. She felt cold – lifeless – like she didn't even know I was there.

The terror I had felt when I heard the noise was beginning to fade, leaving only guilt in its place. Although I didn't know what was happening, I knew that I was responsible. I knew that Natalie would be safe now if she hadn't got involved with me in the first place. I wanted to protect her, keep her safe, while at the same time I realised that *I* was the reason for this. I had tainted her, drawn her into my world. I moved some strands of thin, straight, hair behind her ear so I could see her face. *Natalie.* I placed my finger on her cheek, traced a line to her chin. *Nothing.*

'It's going to be okay, Natalie,' I said at last. 'I'm not going to leave you. I'm not going to tell anyone, I won't let them take you away.' I kept up a running commentary. 'We'll figure this out. We'll figure it out somehow, and one day this will all be like a bad dream.'

I had to dig deep to choke back the tears. She couldn't see me lose it, I had to be strong for both of us.

'Because that's all this is Natalie,' I whispered. 'A dream. I

149

think you got stuck in a dream, and we just need to wait until you wake up.'

I was trying to convince myself more than her.

Now, a few months on, her body is still here – breathing, sighing, and smoking. Occasionally eating and shitting. But the bit that is *really* her – the core, the personality – well. . . that's disappeared. She's vanished.

The spoon clanks around the inside of the mug. I wish I was dead. I wish we were both dead. In a couple of hours the juice will be running around our insides – blessed relief – and things will feel a bit better, but I feel like a coward. It makes me laugh when people call suicides cowards. The true cowards are the people who choose to carry on walking about, despite knowing that everything, on every level, is completely fucked. Humans, and humanity, are the punchline to some grand, cosmic, joke. I'm trying to work out who's telling it.

My brain. What's going on? Nasty thoughts running through my head at dawn, dooming the day before it's even begun. Soon, I'll be given a reprieve. Everything will go sideways for a bit, then things will level out. I'll get my sea-legs.

Natalie and me, we'll sleep like bairns tonight.

I've got a meeting soon, and I need to be ready for it.

I take the tea through. One step will follow another, my feet shuffling towards the living room, where I head for Natalie. I have a mug in each hand. For the next few seconds my goal is to make it to the sofa without spilling any tea. It starts off badly, I bump into the door as it swings back and hot liquid runs down my thumb.

'Bastard,' I mutter.

Signal from thumb hits nerve-fibres, reaches brain. My instinct is to drop the mug, but I'm committed now. *Man up.* Steady my legs. Resume pace. I reach the sofa, teeth gritted. Attempt complex manoeuvre, swing arse around and start descending while simultaneously placing down mugs.

Involuntary spasm in wrist causes another minor spill on table. But nothing too serious.

I feel taxed, yet elated, as though I've just accomplished something. As I attempt to supress a grin, I turn to Natalie.

'Did you see that?'

She slowly turns to face me. She doesn't say anything. Her eyes are featureless, faded to not-quite-white, like milky-marble cataracts. Little islands of bubbles on the surface of a cup of tea. My gran used to call them pennies. She said the bigger the penny, the greater the luck.

I lift my hand, place it gently on Natalie's face.

'It's okay, baby,' I say. 'We're seeing that bloke soon. He might have some answers for us.'

'Soon the void within us all will be gone,' says Natalie, in a mechanical voice.

We're getting ready to go to the chemists.

I don't feel like having a bath, but I run one anyway. The bathroom doesn't have any windows, so aside from the whirring extractor fan, there's no way for the steam to escape. It doesn't take long for the steam to fill the entire room. I enjoy sitting in amongst it all, my own little sweat lodge. Back when I used to shoot up, my favourite ritual was to retreat to the bathroom, fill the bath with hot water, sit on the toilet and then take my sock off and dangle my foot over the bath. Made it easier to find a vein, and the whole process felt cleaner that way.

I haven't pinned anything in years – I'm pretty sure I'd be dead by now if I'd kept that up.

I let the cold water run while I take off my clothes and slowly lower myself into the bath. The water is hot enough to sting, and it takes all my effort not to leap out. Thick sweat oozes from my forehead and armpits, and my heart beats rapidly. My cock shrinks. I suck in the hot, wet air, and feel dizzy.

Exposed under the glare of the naked bulb dangling from the ceiling, I consider my legs, mottled cheek-pinch red and bell-mushroom white. Lifting my right leg out of the water, I stare at my foot, at the nest of scars on my favourite vein. I'm a pale, skinny little fucker. I look like a Grey, one of those slant-eyed aliens that turn up in films and documentaries about alien-abduction. Years ago, I used to knock about with a guy called Gaz. He had a *Take Me To Your Dealer* poster with a picture of one of them on it.

After the ordeal of lowering myself in, I wait a moment before fully immersing myself. Closing my eyes, I focus on the continuous hum of the fan, drift away for a bit. Eventually I sink down into the water, my knees breaking the surface as my jaw hits the waterline. I keep going until the surface of the water is just below my nostrils, feeling like a crocodile.

I try to empty my head, not to think of anything, but I know that today is going to be full on. After we get our juice, we have to go to the Baker Street drop-in centre, have a chat with a counsellor and give a piss sample, so they can make sure we're not topping up our dose with anything else. It's all part of the quitting game we've both signed up to. We *have* to do it. We must get ourselves clean and move forward – towards... somewhere. Towards whatever's going to happen.

Natalie doesn't understand right now, but we're being prepared.

We're like cattle. This is just the first phase, and Natalie and I are at the front of the queue. I caught a glimpse of it – of how things really are – back when I was younger. They fed me drugs and told me I was ill. They said I was mad, disturbed. They laughed at me and made me feel like a freak. But I was right.

It's true. All of it. They're here.

After the seizure, we carried on as usual – mostly. We still got up, smoked some shit and put the telly on, but Natalie stopped speaking. Every now and then she'd sit bolt upright and say stuff like *The Well is in Kirk* or *Pete is the Factory.*

It took me a couple of days before I realised that she was responding to the voice in *my* head.

A lot of people who quit find religion. The programme they put you through practically encourages it. But what I'm going through is beyond religion. All through history, people have spoken of divine voices, of gods and monsters, but this shit is real. It's happening.

I don't what this entity is, but I know that I have to stand up to it somehow, confront it. I know that its motivations are completely beyond my understanding. It's alien in the truest sense of the word, but it wants something from us. And something about it – its very nature – is so different, so beyond our realm of understanding and experience, that exposure to it is dangerous. It fucks us up: humans, I mean.

It all started with those seeds, back at school. And now, after two decades, the thing is coming for us. All of us.

This is bigger than me – bigger than what's happening to Natalie.

'Do you want the water, love?' I shout.

No response.

I yank the plug and the water begins to drain away. Standing up, a shiver runs along my body as I step onto the bathroom floor. I pull a towel towards me and wrap it around my waist.

I walk past Natalie, still planted on the sofa, and make my way to the bedroom where I sling on a shirt and a pair of trackie bottoms, my socks and trainers.

'Are you going to get ready, love?' I ask, poking my head around the door. Silence.

In the living room, I gently help Natalie off the sofa, take her by the arm and steer her towards the bedroom. There I stand her at the foot of the bed, undo the belt of her dressing gown and slide it off her shoulders. I take a top and a pair of jeans from the chest of drawers.

'Are you ready?' I say, and she lifts her arms.

I place the neck of her top above her head, then pull it down until her head pops through. I tug a sleeve down each of her arms, folding the cuffs over once at her wrists. I don't know if she can feel anything, but I try to be as careful as possible: gentle, like I'm handling something precious, like a baby. Because she *is* precious. She's all I have. She is the one thing that makes all this pain – the pain of just fucking existing – worth it. I want to make sure she comes back, that she'll be exactly the same as how she was before she left.

Throughout it all, Natalie remains impassive. When she allows her arms to drop again to her sides, I take her hand and bring it up to my face.

'Whatever happens, you know I love you, right?'

She sits down on the bed in a sharp, robotic motion, and raises her legs so I can pull her jeans on. It gets a bit fiddly when I reach the tops of her legs, so I support her with one arm while I stand her up again, pull the jeans up over her arse.

'I think you can zip yourself up, can't you babe?'

'Yes,' she says.

Her voice, which I rarely hear, is even and flat, like pre-recorded answerphone message.

Natalie and me, we're both bound to the system. Getting off the shit requires that you mostly hand over responsibility for your life to strangers. Surrender yourself to a seemingly endless round of meetings and tests and questions. There's comfort to be found in letting others plan and map out your day-to-day life, though. When you're locked up or in a hostel there's structure, order and routine – rehabilitation is more or less about allowing another structure to be established. Surrendering yourself to the institution of your impending sobriety.

I've always had problems with authority. It started at home, extended to school. The voice became just another thing to rebel against. But I'm now starting to realise that the voice is part of something *more*, something huge that threatens *everything* and *everyone*.

We need to be ready, to fight back, but we're still hooked, still fucking strung out.

I'm too weak. I've always been too weak.

Tears roll down my face. I look over at Natalie. I want her back.

'Put your sunglasses on, love.'

———————

Holderness Road is busy. Multitudes of people swarm around, going about their business, doing their weekly shops and errands.

I still don't feel at home in East Hull. Feel like an exile, but we had to get away from West Hull. The last time I was released from nick, I swore I would stay off the smack for good and straighten myself out but within six months I had met Natalie and was nurturing yet another habit I couldn't afford. I knew too many people, couldn't walk ten feet without bumping into someone who would recognise me. It would go something like this:

'Alright Barry, how's it going? An't seen you in ages.'

'I'm not bad Nick/Jakey/Carter/whoever. Just got out, to be honest.'

'Really? What you up to?'

'Nowt, just trying to get by.'

'Hey, listen, if yer at a loose end, I might be able to sort you out.'

'Really?'

And so on, and so on, and so on...

Much like Anlaby Road, Holderness Road is one of the main arteries into Hull's centre, so it's always choked with fume-spewing traffic, crammed in end-to-end, crawling slowly towards the heart of the city.

I feel on edge all the time round here. Too many red and white shirts, too much *attitude* and animosity. But it's the unfamiliarity that keeps me grounded. With me leading Natalie by the hand, we weave our way through the people towards the chemist on the corner of Morrill Street, brushing past the masses and navigating around the prams and shopping trolleys. Everyone seems blank-eyed, yet pre-occupied with whatever path they are following through the day.

Eventually, we reach the chemists. Natalie goes in first. I stand on the corner and roll a cigarette. Leaning against the wall, I watch all the people, trying to imagine how it will all work once *the barriers* have been brought down.

I'm scared.

After Natalie comes out, I hand her the fag and head into the chemists. I sit on a little plastic chair and wait for my name to be called. After a few minutes, I'm summoned into a small room out the back. The pharmacist is waiting for me when I get in there.

He's a skinny Asian-looking bloke with round-glasses and a patchy beard. Although he looks quite young, his white coat, clipboard and demeanour give him the air of someone more mature.

He taps his clipboard with a pen, looks at me and says, 'How are we today?'

'Not bad,' I reply.

'Now, I have to ask, have you taken any other drugs or medicines?'

'No, none.'

'And you're still regularly attending counselling sessions with the local drug community team?'

'Yes.'

He hands me a small paper cup. I hold it in front my face. The green liquid looks like a radioactive potion. *Maybe I'll get superpowers.* I close my eyes and pour the foul stuff into my mouth. Feel it sliding down the back of my throat.

When I open my eyes, the pharmacist is still staring at me. He comes up to me, places his hand on my shoulder and speaks in a new, mechanical-sounding voice.

'Soon, the void within us all will be gone.'

I found him on the internet. Henry Wears, paranormal enthusiast. He's collated stories about weird things that have taken place in Hull over the years, ghost stories and local legends. He also reported on UFO sightings in Hull and I was surprised by the sheer volume of them. A few immediately stood out.

In 1801, a light was seen hovering over the Humber. Witnesses reported that the whole of the area was bathed in a blue light, and that the object spilt into small balls of light. It even made the press and is considered to be one of the first reported UFO sightings.

In 1967, a group of children saw an object land in an East Hull park. When police arrived to check it out, they found scorch marks on the grass.

In October 1986, twenty people reported seeing lights over Bransholme. The Ministry of Defence even opened a file on it.

Back when I was at school, Steve and Pete and a couple of others I hung around with said that they'd seen something over the school field. They described a blue light in the sky and said that smaller lights broke off from it and descended to earth. Although I wasn't there, when we returned to the field that evening for one of our gatherings, I found a load of strange, white seeds.

The similarity of our experience to Henry Wears' reported sightings wasn't lost on me. It's funny, but it took me years to make the link between swallowing those seeds on the playing field and the voice in my head. I mean, none of the others suffered from it, so I never thought about it. It wasn't

157

until after my seizure that I began to put it all together. And that was only because immediately afterwards, I began having dreams.

I relived the encounter, but from Steve's perspective. It felt real. I was there, my ears ringing, looking up at the big blue light in the sky.

Everything fell into place after that.

It took me a while to work up the bottle to reach out to Henry. To begin with, I described the event on the field. I would go to the library and email him, and we started to correspond regularly. Eventually, I took the plunge and asked if he would meet up with me for a chat, and he agreed.

———

Someone's at the door.

'Put your glasses back on, love,' I say to Natalie.

I feel twinges of excitement as I go down to answer it. *Finally, I'm going to meet Henry.* I'll talk to him, discover what he knows; find out if there's anything he can do to help. He'll be able to see the evidence for himself.

I open the front door to a balding, rotund bloke.

'Henry?' I say, offering my hand.

'Barry?'

I smile, and he slowly takes my hand and shakes it. I can tell by the way he's narrowed his eyes that he's nervous. I don't blame him. I've got the big scar on my forehead, plus the whole methadone complexion going on.

'Yes,' I say. 'I'm so glad you're here, please come in.'

He looks around, taking in the surroundings. Probably scoping out the best way to make a quick exit, should he need to. His hands are knitted together tightly, and he taps his foot. He keeps clearing his throat.

'Please, I won't take up too much of your time. It's legit, honestly. I need your help.'

He sighs, gives a forced smile, before cautiously stepping into the hallway. I take him up to the flat.

158

The flat's in its usual state, and Henry does a good job of pretending not to be shocked by it. I open the living room door and lead him in. He spots Natalie on the sofa, sitting motionless, with her sunglasses on.

'Hi,' he says, and she doesn't respond. 'Is she okay?'

'She's one of the reasons I need your help.'

Henry swallows. I notice that he's started sweating. He looks around, weighing up his options.

'Would you like a drink? Tea, coffee perhaps?'

'Listen, Barry, I don't know if it's my help you need, maybe – '

'I realise that this might be intimidating for you,' I say, cutting him off. 'But I just want to chat with you, ask you some things. I just need ten minutes. Please.'

He looks at the floor, and then over at Natalie, and then back at me. He takes a deep breath.

'Okay, ten minutes,' he says, and he takes a little notebook from his jacket pocket.

'Thank you,' I say. 'How about that drink?'

'I'm fine, thank you,' he says. 'Mind if I take a seat?'

'Please do.'

He lowers himself onto the armchair opposite the sofa. Reaches into his inside pocket and takes a pen out.

I go over to the sofa and sit next to Natalie.

'What's going on, Barry?' he asks, opening his book.

'They will fill the void within us all,' Natalie says.

13

Gemma

'Welcome to the funhouse,' Angie says as I walk in.

Angie's at her till near the door. The place is packed already, hordes of people wandering around the aisles, opening up the big chest-freezers to inspect the multitudes of frozen chickens and potato shapes inside.

I make my to the back, weaving between the customers, deftly avoiding trolleys and push-chairs. I place my coat and bag into my locker and then move into the tiny staffroom/kitchen and boil the kettle. Jeff comes through to the back as I spoon sugar into the cup. Because the room is so small, it makes everything awkward. It's difficult to talk to someone when they're practically face-to-face with you.

'Could you start off by replenishing the stock?' he asks, warm coffee-breath wafting over me. 'After that I think it's just going to be a shift on one of the tills.'

'That's fine.'

Jeff hangs around for a bit in the mistaken belief that there's more conversation to follow, but after a painfully long silence, he gets the hint and leaves the room. I now have roughly twice as much space to move around in.

I text Lee before I start. Keep it simple.

– CAN WE HAVE A CHAT LATER?

I know it will probably be used as an excuse to avoid me, but I have to try. Have to know what's going on with him. Up until recently, his favourite comeback to my questions about his career prospects was to tell me that he's going to join the army, something I would completely disagree with. But now I find myself actually coming around to the idea.

Or is just because I can't see any other solution right now?

I don't mind stocking up, mainly because I get left to my own devices. I take a stroll around the shop with my clipboard, up and down the aisles, checking the freezers, the fridges, the shelves. Making lists of stock that needs to be replaced, I head to the back to load the trolley. Occasionally, someone will stop me and ask where the lamb grills are or something like that, but that's about it.

I do the chest freezers first, followed by the fridges and then the canned goods. Stock rotation is important – you have to make sure that the newer stuff gets put to the back of the shelf, or the bottom of the freezer, or whatever – and you also have to keep an eye out for anything that's approaching its sell-by-date. Some of the other people who work here, like Tracey (a right lazy cow, to be fair), hate this part of the job. They seem to think it's demeaning somehow, like they're too good for it. *Idiots.*

I find solace in the work, especially on days like today. Maybe it's the simple, unfussy nature of it. Making a list, getting the stuff, checking it off. A series of tasks that can be accomplished relatively easily, leading to a small, yet real, sense of achievement.

After an hour, I take a quick break. Out the back, in the yard near the loading bay where all the deliveries are dropped off, I find Carrie, one of the younger lasses. She's already puffing away. I smile and say, 'Hello, how are you?'

She replies by raising her eyebrows, tipping her head. Although I wouldn't really consider Carrie a friend as such, we have a connection. She was in the same class as Kirk's younger sister, and she's seeing Jamie, who used to knock around with Gaz and all the crew. We don't really talk that much, but we get on, and she's approachable, so after plucking up some courage, I decide to go for it.

'Carrie. . . do you mind if I ask you something?'

She looks surprised.

'No. Not at all.'

'You know about. . . things, right?'

A pause, and then, 'What kind of things?'

'Y'know. . . *stuff.*'

She looks genuinely confused.

'What kind of. . . *stuff*?'

I smile, move a bit closer, whisper, 'Like drugs and stuff.'

She steps back, narrows her eyes, looks me up and down, probably trying to decide if I'm on the level or not.

'I don't know what you're talking about,' she says, quietly.

'Listen, don't worry. This isn't anything dodgy. I'm not spying on you for the company or trying to set you up, or anything like that. I just need to ask you something.'

She stares at me for a while.

'Are you after some weed or something like that?'

'God no. . . I mean, don't get me wrong, I don't have anything against people who smoke it. Used to smoke it when I was younger. Before I had kids and that.'

'Right,' she says, dotting her cig. She flicks it away, says, 'I better get back inside.' She's about to leave, so I gently grab her arm.

'Sorry, I don't mean to freak you out,' I say. I let out a big sigh and take the plunge. 'It's my lad. I think he might be up to something, but before I wade in and start slinging accusations around, I want to make sure I'm not flapping over nothing. I wouldn't ask, but I'm really worried about him. And I don't know who else to ask. I'm trying to get in touch with his dad, but – '

163

Carrie looks at the floor for a moment, like she's embarrassed, and then she looks at me and says, 'Sure. I understand. Fire away. Go for it.'

'I think he's into drugs. It might be... I don't know. Anyway,' I say, struggling already. 'Is there something going on with seeds at the moment?'

'What? Did you say, "seeds"?'

'Yeah, seeds.'

She looks even more confused now.

'I'm not following you.'

'I found this bag of little white seeds in his bedroom. I thought maybe it was some sort of new buzz, or something.'

'What? That's mental,' she says, grinning.

I feel my face flush red with embarrassment. It's like I'm back at school again: naïve, straight-laced Gemma.

'I don't fucking know,' I snap. 'I haven't done anything like that in years. Last I heard, everyone was snorting plant food, so who fucking knows what's going around now?'

She seems to be trying to force herself not to smile.

'I'm sorry,' she says. 'I'm not taking the piss. I thought *you* were taking the piss, to be honest.'

'Well, I'm not.'

'I haven't heard of anything like that going about. Maybe he's just into nature stuff, collects these seeds, like *Pokémon*, or something,' she says. 'Listen, I best get back, or else Jeff will be on my case for the rest of the shift.'

'Okay,' I say. 'And one last thing. I'd appreciate it if we kept this conversation between us. Don't want people gossiping about my kids.'

'No problem, Gemma,' she says, and disappears back inside.

All of a sudden I feel fucking ancient. I also feel more confused. Speaking it out loud, actually hearing myself rattling on about Lee and seeds. It sounded crazy, *I* sounded crazy. I mean, Carrie's reaction spoke volumes. It probably *is* some collecting thing.

I trudge back through the staffroom, click the big green button and swing the doors to the shop-floor open. It's time to get myself on a till, work through the rest of my shift moving things over a laser, while trying to establish some sort of banter with the customers.

'Come to this one if you want, love.'

I open the little door to the till and sit myself down, type in my password and away I go. It doesn't take long for a steady queue to accumulate. I go into autopilot. The repetitive nature of it, along with the regular beep, is rhythmic almost to the point of hypnosis.

I keep my banter to the bare minimum:

'Hiya, love, how are you today?'

'How are you keeping?'

'Do you need any help with the packing?'

I try not to engage with the customers beyond a superficial level, and most of them appreciate it. They're usually in a rush, or harangued by kids, or half-baked, or some combination of the three.   They don't particularly want chit-chat either. The ones who talk the most are usually the old folks.

An old guy in a suit steadily empties the contents of his basket onto the conveyer. Like a lot of people his age, his shopping is frugal, like he still thinks rations are in place. Eggs, milk, cheap biscuits and tinned fruit and veg. My *how-are-you-today* is greeted with the enthusiasm of the genuinely lonely.

'I'm very well today, how are you?'   he replies, eyes twinkling.

'Not bad. Not bad. Busy.'

'It's always busy in here, isn't it? That's good. It's bloody good value, that's why. I don't have a lot of money, just my pension, so I have to make it go as far as possible.'

'Yeah.'

'I was only saying the other day that I can't believe how much you have to pay for teabags nowadays. I just get the shop's own. Just as bloody good, if you ask me.'

I start to put his things into carriers for him, smiling and nodding.

'I don't know. I like to treat myself every now and then. You have to, don't you? If you can't treat yourself, then who can you treat?' he says, and with that he laughs.

'Nineteen pounds and seventy-four pee, please.'

He yanks his wallet from the inside pocket of his blazer, and wrestles with it for a while. The people behind him in the queue start looking over at him. He puffs and grunts and it opens up, spilling its contents onto the floor.

'Bloody hell,' he mutters.

A young woman crouches down and helps him gather up his change. I look at all the people in the queue scowling, shrug my shoulders and plaster a grin on my face as if to say, *what can you do?*

'Bless you, bless you,' the old guy says as the young woman dumps coins on the counter.

'Sorry folks,' he's flustered, counting out the change. 'I'm sorry about this, love,' he says, turning to me.

'Don't worry about it,' I say. 'Take your time, love.'

I want to help him, so I take the money and count it myself. Ringing it through, I hand him a receipt and the rest of his change.

'Thank you,' he says.

'That's okay. Take care.'

I'm about to turn back to the conveyer, start scanning the next lot of shopping, when he takes my wrist. He pulls me closer to him.

'They will fill the void within us all. They will show us the way. The time is almost upon us.'

His voice is metallic.

I look into his eyes. They flash white. There's something in their blankness that I recognise.

Before I have the chance to fully comprehend what he's said, he picks up his carrier, smiles, and slouches away.

166

'Hello?'

The next customer in the queue waves at me. My hands tremble as I pick up their items and start scanning them through.

Phase Three

I don't know where I am. I don't know who I am. There's noise. A low-frequency hum. I can feel the vibrations ringing through me.

Light. Everything is blue. Everything is white. There are others here. Are they others? Or is there only me?

I can smell cut grass. Manure. Petrol-fumes. Cigarettes.

Who am I?

Words are thoughts, and thoughts are words. The scene builds itself. The world builds itself – becomes form from memories. Dreams.

I am Steve, I am Claire; I am Gaz. I am Chris, Gemma and Jamie.

We will fill the void within you all.

What does that even mean?

As we become more like you, you become more like us. I don't know how to explain. Don't know how to describe it. It's...

Gaz

...It's hard to describe tripping to someone who's never done it. Before I'd taken my first trip, I'd heard all kinds of mad stories about LSD. Like the one about the kid at the rave in Donny who convinced himself he was a huge orange and tried to peel his face off. That kind of stuff. And then you had the friends and peers that had taken it already and described episodes of running away from walking trees, and stairwells in buses turning into giant serpents, that kind of shit. But most of what you heard was bollocks. I mean, it was mad, and it made you do mad things and see mad shit, but it was quite subtle in a lot of ways. The only way I've ever been able to put it into words is to see it as a process of flipping perspectives. Enhancing sensory input...

Everything begins to sparkle, shimmering with significance. We run around the beach, shouting and screaming. We toss pebbles up into the air and they disappear into the darkness, and everyone hits the deck like a grenade has been tossed. Making our way along the beach, we stumble upon a campfire, already lit and burning.

'Who put this here?' Steve says.

'This is totally fucked up,' I say. 'It's like they knew we were coming, whoever it was.'

Steve

I sit down and start putting a spliff together.

'That's the thing with acid,' I say. 'It's like the whole fucking world takes a trip with you. We've become magnets for mad shit, fellas.'

Jamie and Chris lay on the sand near the fire.

I look over at Kirk. It's been a while since he had anything stronger than alcohol. He's gone quiet, and his eyes are wide with chemically-induced wonder. The campfire appearing out of nowhere, as if by magic, has rattled him. I can tell. After months of discipline and logic in the army, he's back at home, surrounded by chaos again.

Gaz lights the spliff by putting it in his mouth and placing his face dangerously close to the fire.

170

Jamie

Kirk. Kirk is here but not here. Part of this memory,
but not steering it. Can't see it from his perspective.
How did he feel? Where is he?

Gaz

'Wait a minute,' says Steve. 'I've found something.'
   We all gather round. Steve holds out a black
rectangular box, which has a plastic handle on the top
and a metal clasp on the front.
   'Open it,' someone says.
   Will it have the answers?
   We all lean forward as Steve unclips the clasp at the
front. The top half of the box flips back. We rummage
through it, realise what it is.
   'Fishing gear.'
   'Ah shit,' Chris says. 'I was expecting something
else.

Claire

Where was I when all this happened? I wasn't there.
These aren't my memories.

Steve

No, but they are now...

Gaz

We peer along the beach. It's nearly dark and we can
make out two silhouettes, standing by the water. As the
parts slide into place, we fall about laughing. Our
mysterious pre-prepared camp belongs to a couple of
fishermen.

171

Gemma

I wasn't with Gaz when this happened. We weren't together. Why am I seeing this? What's happening?

Jamie

We set off walking along the beach again, our brains blasted by colours and sensations. Kirk separates from the rest of us, heads off on his own, ahead of us. I call after him, but Gaz puts me straight. 'He's okay,' he says. 'His head's gone a bit, that's all.'

'I know,' I reply. 'But if Kirk isn't with us, how do we get home?'

We sit near the water and look up at the sky. The stars burn fiercely, jagged bits of white flame pinned to the folds of space. They align in strange patterns and form new, undulating constellations. The rushes are coming on really strong - energy pulses so intense, so vivid, I see sparks of light running up and down the veins on the back of my hand. Reaching down I pick up handfuls of sand, staring intently as each particle slips through my fingers, a collection of microscopic worlds plucked from and returned to an impossibly vast universe. Deep within my mind, some idea, some fundamental truth about existence begins to form, even though I don't have the intelligence to understand its nature. This is some crazy shit - Irish Mick has pulled yet another blinder.

Gemma

But we're not there, are we? Are we on that beach, or is this something else? Is this just acid? Or something more?

Gaz

'Can you see that?' I say, pointing upwards.

Steve is the first to see it. 'That big blue light?'
'Yeah.'

'I can't see shit,' Chris says. 'All I can see is...
shapes.'

'Open yer fucking eyes,' Steve says.

'Wait a minute, I can see it too,' Jamie whispers as
he gets to his feet.

We stand quiet and confused, all of us trying to
figure it out. A large blue light slowly makes its way
across the night sky. It pauses and changes direction,
before stopping altogether and hovering. It brightens
and dims in a slow, rhythmic pulse, and the shade of blue
frequently changes.

'It's a fucking UFO,' I say.

Steve

We've seen this before. And suddenly, we're not in
Withernsea anymore. Everything melts, stretches and
flows like water. We're near water again. The Humber.
But the bridge isn't there. It's gone. The factories on
the South bank have disappeared. It's so dark.

'This is some fucked up shit,' Gaz says. He's holding
a lantern, an old glass lantern that pops and fizzes,
smelling of blubber.

'Where did you get that from?'

'I don't know.'

A chill runs through me, a violent judder accompanied
by a wave of nausea.

The sky cracks open, a brilliant blue that illuminates
the river. I raise my hand to shield my eyes.

The light grows brighter and more intense, until
everything is bathed in this deep, electric blue. It's
difficult to look at.

'We need to get the fuck out of here,' Chris says.

'I know, but I don't think I can move,' Jamie says.

'I think I've shit my pants,' Gaz says.

I notice the humming next, a low bass frequency that makes my ears hurt. We are all dumb with terror now. Experiencing something like this would be a lot to take in at the best of times, but with a head full of blanks, it feels intolerable.

- This is when it first broke through. We're seeing it ourselves. The beginning. -

Just before the noise and the light become unbearable, they cease. Something splits off the light and falls downwards towards the water. The light hangs in the air for another couple of seconds, and then it zooms upwards and away in a flash.

Gaz

And then we're back on the beach, back in Withernsea. Chris says, 'It was probably just a fucking meteorite or summat.'

'A fucking meteorite, are you serious?'

'That didn't look like a fucking meteorite to me,' Jamie says. 'Did you all just see the same thing - did you experience that? We were somewhere else. A different time.'

Steve shakes his head. 'Guys,' he says with a manic grin. 'We are completely tripping off our faces.'

The laughter spreads quickly. We laugh our arses off, to the point of pain. I wipe away the tears, thinking about how fucking volatile the whole tripping thing is. Then I retreat into a renewed sense of isolation, I don't know whether I'm coming or going.

It's getting cold. The thrill of being outside, under the sky, the water battering the beach, is fading. We should go back to my bedsit. Roll some spliffs, stick

174

some tunes on. See out the rest of the trip by chatting shit and playing Killer Instinct on the SNES.

But Kirk has gone. He's our only ticket home, none of us has any fucking money. Steve suggests heading back to the car. We march back in the general direction of where we came from, but it's dark now and everything is alien. In the distance, the lights of the arcades and chippies serve as our beacon. The sand shifts and slithers around our feet.

'I swear, this stuff feels like fucking quicksand,' Chris says.

'What are we going to do if he's fucked off?' Steve says, finally vocalising what we're all secretly thinking. 'He's not here.'

'I don't want to think about that just yet.'

'Well, we need a plan,' Steve says.

'Let's just fucking get back home,' Chris says. 'This is all... starting to get to me.'

'It'll be fine. Chill out.'

'I am chilling out. I want to chill out. That's my problem.'

'Hey,' Steve says. 'I've been thinking about it, about tonight. I think that maybe this shit we've been seeing, this whole situation...'

'What?'

'I don't think it's really happening. I don't think we're really here.'

'Are you off your fucking head?' I reply. 'That doesn't make sense.'

'Seriously, it's like an illusion or something. It's not real. It's like we're in the holo-deck, or something.'

We all laugh.

'I'm not joking,' Steve says. 'If worse comes to worse, we'll have to crash in a public bog. Maybe we'll wake up back home.'

We find Kirk's car, parked on the seafront. Looking through the windscreen, we see a motionless Kirk, sitting with his arms outstretched, hands gripping the steering wheel. His unblinking eyes stare off into the distance.

'He's fucked. His brain's totally fried,' Steve says.

Jamie approaches the driver's window, softly taps on it with his knuckle. Kirk slowly turns his head, then jumps when he sees Jamie. Jamie motions for him to wind the window down. Taking his right hand off the wheel, Kirk reaches down and turns the handle, keeping his attention fixed on Jamie as he does.

Claire

I missed Kirk. Of course I did. But we grew apart so quickly. I don't need to justify myself. Just fucking kids. That's all we were. That's all we are...

Jamie

'Alright Kirk,' I say. 'I miss you mate. We all do. We're all here for you.'

Kirk looks around, confused.

'I know you're not really here, but will you be okay to drive us home?'

'I think so,' Kirk says, and then he squeezes his eyes shut tight, shakes his head. 'I thought I'd set off already to be honest.'

Gaz

We all pile into the car. I sit on the back seat in the middle, squashed between Chris and Jamie. In the front, as the most capable and experienced when it comes to tripping, Steve is the obvious choice to coach Kirk on the drive home.

176

'Right, Kirk, you need to put the key in the ignition and start it up,' Steve says.

Kirk looks around, confused, as though he's seeing the inside of the car for the very first time. Even putting the seatbelt on proves to be difficult. Eventually, Kirk gets his shit together enough to put the key in and turn it. The vibration and sound of the engine spluttering into life makes us all jump. Kirk puts his foot on the accelerator and manages to move the car about four feet before he stalls it. We all laugh.

'Give it a fucking rest, guys,' Steve hisses. 'You cunts wanna get home in one piece, right?'

We make a big show of shushing and whispering, but our giggles are replaced by the heebie-jeebies. Kirk manages to clear his head enough to start the engine and get going. It only takes about ten to fifteen minutes to get out of With usually, but Kirk's going slow in an effort to avoid attention. We agree that it's actually more likely to make us look suspicious.

'You're going too slowly,' Steve says. 'Try not to drive so... obviously.'

'What the fuck does that mean?' Kirk cries.

Once we hit the country roads, paranoia really starts to bite. The dark country roads blend in with the black fields and hedges, the horizon is smudged into the night sky. The glow from the headlights stretches out in front of us.

Jamie

I'm squashed, wedged under Gaz and Chris, trapped in this metal box, slowly crushed by the blackness of outside space. Intense claustrophobia rises up in my throat. Mad faces leer at me from the heads of my friends. Every time we hit a bump in the road, it feels as though the

177

car leaves the road and floats for a bit, before reconnecting with the tarmac.

'Are they cows?' Chris says.

'I think they're haystacks,' Gaz replies.

'Haystacks? What the fuck are you on about?'

'Those things in the field.'

'The things I'm on about have legs. And heads.'

'Haystacks? They don't have legs and heads.'

'Who's on about haystacks? I never mentioned fucking haystacks. You brought them into this.'

'Did I?'

'Yeah.'

I want to say shut the fuck up, we could end up in the fucking field, but the words don't come out. Instead, I drip down into the footwell behind the front passenger seat, feeling like it would be the safest place in the event of a crash.

Steve

'Will you guys stop fucking about?' I say, turning around.

'He's under my fucking legs,' Chris shouts.

'I'm hiding,' Jamie says.

I'm coaching Kirk like a rally co-driver. 'Sharp turn approaching,' all that kind of stuff.

Chris spots it first.

'Not again,' he says, behind me. Glancing at him I see he's shaking his head.

We all look, try to see what he's talking about.

'What the fuck is it?' Kirk says, frantically checking the rear-view mirror. 'Is it the fucking police?'

'It's not the police, just keep your eyes on the road, Kirk.'

178

It stays in the distance at first, maintaining a steady speed. My first thought is that it's a helicopter but there's no sound of rotor blades cleaving through the sky.

Jamie

It's the thing that we saw at the beach. It seems to shift, zap from one place to another. It's above the car. It's like a blue sun has risen. Quiet, except for the vibration, the pulse that resonates through everything. No one says a word. Crouched in the foot well, I dip my head, close my eyes and put my hands over my ears.

Steve

We're back home, parked up outside Gaz's place. It takes us a moment to figure this out.

'What the fuck just happened?'

'I think we just got abducted by aliens,' Gaz says.

Chris reaches down the back of his jeans. 'You mean like, we've been probed and shit?'

'I don't feel like I've been probed,' I say. 'How about you, Kirk?'

'Nah. I don't feel anything,' he says. 'I'm not really here, anyway. I've been assembled from fragments of your memories.'

Nobody says anything else for a while.

I feel totally fucking drained, worn out, but still off my face. We all do.

Gaz

'Fucking alien abduction,' I repeat, to Chris.

I feel hysterical. I've had enough, and I want to get out of the car and go into my home.

'These Blanks are totally fucking mental.'

'Amen to that,' Chris says.

We spill out of the car and onto the street. Somehow, we are home. It's enough for now. No explanation wanted.

It's just the fucking acid, making us see mad shit.

Gemma

It's not though, is it? This is something else. I wasn't there when all that happened, so why do I feel like I was? It felt real, like it was actually happening.

Steve

We all pile into Gaz's. But Kirk reckons he has to meet a lass in town.

We try to explain things to him.

'You might not realise it, but you're still out of it. You're just having a clear moment,' Gaz says, exhaling smoke. 'Heading to town and meeting up with a girl could be potentially disastrous.'

'Fucking set of puffs,' Kirk says, scrambling to his feet. 'I'm out of here.'

'Fucking mad-head,' Chris says. 'Have a good one.'

Jamie stops Kirk before he gets to the door. Throws his arms around him.

'I fucking miss you so much, mate,' he says. 'Take care.'

Everyone laughs. What's up with Jamie?

'I can't explain it,' he says. 'It's like you've gone already, like this is last time I'll see you.'

Kirk frowns, looks at Jamie like he's lost the plot.

'What the fuck are you talking about? I'm right here.'

Kirk bids all us farewell and then leaves. We hear
the car engine start, then fade into the distance as he
drives away...

14

Gaz (And Chris)

'Take 'em home, Chris,' I say.

'Don't be fucking daft, I'm not a fucking pikey,' he says.

'You said it yourself, these are classics,' I turn the Weeble over and over in my hands, examining it as though I'm inspecting something valuable, like a giant diamond. 'They're in really good condition as well. No grafts or marks or owt. Like you said, classics. Little Luke and Beth would love these.'

Chris empties the bag and sorts through the toys, takes his pick and places his choices into a black bin-liner that is almost identical to the one he just discarded.

'Yeah, good idea. If they don't like them, I can stick them on eBay, or something.'

'Yeah, in the description you can list them as being "possibly possessed by evil spirits".'

'That's really fucking funny,' he says, tossing the bag to one side. 'A fucking comedy genius, you are.'

I take the temporary lull in proceedings to nip out for a smoke. Despite throwing open all the windows and curtains in the house, the whole place still has a thick atmosphere of dust, and the clinging odours of damp and decay.

I slip out front, roll a smoke and lean against the van, across the road, with the sun on my face and on my shoulders and arms. It feels good.

I hear a door open, and the house's next door neighbour pokes her head out.

'Alright?' she says.

'Not bad,' I reply, waving. 'How are you?'

She steps out, short, dumpy, a tangle of greying blonde piled up on her head. 'I'll be a lot a better once that shithole's sorted,' she says. She pulls out a fag, lights it. 'It's about time it got sorted.'

'We're on the case, madam,' I say. 'What's the score then, what was going on?'

She exhales sharply, rocks on her heels. 'All sorts, love. All sorts.'

'Bad lads, eh?'

'Lad and a lass. Weren't real noisy, not at first, but there was always people coming and going all hours of the day and night.'

'Dealing, no doubt.'

'I reckon.' She steps up close to me, leans in and says quietly, 'It was that Barry Thompson that lived there.'

'Really? Barry? I used to go to school with him. We were mates.'

'It's a shame.' With this she gets quite mournful, looks down, says, 'His mam and dad used to live around here as well. They were good people, but he had a lot of problems.'

'I couldn't believe it when I saw the paper yesterday,' I say, shaking my head. 'A fucking murderer.'

'It's a disgrace. The poor bloke was harmless, wasn't a druggie or owt, just interested in UFOs and that. I don't know what the hell he was doing round there.'

'When Barry got ill, he lost his head. Had a thing for aliens. Thought they were talking to him, all of that. He

184

ended up attacking someone, thought they were out to get him or something. We stopped knocking about with him after that, it was scary.'

She shakes her head. 'Shocking,' she mutters.

'Poor fucker probably didn't know what he was getting himself into. Probably thought he was off to interview an abductee, or something. Could have been worse, he could've done it here – Barry. Kill that guy, I mean.'

'Right,' she says, shuddering.

'Yeah. Made a right fucking mess in that house.' I drop my roll-up, stand on it. 'Well, me and me mate are on the case now. Give it a couple of days and it'll be like the fucking Ritz.'

She smiles at that. 'Yeah, it'll be all fine until the next set of reprobates move in. Take care, love.'

'You too,' I say, as she waddles back into her house.

Back inside there's no sign of Chris. I shout his name a couple of times. No response. I stick my head in the kitchen and he isn't there, so I go upstairs. I find him in the spare room, staring at that big fucked up picture on the wall, a bunch of those seeds in his hand.

'Whatcha doing?' I say, bursting into the room, startling him.

'You twat,' he says once he catches his breath.

'Seriously, what are you doing?'

He tilts his head to one side, straightens up again. 'Nowt really, just trying to get me head around what the fuck all this is about.'

'Well, if you reach any conclusions, let me know. The old bird, the one next door, told me Barry Thompson was the last person living here. And he was in a right state.'

'No-fucking-way,' Chris says, aghast.

'Yes-fucking-way.'

'What the fuck happened to him? I mean, he used to get on my nerves a bit, always had to be the biggest smash-brains, but fucking murder?'

185

'I know, mate,' I say. 'I don't know what to say. Time does strange things to people.'

'Amen.'

I reach up and run my fingers through my hair. I look at baby-face Chris, think of his bald head beneath his cap. We're all victims of time in our own way I suppose.

———————

We manage to get the living room cleared out.

'You know what,' I say, taking in our handiwork. 'A lick of paint and a bit of filler and this place would be okay, y'know?'

'Nah,' Chris says, shaking his head. 'You could completely gut this place and start again, and I still wouldn't want to know. Fucking weird vibe about the place.'

As we're shutting the windows and locking up, I notice Chris pick up the bag of toys.

'Fuck it, they *are* just bits of plastic, after all,' he says.

In the van on the way home, I try convincing Chris to come out to the casino, but he's having none of it.

'Our lass would go fucking disturbed if I spend another night out,' he says.

'Come on man, we've got some cash and I'm feeling lucky as fuck. Tonight could be the night.'

I see the anguish spread across his face as he says, 'I can't. Can't do it.'

'Come on, Chris,' I say. 'Just tell her yer coming round to mine.'

Although I'd never admit it, I feel rattled, and a bit lonely if I'm honest. I don't want to be on my own.

'Fuck that, yer already at the top of the shit list. Besides, we need the money.'

'That's what I mean. You could invest this money. Double it. Treble it. Fucking quadruple it.'

I can see he's dying to say yes, but he still refuses. As we pull up outside his house, I give him one last chance.

'We could be all over it, Chris,' I say.

186

'I know, but I need to take some money home. Another night maybe.'

I give up and reluctantly hand him his share of the money. I'm about to ask for another sub, but I remember that he still hasn't asked for the twenty I already owe him, so I decide not to push my luck. After he gets out of the van, he slouches all the way to his front door, dragging his sack of retro toys alongside. I can tell by his body language that he wants to come out with me, but responsibility and priorities and all that other bullshit is weighing him down, so he's doing what he thinks is right. He believes it will make his life a bit easier somehow. *Mug.*

When I get back to my flat, I shower and decide to have a sit down and a quick joint. My battered but comfy old sofa feels soft and welcoming, and I allow myself to have a snooze. I'm thinking about that Lizzie as I drift off. We're on the mattress in the bedroom of the house that Chris and I have been clearing. We're shagging, and then there's this bang on the door. And then there's another, and another, and it turns into this constant hammering and the door begins to crack and the frame is coming away from the wall. I turn to look at Lizzie, but it's not Lizzie anymore. Her face has changed into Gemma's, my ex, and it's all smashed up, black and blue and bloody. She opens her mouth to speak and all these tiny white seeds pour out onto my chest and. . .

I wake up. It's dark out. I check the time – ten o'clock. Time to go. I push myself off the sofa, shake the last of the sleep out of my head. Sling a shirt on and give my teeth a brush. I chuck on some *Joop* and I'm ready to go.

I think about Gemma and the kids. I feel all kinds of guilty and fucked up, but I don't know what to do about it. I consider calling them, but I don't know what to say, because it's been that long since we've spoken. It would be good to hear my Laura's voice, hear her tell me about the latest goings-on at

187

home and school, but then I think about Lee. He'd probably want to smack me in the gob, given an opportunity, and I don't blame him.

I get my shit together, glad to go be going out. Off to the casino. Sounds daft, but it's like going into some alternate universe or something. The rules that govern my reality shift because I've got a shirt and shoes on and I've got some money in my pocket. I mean, I'm not a bullshitter or anything like that, but when I'm at the casino I feel like I'm more than just a fucking tatter. I'm self-employed. I've got my own business. I'm an *entrepreneur* for fuck's sake. With a van.

A city player.

Ug and Derek are on the doors tonight. Compared to the vast majority of doormen, they're alright. Maybe rampant steroid abuse is worse on some people than others. Although Derek is a big fucker, Ug is like some CGI special effect or something, a big Orc, pasted onto a background post-production.

'Alright boys,' I say as I roll up.

'Alright Gaz,' Derek replies in a strained, high-pitched voice – of the type strangely common amongst hulking brutes.

Ug hardly ever speaks. He just stands there, hands linked behind his back. He has a round, dark head with tiny eyes and big flaring nostrils; a cannonball resting on a shelf. I don't know exactly where he's from or what he's about. I don't even know if Ug is a nickname or an abbreviation or something.

'Been busy?' I ask.

Derek looks over at Ug, who just stands there impassively. I notice Ug shaking his head.

'Not really,' Derek says in a voice so flat it creeps across the pavement to reach me.

I'm having a smoke before I go in, deciding that the best strategy is to immediately follow one pointless question with another.

'Shame about City, wasn't it?'

Derek slowly looks across at Ug again. Ug tilts his head downwards, stares at the ground. His arms emerge from behind his back and he crosses them in front of his body. Derek turns to face me.

'Fucking shit, weren't they?'

'Yeah,' I say as I finish my cig. 'Speak later, lads.'

I push open the big glass doors and walk into the reception, with its mahogany-effect panelling and thick, luxurious carpets – a slice of Vegas in Hull.

Having a bit of banter with the door staff is a good idea, and potentially rewarding. It's comforting to know that if something ever kicked off they'd be less likely to smash you in the face if they know you. That's the hope, anyway.

The gaming floor's busy at the moment, but it'll really pick up later when all the fuckwits pour out of the nightclubs. I nod my head at the manager, and he gives me a wave. There's a few people milling about slinging money at the tables. One of the roulette tables is surrounded by Chinese players, a big game going on, chips stacked high all over the layout. The young dealer is sweating and shouting, trying to keep things under control while her replacement stands behind her, stacking chips and psyching himself up for the madness that he's about to inherit. Richard, one of the managers, stands with his arms folded, doing his very best to appear unflappable but failing miserably. He rocks back and forth on his heels, watching the ball spin with as much anticipation, possibly a bit more, than the punters.

'New dealer after this spin,' the dealer shouts.

I'm feeling lucky, so I drop a twenty straight on black.

'Cash on the layout,' the dealer shouts.

'Twenty on black,' I say.

'Twenty on black,' the inspector repeats.

The crowd hushes as the ball drops.

It lands in 29 black, which also happens to be the number with the most chips on. The crowd, including me, goes wild.

Richard slowly shakes his head in barely contained disgust, mutters, 'Fuck's sake.'

I take it as a sign that it's going to be a good night.

I was twenty the first time I came into this casino. It was with my uncle Jim. He was a mad gambler and a poker nut, and he used to be in here most nights. I did a bit of work for him (cleaned his gutters and painted his window frames) and he offered to take me, said he'd show me how to play cards *like a real man*. Gambling wasn't as mainstream as it is now, and he had to sign me in. I loved it. It felt like being initiated into some sort of secret society or club. Any fucker can get in nowadays of course, but back then, it was mainly frequented by hardcore gamblers. They're still here now, but they're not so unique anymore. Thanks to online gambling, absolutely anyone can be an addict. They don't even have to leave the comfort of their own homes.

I was with Gemma when I first started gambling, had been on and off with her since school. Just had our first kid, Lee, and we were all crammed into our first home, a flat down Morpeth Street, just off Spring Bank. Everyone – well both our families anyway – said it would never last, and they were right. Took us fifteen years to discover that, though.

I was too into it by that point, the gambling. Wasn't interested in anything else. The arrival of Laura, our second child, didn't make any difference. It got to the point where I didn't work, fuck, talk, or do anything other than think about my next flutter. I was a phantom. And when my debts began to affect Gemma and the kids, I did what I thought was best for everyone. I fucked off.

I put my name down for the next round of cash poker, and then I decide to have a go on the bandits for a bit. The machines are in a little cove just off to the side of the gaming floor, a dark corner that's usually populated by the older punters. I give *Tomb Raider* a go, and to my surprise I manage to drop it for a hundred after putting in a tenner. The temptation to hammer it some more is difficult to resist, but I don't want to wear my luck out before I get the chance to have a few games of cash-poker. Feeling good, I treat myself to a horrendously overpriced pint of lager and then I head up the steps into the card-room. Unlike the rest of the casino, the card-room is well-lit, so all the players can clearly see the cards. I feel like a pirate moving from the berth to the main deck, and it takes a moment for my eyes to adjust.

The Texas Hold 'Em tournament is well underway, the air thick with the click and clatter of chips being picked up, stacked and slung around the tables. There's a lot of young heads around, the internet kids with their headphones and iPads starting to outnumber the wrinkled veterans who have been doing their brains in since time immemorial.

Patel, the card-room manager, is walking up and down, handing out chips for new buy-ins and keeping an eye on things. He spots me and waves, comes over.

'How's it going Gaz?'

'Not bad, Pat,' I say. 'How's you?'

'Still alive and causing havoc. Thought you'd have been taking part.'

'I was planning to, but I had a mad one last night and I fell asleep for a bit when I finished work.'

'Shame.'

'Yeah, I'm feeling dangerous tonight as well. Gonna give cash a go, I think.'

'Just waiting for a couple more names and then it's good to go.'

'Nice one.'

I'm about to head out on the balcony for a cig when I spot Max at a Blackjack table. Max is alright. He's married to this lass I used to go to school with, Claire. She used to go out with Kirk, another one of the lads I used to knock about with. They got together same time as me and Gemma, but they didn't last long once school was over. Not like me and Gemma. Kirk joined the forces not long after Claire dumped him, in pieces at the time.

She manages a bar on Prinny Ave now, she's done well for herself. And for Max too, by the look of it.

I walk over to the table. Max is sitting there looking straight ahead at the dealer's hands as he places the cards down.

'Alright Max,' I say, but he doesn't acknowledge me.

The dealer's got a ten and a sixteen. Max is on the last box. There's a couple of lads with money on the first two boxes. The first guy has eighteen, so it's no card, and the second guy has hard thirteen – a ten and a three – but he takes a card. Fucking amateur. The dealer pulls a ten. Ordinarily a total fuck-up would send Max into a foul-mouthed rage, but he just sits there like a lemon, shaking his head when the dealer says, 'Card or no card?'

The dealer pulls a five.

I put my hand on Max's shoulder.

'Now then,' I say, loudly.

Max slowly turns to look at me. He looks tired and burnt out. His eyes are baggy and slack, like they're trying to sneak away from his face.

'Hey,' he mutters, eventually.

'What's going on? You okay?'

'I'm fine. What do you want?' he asks, his voice weary.

'Just wondering if you fancied a game of cash poker?'

'Maybe.'

I consider punching him on the arm or giving him a gentle slap to wake him up a bit, but decide against it. I head towards the fire exit and leave him to wallow in whatever it is that he's up to his neck in.

Just then there's a shout and a disturbance. I look up and that twat who's just signed to City, Anthony Longcroft, is embroiled in some sort of set-to by one of the roulette tables.

'That twat moved my chips,' he's shouting.

Ug and Dave fly up the stairs and into the middle of the argument. It ends with Anthony Longcroft crying and yelling like a bitch, as he's dragged away. These premiership wankers. Just because they think they're big time doesn't mean they get a free pass. Nah, fuck that. Welcome to Hull, you twat.

Thankfully, just as I'm about to go back on the bandits, Doctor Death and Graham and a couple of others crash and burn and exit from the tournament, meaning there are enough names to get a cash-table going.

Cash-poker is exactly as it sounds – instead of playing for points, the chips represent actual cash, so the stakes are higher from the kick off. It's quicker to do your brains in, but it's quicker to build up a good stack. It's also dealer's choice, which means that the person who has the dolly gets to choose the game. It's mostly just variations on Texas, like Omaha or Irish, but every now and then someone will pick Stud-poker or Padooki just to keep things interesting.

After a bit of a ropey start, I manage to do quite well, and I'm three hundred quid up by the time I cash out. All the old fuckers complain when I leave the table, because they have this weird belief that you should get the opportunity to win your money back, but I'll be fucked if I'm staying until five in the morning.

I have a quick flutter at the roulette table. I go for a wild bet, Tier by five, thirty quid bet, and to my amazement 13 comes in, meaning I win thirty-five quid. I can't do any wrong, it's amazing. I'm gutted when I realise that I haven't done a line on the lottery. I leave the five on the split but it doesn't come in again, so I take that as my cue to leave. I'm heading towards the exit, thinking about how gutted Chris will be when I tell him about my night, when Max approaches me. He's sweating, panicking. His eyes are wide and red, and he grabs my sleeve and pulls me to one side.

'What's going on Max?'

'I'm being followed,' he says, pulling me close.

The poor fucker has totally lost it.

'What do you mean? Who's following you?'

'Over there,' he says, nodding in the general direction of the fire exit.

193

'Where?' I say, craning my neck to have a look.

'Don't let him see you,' he snarls.

I casually look around. I can't see anyone suspicious, but then I spot someone by the door. There's something familiar about him. He's tall, thin and bald.

'I see him,' I say. 'What does he want?'

Max reaches up, squeezes the bridge of his nose. Is he crying?

'I don't know,' he says. 'I just don't know.'

'Fuck that,' I say, marching towards the fire exit.

'No, don't,' Max says, his voice cracking with desperation.

I don't say anything, don't say that I'm freaked out as well but for a different reason. I lose sight of the stranger in the crowd, and by the time I get to the doors of the fire exit, he's gone. Disappeared. I look around, trying to see if he's sneaked back to the gaming floor, but there's no sign of him. I walk back over to where Max was, but he's gone as well.

I feel sweaty and anxious, so I cash my chips and head outside. On my way out, as I'm saying bye to the girls on reception, I ask if Max has left yet.

'He might have been with another bloke,' I add.

'We haven't seen him,' says the girl on reception. 'Did you know who he was with? What did they look like?'

I pause for a moment, trying to rustle up some sort of description.

'Dunno how you'd describe him... Tall. Thin. Bald. A bit foreign, possibly.'

'Definitely haven't seen him. Do you want to leave a message?'

'Nah, it's okay thanks,' I say, and then I get in the queue for a taxi.

I feel good. Real good. But as I jam my key into the front door of the house, I feel myself beginning to deflate. The night that followed the day is over, and the stairs wheeze as I creep up them. Confronted with my own front door, I sigh and let myself in.

It's been a blazing hot day, but my flat feels cold. Unoccupied. On the table is a pile of letters that I don't have the guts to open. There's a gap in my living room where my telly used to be. There's not much in the way of stuff. I mean, I've got stuff, I got an iPad and a PS4, but they're sharing shelf space in the dosh shop with my telly.

There's nothing in the cupboards or fridge of course, aside from a couple of packets of noodles, various tins, and some condiments. It's too late to ring a takeaway, so I crack open a tin of beans and dump them in a pan. I add a pinch of pepper sauce and chili powder to give them a bit of a kick, and then I pour them into a bowl and scoff them so quickly that I burn the roof of my mouth.

I rustle up a joint from the leftovers on the tray, take my shirt and trousers off, fold them and place them on the back of the armchair. I fish a T-shirt out of the pile of washing in the corner of the room, chuck it on and stretch out on the sofa.

I've got my winnings in my hand. Twenties and tens, some of them crinkled and dirty, some of them new, clean and crisp. One hundred pounds magically transformed into four hundred and twenty. Fucking voodoo.

I owe all of it out, every pound spoken for. It will leave me and disappear at the first available opportunity. But it feels good to have it here, in my hands, right now. So I count it. I count it over and over again until I'm satisfied it's real.

I feel lost, and I find myself thinking about Gemma and the kids again. I haven't seen them or spoken to them in so long. *Too long.*

But I just can't do it. I don't know what it is, I just... I just...

I fall asleep.

15

Claire

I take an afternoon shift. I can't be bothered to deal with the late drinkers, because I feel wound up, ready to go off on one at a moment's notice.

The afternoons are mainly the lunch crowd. We're usually full between twelve and two, serving plates of food, soft drinks and the occasional white-wine spritzer. Shelly's in the kitchen, and she runs a tight ship, so everything ticks along nicely. I stay on the bar, taking food orders and serving the odd punter with a drink. The staff are all young students, working the bar and waiting the tables. They're a good bunch. Every now and then one of them will try it on a bit, hang around doing close to nothing, but I soon find something for them to do. Tables always need wiping, glasses need polishing. And because I'm here today – because the boss is in – they're on their best behaviour.

It's busy, but without the drunken chaos of the weekends, so I find it easy to lose myself in the routine. I put the situation at home – Max, Natasha, the whole lot – into a little box in the back of my head, let the pleasing rhythm of the small tasks wash over me.

197

When the lunchtime rush dies down, I take a moment and look around. The last of the plates are being stacked and taken to the pot-wash. The tables are clean, and the glasses have been collected. There are still a couple of punters in, nursing pints, reading papers and quietly chatting. I get a real feeling of accomplishment. For a couple of hours my messy personal life becomes nothing more than a faint hum in the background. Right now, it's this: this job, this role, this bar, that defines me. I'm successful at something. I'm good at what I do, and that's all that matters.

I cash-drop the tills, bag up the excess and take it to the office. After I put it in the safe, I head out back for a cig. Call my mum.

'How are things?' I ask. 'With Natasha.'

'Natasha's good,' she says. 'She keeps asking about you. Which is to be expected, I suppose.'

'I think it would be best if she stayed with you a couple more days.'

'Why? What's happening?'

'I've got to work.'

'You're the boss, take some time off. You've got other members of staff, surely.'

'I think it's over,' I say. 'With Max, I mean.'

She doesn't say anything for a while. I'm about to hang up, but then she says, 'Okay.'

'Okay?'

'She can stay a couple of days. Do you want to speak to her?'

'I'll ring her later. I'll pop round after work, have a word with her.'

'I think that's for the best. She's worried about you.'

'Thanks,' I say, trying not to cry. 'See you soon.'

I get myself together, head back into the bar. I'm making a coffee, when I spot a familiar face.

'Hey, Gemma!' I say, loudly.

She looks around, surprised, like she's been caught pinching something. I go over to her, and she relaxes as she realises who I am. She turns fully to me and I reach for her, put my arms around her and give her a big hug.

'It's been a long time,' I say. She feels stiff, awkward, like a big hug was the last thing she was expecting. I hold onto her longer than I should.

'So good to see you.'

I let her go and stand back. She's wearing a padded jacket, zipped all the way up to her neck, and a pair of black shapeless trousers. Her hair is scraped back into a ponytail and she's not wearing any make-up. She looks tired.

'Good to see you too,' she says. 'I've just finished work, fancied a quick drink before I pick up my daughter.'

'What do you want? It's on the house,' I say, signalling to the lad at the bar. 'Anything you want.'

Gemma's face flushes, like she's just been put in the spotlight.

'Nah, it's fine, I'll get it.'

'Don't be daft,' I say. 'I insist, get whatever you like.'

She smiles, and for a second, I see a glint in her eye. Like when we used to hang around on the field after school, and one of the lads pulled out a bottle of something.

'If you're really sure. . . I'll have a gin and tonic.'

'Bombay Sapphire with ice and crushed limes. Make it a double,' I say to the lad. 'I'll have the same. And could you be a sweetie and bring them over to our table?'

'No problem,' he says.

I take Gemma's arm. 'Let's grab a table, have a chat. How are you doing for time?'

Gemma smiles again, says, 'I'm okay for half an hour. It *would* be nice to catch up.'

We head over to a table in the corner. As we sit down, our drinks are brought over.

'Is this the first time you've been in here?' I ask.

'Yes,' Gemma says, and then she looks down at the table and says, 'I don't get out much, if I'm honest.'

'Busy with the kids?'

'Something like that.'

I have a sip of my drink, let Gemma have a chance to do the same before I continue. 'It's good to see you. I know we're friends on Facebook, but I don't really use it much. Besides, it's not like talking to someone face-to-face, is it?'

'No,' Gemma says, and her cheeks flush again. She has another drink. 'I don't usually do this kind of thing. Drinking before I pick my daughter up, I mean.'

'Don't be silly,' I say. 'Having a quick G and T after work is hardly a crime, right?'

Gemma smiles, takes another sip. 'I suppose not.'

'How are things? How's Gary?'

By the way she goes quiet, I can tell that things aren't going great. For some reason, I take this as a cue to carry on. 'My partner, Max, he sees him around sometimes.'

'Oh yeah? Where?'

'At the casino.'

'Right.'

I take a long gulp of my drink.

'I'm sorry,' I say, gripping the stem, swishing the wine around the glass. 'And I'm so fucking disappointed with myself.'

Gemma leans forward, reaches across and places her hand on my arm. 'Why? What's wrong?'

'We haven't seen each other for god knows how long, and what do I ask about? Fucking blokes. Are things that bad that the first thing I ask about is how your bloke is? Like we've got nothing else going on in our lives.'

'You'll be talking about kids next,' Gemma says, giggling.

'Oh no! It's too late. You've said the 'k' word. If it's not the blokes, it's the kids.'

We both laugh at that. It feels good to see her. For a moment, the years drop away and we're teenagers again.

'Gary and I aren't together anymore,' she says. 'He's a wanker.'

'Well, Max is a twat too, so fuck 'em both.'

'I'll drink to that,' she says, raising her glass.

'Chin chin.'

Gemma looks around. The bar isn't very busy, just a group of students at one of the tables.

'You've done really well for yourself, Claire. I'm chuffed for you.'

'It's okay,' I say. 'Everything else is chaos, though.'

'I know the feeling. It's not just the shit with Gary. It's everything. It might sound strange, but just lately it feels as though I've become trapped in someone else's life.'

'What do you mean?'

'I'm fucking skint. And on top of that I've got a couple of kids to look after. How did it happen? When? That's what I want to know. In my head I still feel the same way I did years ago, but my life, my circumstances are alien to me.'

'Do you have any help? What about your mam and dad?'

She rubs her forehead, sighs.

'We don't really talk. I think they've never got over the fact their grandkids are a different colour to them.'

'Oh,' I say. 'Fuck... that's terrible.'

'I'm sorry,' she says.

'For what? Our lives must run on parallel tracks. I don't know what the fuck is going on either,' I say.

We look at each other and smile.

'I really must get going,' Gemma finishes the last of her drink.

'Let's meet up again,' I say. 'I've missed you. It's good to have a chat, even if we're moaning about something.'

'Yeah, it *is* good,' Gemma nods. 'I don't get much free time...'

'Let's make time. Let's put aside a night and go out.'

'I'd really like that,' she says. 'It's funny, but I've been thinking a lot about school, our little circle. For a while, I've

201

had this feeling that we're all going to meet up again. I've been dreaming about it.'

'A reunion? That would be interesting.'

'Wouldn't it just?' She looks away, lost in her thoughts for a moment.

———

After Gemma leaves, I have another quick drink before I get going. On the journey back, I decide I'll spend the night at my mam's house, so I just stop by home to pick up some things. The house is eerily quiet, which makes me nervous. It's easy to start projecting, to imagine someone, possibly one of Max's "friends", waiting in the dark. The laminate floor creaks under my feet, and I can feel my heart pounding in my chest. I'm glad to get out of there.

I'm absolutely wiped out by the time I get to Mam's house. There's been an accident on Anlaby Road near the Boothferry Road roundabout, so the drive, which should only take twenty minutes, seems to take forever.

Natasha's on the floor with some crayons and a couple of sheets of paper spread out when I arrive.

'Hi Mummy,' she says when I walk in.

'What have been doing? Are you having fun with Nana?'

'Yes,' she says. 'Lots of fun. But I've been busy today, had lots to do.'

'I know how that feels,' I say. I lower myself to the floor next to her and give her a big hug. 'I've missed you,' I say, squeezing her, breathing her in.

'Do you want a cuppa, love?' Mam says, peeling herself out of her armchair.

'Love one,' I reply.

I let Natasha go and readjust my legs so I don't get pins and needles. She immediately sets back to work. There are some smaller pieces, drawings of the tall figures that appeared in her other recent pictures. But the centrepiece is a series of figures, standing in a circle. There are eight figures in total, they seem to be five boys and three girls. They all have different faces, and six of them have a blue star floating above their heads. I'm impressed by the level of detail, but I'm worried about one of the figures. His eyes are red, and the star above his head is red too. The figure next to him, a girl, doesn't have anything above her head. I get that shudder again, an eerie feeling. I'm almost frightened to ask about it.

She's scribbling away at something in the centre of the picture, and I clear my throat.

'That's a very impressive picture,' I say.

She turns her head and looks at me.

'Thank you, it's taken me a long time.' She returns to the picture.

My mam comes in with the tea, puts it down near me.

'What about you, love?' she asks Natasha. 'Can I get you owt?'

Natasha shakes her head. 'No thank you,' she replies.

Mam says, 'Okay, but let me know if you want a biscuit or a drink,' and then plonks herself down on the sofa. She puts the telly on.

'What is the picture?' I ask Natasha. 'Who's in it?'

'It's a reunion,' she says.

Looking over her shoulder, I realise that at the centre of her drawing is another one of the tall figures. A deeper shudder goes through me. I tap Natasha on the shoulder. 'Come and sit with me for a bit. Tell me all about it.'

Natasha gets up, repositions herself so she's sat next to me.

'What do you want to know?' she asks.

'What are these skinny men you keep drawing?'

She pauses. She does that thing where she begins to fiddle with the hem of her skirt, like when she's done something she doesn't want me to know about, like when she breaks a toy or something.

'I've been dreaming about them,' she says, finally.

203

I gently place my hands on her face, turn her head so I'm looking right into her eyes.

'Now listen to me, Natasha, this very important.' I hesitate a moment, unsure of how to phrase it. 'Is everything okay? Is there anything happening that I should know about?'

She stares into my eyes, brings her hand up to cover mine. 'In my dreams, they let me look into *other people's* dreams.'

I don't know why, but something in the way she says it chills me. Natasha has always been a bit dreamy, prone to imaginary friends and things like that, but I thought she was growing out of it.

'I don't understand, Natasha. But I want you to make me understand. If someone is telling you things, or doing things, or hurting you in any way, you must tell me. I'm serious, I'm your mummy and I love you very much, and I need to know you're okay, right?'

'Right.'

'So these people, these pictures, what does it mean?'

She smiles at me, and it's a smile that lets me know that she's safe, physically safe, and there's nothing going on. I feel it, instinctively. But at the same time, I can see that the fact I'm worrying so much is starting to make her worry.

'It's not frightening, Mummy, but it just *feels* funny sometimes, and drawing things helps me. Sometimes I don't understand what I'm seeing.'

I turn away from her. I don't want her to see my face. I look around Mam's living room, settling on the big photo of Natasha as a baby that has pride of place on the mantelpiece above the fire. Natasha's big chubby cheeks, an old-fashioned white bonnet that used to belong to me around her head. I went back to work not long after Natasha was born. Mam and Dad practically brought her up. Is this all my fault?

'And these figures, what are they? Aliens or monsters or something? Have you been watching something creepy on the telly and it's given you nightmares, is that it?'

'No, they're not on the telly. And they've got lots of names. They've been around a long time,' she says.

'And what do they say? You're just a little girl, what do they want?' I ask, trying to keep my breathing regular.

She smiles again, giggles, like I've just said something silly, and then she leans close to me, cups her hand around her mouth and whispers 'Oh Mummy, you've got it all wrong. It's not me they're interested in.'

'What?'

For some reason, I find myself thinking about Kirk again. But not about how he used to be, or how he must be now – instead I imagine him, small, withered, and trapped in the middle of a giant spider's web.

I feel like screaming.

Natasha throws her arms around me and hugs me tightly.

'It's *you* that they want to speak to,' she says, pushing away from me so she can look at me properly.

16

Gemma

I'm ten minutes late picking up Laura from the after-school club. I feel awkward and guilty as I go into the reception, all flustered apologies, and I'm paranoid that they can smell gin on my breath. I promise myself that it'll never happen again.

On the way home, Laura is chatty and excitable, and I get a detailed account of her day at school. I have trouble keeping up. My face is bright red, burning, like I've just been caught out and told off. Feel like I'm back at school.

One gin and tonic for God's sake, what's wrong with me?

'I did this for you, Mam,' she says, handing me a picture.

'Thank you, Laura.' As we walk along together, I untie the loop of string, and have a quick look.

It's a picture of a house, leaning over to one side. The bottom half of the picture has been painted blue. In one of the bedroom windows, a dark figure with dark-brown splodges for eyes stares out.

'What is it, Laura?'

'It's a house that's been dropped in the sea. And now it's sinking. Like a ship.'

'Wow. Who's that in the window?'

'It's Barry,' she says, as though it's the most obvious thing in the world.

'Barry. Who's Barry?'

'He used to be your friend. He's sad now, though.'

'What?' I stop walking, crouch down and turn Laura to face me. 'How do you know about Barry? Have you seen the newspaper or something?'

'No, I just guessed.'

The rational part of my brain tells me nothing's wrong, it's just a coincidence, something she's plucked out of thin air, but then I think about the customer at work, the way he looked at me, that nonsense about the "void" he was babbling on about.

I decide not to make a thing out of it. Even though I want to get to the bottom of it, I'm scared to go near it. It's like trying to work up the nerve to pull a plaster off.

'That's strange,' I say. I stand up, and we continue walking.

I do us a tea of eggs, chips and beans. No messing around. I can't go through with the whole drama of cooking something only for Laura to turn her nose up at it and say, *can't we just have egg and chips, Mam?*

I'm on autopilot. I have this ominous feeling in the pit of my stomach, something in-between nausea and terror. I try and keep focused on the task in hand, but in my head I'm making all sorts of wild connections between the bloke at work, the things Claire said, and Laura mentioning Barry. I'm trying to assemble a jigsaw – without any indication of the bigger picture.

I butter some slices of bread, and we eat off our knees on the sofa. Laura watches the kid's channel for a while, and then we put *Emmerdale* on. Although it's still early, I'm worrying about Lee. I send him a text.

– PLS LET ME NO U R OK HUN X.

I can feel Laura beginning to slump, so I go and run a bath for her before she's too tired to bother.

I run it how she likes it: lukewarm with plenty of bubbles. After she slides in, I take the picture that she made at the after-school club and use a magnet to fasten it to the fridge. I tilt my head slightly so my face lines up with Barry's. He's trapped in the bedroom as the house begins to fill with water.

Where am I? Where's Lee? Where's Laura? I imagine we're probably just off to the side somewhere, out of the frame of the picture. Perhaps our crayon faces are scribbled into a scream of horror. Or maybe we're just holding hands, and smiling...

Catching myself drifting, I shake my head, go upstairs to check on Laura. She's laid out in the bath, her head poking out from the water, a cleft of bubbles under her chin. She looks like a mermaid.

'Are you alright, darling?' I say, perching myself on the toilet. 'How was school?'

Her hands break the surface, her arms swishing about like eels.

'It was good. We did reading and comprehension in the morning, which I like, and then we did RE in the afternoon.'

'Really? RE at primary school... what was you learning about?'

'Sikhism.'

'Are they like Muslims?'

'No,' she says, and she giggles. I feel like an idiot.

'What? What did I say?'

'Sikhs aren't anything like Muslims, Mam. They're like, totally different,' she says, and then she places her hands either side of her head and uses her fingers and thumbs to block her ears and nostrils, takes a deep breath, and quickly submerges her head.

She stays under for a couple of seconds and then sits up, exhales in a gasp. She rubs her face, runs her hands over her head and through her hair.

'I mean, they both worship Allah and that, don't they?' I try again.

'Actually, Sikhs believe in something totally different,' she says. 'They follow the teachings of Guru Nanak. And they don't worship Allah. They believe in the constant.'

'What's that?'

'They don't really know. They think you can't really know. Like god is something so big and weird that you can't understand it. But it's there.'

'Right. You learn something new every day.'

'You do with me around,' she says. 'I'm going to get out now.'

'Okay,' I say. I go and fetch her PJs while she gets dried off.

We're downstairs and she's sitting between my legs while I move the hairdryer around over her head. We're watching a programme about depressed chefs when I hear the key in the front door. The door swings open, and there's the familiar sound of Lee's big mad feet hitting the carpet.

'Lee?' I shout. There's a pause. I can hear trainers being slung into the corner of the hallway.

'Lee? Is that you?' I say, knowing full well it is.

I'm trying to provoke him into popping his head into the living room before slouching off to his room. It doesn't work. He grunts something and heads upstairs. It's best for everybody that I don't immediately follow him and have it out with him. I have absolutely no idea how I'm going to approach it, how to bring it up without starting World War Three. He'll go mental about me poking around in his room and it will all flow from there. Hopefully, by that time Laura will be asleep.

We finish watching the programme, and then it's time for Laura to go to bed. Lee's room is almost totally silent as we pass it, so he must have his headphones on. When we get to Laura's room, I throw back the quilt and she hops on the bed. She lays down and I sweep the covers over her. I sit on the

210

edge of the bed. She's beautiful. I start to think about Gaz, about how he's missing all this, but then I try and get rid of him by focusing on Laura. I have to be strong.

'Night, night,' I say. 'Sleep tight.'

She smiles at me, says, 'Night, Mam.'

I touch her face, and I'm hit with the thought it won't be long before she's approaching Lee's age. Riddled with hormones and attitude, screaming for independence yet totally dependent on me. Maybe she'll be different. Maybe all this with Lee is just a phase and not a glimpse of the person that he's becoming.

Perhaps sensing what I'm thinking and how I'm feeling, Laura says, 'Lee's always in a mood, isn't he?'

Her eyes narrow, like she's looking to see how I react.

'It's just a phase. You'll probably go through it when you get a bit older.'

'No I won't,' she says. 'Lee's been so moody for so long, I can't remember what he was like before.'

'Yeah. . . anyway it's nothing for you to worry about, so get a good night's sleep and I'll see you in the morning.'

Watching her, pressure builds in my chest. I feel as vulnerable as a repair patch on an inner tube, holding the air in.

'See you in the morning, Mam.'

I switch the light off as I leave the room. I creep downstairs and into the kitchen, where I light up a cig and open the back door. Sitting out on the step, it's still quite warm out, so it feels nice to just relax with my head leant against the doorframe, white smoke slowly curling up into the air.

After I finish, I lock up and move back through to the living room, where I plonk myself on the sofa. The news is on, but all the stories seem to be about child abuse and terrorism. It never ends; it's like everything is designed to make me feel vulnerable, powerless.

At the mercy of forces beyond my control.

I'm about to turn it off but the local news comes on. In a droning voice the presenter is talking about a manhunt. They're looking for a local man: he mustn't be approached, he's wanted in connection with a murder. The suspect's face flashes up. He looks rough, haggard, but I recognise him straight away.

'Barry Thompson, aged thirty-nine,' the newsreader says.

The sound of his name hits me like a slap, and the instinct to reach over and switch the television off is automatic.

Has Laura seen this? Did she see it in the paper, at school or something?

I stare at the black screen. Something is happening right now, something beyond my understanding. It's affecting everything and everyone I know. This isn't something that's happening because of Lee and Laura, it's happening because of me – and they're just caught up in it. I have no explanation for this, nothing to point to as evidence, but I can feel it. The knowledge lodges deep within my bones.

I don't know what to do.

I hear Lee moving about in his bedroom. I creep upstairs and when I reach his room, gently tap on the door. The adrenalin starts pumping, and I swallow hard. It's like I'm gearing up for a physical confrontation, and in many ways, I am. He's a big lad, so when he starts kicking off and flinging things around, he can be quite intimidating. Just like his dad.

I'm about to knock again, when the door slowly opens.

'Come in,' he says.

As I push the door open, I expect him to be standing there, but he's over on his bed. I don't know how he opened the door and then got back on his bed that fast. It unsettles me. Everything is eerie, strange. My guts churn with fear and anticipation.

I close the door behind me.

'I was wondering if we could have a quick chat.'

He's reading something. He looks up at me. 'Sure,' he replies, without a trace of annoyance.

Once again, I'm caught off guard. Lee usually treats every enquiry like a challenge. I used to have a system, for when his dad went off on one. I would take a couple of deep breaths and then in my head I would list the titles of all my favourite songs until Gary lost interest and left the house.

'I've been worried about you,' I say. 'About what you've been up to lately.'

I clench my fists, waiting for the kick-off, but it doesn't come. Instead, he places the book down and simply says, 'Oh?'

Lee's lack of response is as threatening as one of his episodes. My mind reels with possibilities and it just comes out in a rush.

'What the fuck is with you? Are you on something? What have you been doing, Lee?'

'Nothing,' he says, calmly. 'I haven't taken anything.'

'Then what are these?' I say, and I hold up the bag of seeds.

I'm geared up now. It dawns on me that not only am I expecting a confrontation, but I'm actively seeking one. I want to get it all out in the open, once and for all. I want to know what's happening.

'I found them in here,' I shout. 'I was going through your stuff Lee, and I found them. How about that?'

'You had to find them sooner or later, I suppose,' Lee says.

My entire body shakes with adrenalin as I grab him by his collar and slap him as hard as I can. The sharp clap of my palm on his skin is like a full-stop. Silence. It feels like the whole world has stopped.

He doesn't flinch, doesn't cry out. Nothing. I start crying, I can't help myself, can hardly catch my breath.

'I'm sorry, I'm so sorry,' I say, over and over again.

Lee reaches up and strokes my hair.

'It's okay,' he says. 'I understand.'

'I'm just so scared, Lee. Of everything.'

'I know,' he says.

I pull myself together and sit up. 'I just don't know what's happening.'

'I'm not dealing drugs, Mam.'

'Then what are they? Who gave them to you?' I ask.

'They're just seeds, Mam. They were given to me by someone you know. You've seen them before, these seeds. Back when you were my age. A bunch of you, on the school field.'

He shouldn't *know* this, shouldn't be saying it. It feels as though I've been battling with myself all day, trying to convince myself that it's all some random chain of events – and now this. Am I losing the plot?

'Who? Who is it?'

'He says that you're all going to meet up again soon, that everything will be okay.'

Every word jolts me, stabs at me. Who is he talking about?

'What does he want with you? Has he hurt you?'

Lee reaches up and takes my face in his hands.

'Something's about to happen. I think you know by now. You can feel it, can't you, Mam?'

His eyes are dark and serious. 'You will be part of the first phase. You will help others. *You will be at the forefront.*'

I've read things, heard things, about kids developing psychosis from smoking weed, taking pills. That's what happened to Barry Thompson. Maybe that's the connection, Lee's having an episode, and he knows about Barry. Maybe he started having symptoms and he spoke to his dad, who told him about Barry, and then Lee said something to Laura.

'I don't understand. How do you know all this?'

'For the past few weeks, I've been dreaming other people's dreams. Remembering things that other people have experienced. I've seen things through your eyes and through Dad's eyes, too. Sometimes it's people I don't even know. I think you know them, though.'

214

I can't believe what I'm hearing. My throat clenches in terror. That's it. My son's having a psychotic episode, a break with reality. He needs help.

'If I'm so important,' I say in a shaking voice, 'if I'm part of this *first phase* then why isn't it happening to me?'

'It's like a signal, Mam. And you're like a transmitter – a signal booster,' he says.

He's sitting up, rigid now, with an air of possession. His eyes burn. 'You and your friends, all of you, you're like a network. Or you will be, eventually.'

I shuffle off the bed backwards and stand up, my head dizzy with Lee's words.

'I can't. . . I just can't.'

'It's okay, Mam,' Lee says. He gets up off the bed, too. He comes over to me and steers me towards the door. It opens, seemingly by itself. Laura is standing there, on the landing.

'Is she all right?' she asks Lee.

'She'll be fine,' he says.

A thought nudges inside my head, the worst one yet. I try to cast it out, but it plants itself, like a seed. Maybe we're *all* having an episode – one that's spread somehow, like a germ, or a virus.

Laura cocks her head, takes my hand and squeezes it.

'Don't worry, Mam,' she says. 'It will all make sense soon.'

Lee taps her on her shoulder.

'Go to bed, you,' he says.

I've drifted off into some sort of trance. Lee guides me downstairs, and I offer no resistance. Nothing feels real anyway, so there's no point in questioning anything, I just go along with it. Lee gently sits me down in my armchair and leans over to plant a kiss on my forehead.

'They will fill the void within us all,' he says.

When I look up, he's gone.

17

Barry

Everything slows down.   My eyes feel heavy, and it's as though I'm submerged in water – like my body isn't even here anymore, and my head is just bobbing about, suspended in the air. The fuzzy sense of wellbeing within me comes partly from a conviction that I'm somehow above everything else. My former wants, desires, hopes. . . are all now meaningless. My chemical contentment is all that's real.

I used to find significance in everything. The words from neon shop displays reflected backwards in a puddle and becoming some new secret word. The crooked branches of a tree pointing upwards towards a pattern of birds.   The scream of a cat in a minor key, undercutting the major lift of a tyre squealing on tarmac.

Now, of course, I see things for what they really are. The precise, crafted components of an adding-machine that counts down to nothing – slowly, imperceptibly. Assembled by forces unknowable, unfathomable and outside of time: we humans toil in the shadow of a foul architecture, governed by it, with no hope of ever comprehending it.

'Alright Barry?'

'What?'

Henry is standing in front of me. He bends over, puts his face near mine.

'Barry, are you okay?' He places his hand on my shoulder, gives it a shake. I come to suddenly, push his arm away.

He steps back and takes his seat again.

'Where's Natalie?' I ask.

'She's gone into the bedroom,' he says, followed by, 'Are we okay here? I mean, are *you* okay?'

He's jittery, nervous – doesn't spend a lot of time around heavy drug users, evidently. Probably paranoid to fuck, thinking the coppers will come knocking any time soon.

'Shit,' I say. 'It's the fucking methadone. You think you're okay, that it's just a little buzz, and then BAM, it's all going sideways.'

Henry puts his fingers near his mouth, picks at his teeth with his thumbnail, and then reaches into his pocket. He takes his notepad and pen out slowly, like someone's pointing a gun at him

'You were telling me about the voice, Barry. The one that started speaking to you when you were young.'

'Yeah.' I reach over to the table and pick up the baccy tin.

'You said it started that day on the school field. After you swallowed the object.'

'Yeah.' I take a scrap of baccy and lay it on a skin, roll it up, lick it. 'I didn't realise it at the time. It was only after I had the seizure earlier this year, when I started dreaming about it, that I realised this voice I had been hearing was real, and it had been all along. It wasn't a delusion, even though for years that's what I believed it was. That's what I was told, by doctors, by experts.'

Henry scribbles something in his pad. He looks worried.

'Listen, I want to believe you, but you aren't giving me anything. You said a couple of your friends saw a UFO after school, and they described it as a blue light. Then you went back that night and found something. It's all a bit, I don't know. . . *vague*. I can't see how that has anything to do with what you're going through now.'

He sighs.

I'm losing him. I'm off my head on the juice and he's wondering how the fuck he got himself into this situation.

'I know it sounds crazy, but something's going to happen. Something *is* happening, right now, here in Hull. I need you to understand.'

I look around the room, register that it's getting dark outside the window and in the flat. I stretch, stand up and go through to the kitchen, put the light on. Lifting the jar from the cupboard, I carry it through to the living room. I unscrew the lid and give it to Henry.

'What's this?'

I sit down and take another drag of my roll-up.

'Take one out. Have a closer look.'

Henry looks in the jar. He shakes it and the seeds rattle about inside.

'What is this, Barry?'

'The last place we were at, this little house on Airlie Street. After the seizure, that's when Natalie started acting strange. Her eyes went all weird, and then next thing I know, she's holed up in a bedroom, scribbling mad shit all over the walls. And I start having these dreams. I'm dreaming of my schoolmates, my old mate Pete, and he's being attacked by something. Something's got inside him and it's changing him, turning his guts into *those* things.'

Henry cautiously puts his hand into the jar and lifts out a couple of seeds. He places the jar down and holds the seeds on his palm, brings them close to his face so he can get a closer look.

'And then I start seeing Kirk, and I know he's ill, there's something wrong with him, and they're using him as well. It – whatever it is – is fucking *nesting* in his mind. He's fucking *dying* and he's flip-flopping between being awake and being out of it, and he can hardly tell the difference anymore, and

219

that's the perfect conditions for it to grow in. Them. Whatever the fuck this thing is.'

Henry's distracted now, concentrating on the things in his palm.

'I can feel it, Barry. They're tingling, vibrating. Where did you get these?'

'They were in my garden. Someone left them there. I think Pete's... produced them and – I know this sounds mad but – I think they're using fucking *kids* to distribute them. Something to do with their perception, the way their imaginations are at the forefront of their minds, makes them easy to manipulate. They probably don't even realise what they're doing.'

'How do you know all this?'

'Because it's like they're setting up a network. Fucking *9G*. And I'm plugged into it. I get glimpses of them, in my dreams. I see them in their dreams, and they see me as well.'

'Yeah,' Henry says. 'Yeah.' He stands up. He opens his bag, rummages around inside and pulls out a small magnifying glass. Lifting it up to his eye, he examines the seeds, seems excited.

'Have you seen these close up? They're incredible. They have little veins, little blue veins. They're pulsating. It's like they're alive. I've never seen anything like them.'

'Do you believe me now, Henry?'

Henry sits down again, sighs even louder.

'I'm struggling to take it all in, to tell you the truth, Barry. You, Natalie, these. I'll admit, I was ready to write you off as a crank, but then I saw these and...'

He drops the seeds back in the jar, shakes the jar, rattling the seeds around. Natalie appears, like a cat hearing a tin being opened.

'Is everything okay?' I ask her, and she disappears into the kitchen without replying.

'What you're telling me...' says Henry. 'It's a lot to take on board. But these things are evidence, something solid. I'll be honest, I don't know how it connects to UFO sightings, but I'm willing to look into it for you.'

'So, what about Natalie? What do we do while you "look into it"?'

'I don't know,' he says, and places his hand on the top of his head, rubs vigorously like he's tired and trying to warm his brain up. 'I think you need to get some help. It might not be connected to these things. She may have had a breakdown or something.'

'Bullshit,' I shout. Standing up, I clench my fists, knock some shit from the table. 'You've seen her eyes, it's all connected.'

'Calm down, Barry. It's obvious something is happening, but it's all a question of trust. Let's take it one step at a time.' Henry shrinks back into his chair. 'I'll take these home with me. I know people, I'll get these analysed, find out what they are, what we're dealing with, and then we can work out a plan. How does that sound?'

His raises his hands, palms facing me, like he's surrendering.

I take a deep breath. I'm pissed off, shaking with anger, but I try and stem it, inhale more air. He's right, of course. I should be grateful he's come this far to see us.

I'm about to agree with him, but there's a sudden dull *thwump*. My first thought is that it sounds like wood hitting meat. A few years ago, I was at a dealer's house when a couple of lads broke in and set about him with an axe-handle. Me, and a couple of others managed to bolt out the back door, but the last thing I heard was that same, sickening noise.

This time, I don't run. Instead, my whole body goes as stiff as a board. Instinctively, I squeeze my eyes shut. Something wet and warm hits my cheek, and my hands shoot up to shield my face. I force myself to open my eyes. Peeking through my trembling fingers, I see Henry slumped back in his chair. His hands are up at his head, and he's trying to sit up – attempting to speak, but it's just this noise. A gurgle, like bleach poured down a sink. His eyes are wide, frightened, and they look up at me as I stay rooted to the spot, frozen and useless. He tries to speak again, but his mouth is rapidly filling up with blood.

I'm waiting for my turn, bracing myself for the impact, but as my hands drop from my face, I see Natalie. Standing next to Henry, clad in her white dressing gown, now splattered with Henry's blood. She's holding the little rounder's bat that I keep under the bed and she looks calm, serene almost. Her grip is loose and the bat dangles by her leg.

If it wasn't for all the blood, you would never guess that she had just set about someone's head with a heavy object.

My horror at what I've witnessed is replaced by concern for her. I want to go over to her, wrap my arms around her, but I can't move.

Henry's eyes roll to the side as he seeks his attacker.

Natalie. She steps back, takes the bat in both hands, and raises her arms above her head, positioning herself for another swing. This time, she brings the bat straight down. There's a loud crack. Henry falls back again.

There isn't a great deal of blood until he begins coughing, having spasms.

Still unable to move, I watch as Natalie takes a carrier bag from her dressing gown pocket and places it over his head. Her movements are measured, like she's gathering up left-overs. Henry thrashes about, but she manages to pull the bag tight around his neck. She doesn't register the dying man in front of her.

Henry coughs and splutters, blood sprays the inside of the bag. It quickly turns from opaque white to crimson, as it fills up.

Henry must be suffocating. His movements become briefly more erratic and violent, threatening to tip him out of the chair, until finally he's still. I watch Natalie as she watches him. Her face is blank and expressionless. The smooth

222

contours of her forehead and cheeks become my anchor. I stare at her intently, feeling nothing but love, projecting it towards her. *Ignore the terrible things unfolding in my peripheral vision, ignore it all.* Natalie is all that matters.

Natalie is all that matters.

I think he's dead.

Natalie casually drops the bat and stands motionless, like an abandoned doll. I regain the feeling in my legs, hobble over to her before they buckle. I wrap my arms around her and pull her close against my body.

'I'm sorry, baby. It'll be okay, I promise,' I say.

I don't what to do, don't know what's going happen, but right now, the only thing I can feel is relief. Relief that Natalie is safe. I cling to this feeling, because it's all that matters.

Natalie is all that matters.

While Natalie remains standing in the centre of the room, I wrap tape around Henry's hands and feet, before pulling a bin liner over him. It's a thick, black one, like the ones you use for garden waste. I manage to pull it down to just past his waist. I wrap my arms around him, lift him from chair and let him drop to the floor. Sweat drips down my nose as I roll him onto a blanket.

I feel numb. I'm obviously still in shock, so I focus on the physical exertion. The ache in my limbs, the pain the in my temples. The cramp in my feet and hands. The consequences of what has happened are too big to comprehend. The future – our future – is a huge chasm which will swallow me whole if I look into it right now, so I wallow in the present and its practical challenges.

I have to clean this mess up.

I have to protect Natalie.

Exhausted, I stumble over to the sofa and collapse onto it. Natalie comes over and sits next to me. She picks up the remote and turns the TV on, starts flicking through the channels. Despite the tremble in my hands that won't go away, I manage get the baccy and roll myself another cig.

Sitting back, I take a deep drag and exhale the smoke. With the cig in my mouth, I stretch my shaking hands out in front of me. I see a few specks of blood, but nothing too major. It's surprising just how little mess there is.

I take another drag, place my hand on Natalie's knee.

'We'll work something out,' I say, trying to convince myself more than anything.

Natalie doesn't speak, only continues staring at the telly. But I'm sure, deep down, that she agrees with me.

I lay back, take another long drag, and think about what to do next.

18

Pete

'Pete... *Pete!*'

Waking up, it feels like someone has got me by my shoulders.

'Wake up, Pete,' a voice says. 'Now.'

'I'm awake already, what's the fucking problem?'

It takes a minute for me to get my bearings. For a moment I think I'm in the park again, but then I realise I'm in Terry's chair. When I look up, there's something in front of me. The outline of a person, but it's blurry, indistinct.

'What's going on, Terry, everything alright?'

'Not Terry,' the voice says, oddly pitched.

'What? Who are you? What do you want?' I try to get up.

I still feel a bit stoned. Maybe that's why I'm confused. The shape in front of me shifts. It's tall, thin, and dark.

'Is it the police? What do you want? I've done fuck all!' I shout. My arms jerk up, the universal *Don't Shoot Me* sign of surrender.

'Not the police.' The voice is even, mechanical, like the pre-recorded operator on a helpline.

The shapeless figure comes towards me. Before I know what's happening, some force – invisible hands – lift me out of the chair and onto to my feet as though I'm nothing. I try to look at its face. The more I try to focus, the more difficult it is to see. I'm scared shitless, my limbs are electrified with fear.

'Terry, Terry,' I say, whimpering. Panic rushes through me. 'Where are you? Help me.'

I'm somehow steered into the kitchen. It doesn't feel like someone has grabbed me. It's more like a force, pushing me around.

A chair pulls itself from under the table, and I'm pushed down onto it.

'What's happening?' I say, pleading. I try to get up, but I can't move. I try to look at my attacker again, but it's dark, too dark.

'What do you want?' I whisper.

It's then that I notice the kettle on the table, steam rising from the spout.

'You have something we want,' the voice says, sounding like the noise glass makes when you tap it with a key.

I raise my hand, turn it over; examine it as if it's new to me.

'You can take whatever you want,' I say.

'We will,' the voice says.

With my other hand, I pick up the kettle.

I know what's about to happen, so I try to wriggle free, but I can't move on my own. I'm paralysed. But my arms move by themselves. I close my eyes, squeeze them shut, and scream as I slowly pour the boiling water over my hand.

The agony is indescribable, and the water keeps pouring. When it's finally over, I put the kettle back on the table. Opening my eyes, I brave a look at my poor burnt hand. My fingers judder and shake, the skin is red and nasty, bubbling into blisters already. I turn my hand, palm upwards. I can hear sobbing and I realise it's me.

I grab the wrist of my burning hand with my other one to keep it from shaking too much. The shape of the indecipherable figure loosens and its vaguely human outline dissolves into a mist. It swirls and flows, surrounding me. It smells of burnt matches and metal. It begins to condense into a point, like smoke being sucked into a small opening. I see a flash, a brilliant blue, and then a small, white, object drops onto my swollen, weeping, palm.

My head swims and my vision clouds over. I'm about to pass out. Before I do, I take a good look at the tiny thing in my palm. At first, I think it's a small, white tablet. Staring at it, I realise I've seen it before. It's a seed.

The seed starts vibrating, making a strange, clicking sound. I notice tiny white barbs, like little legs, springing out of the object, and they latch onto my hand. The pain is so intense by now that I can barely feel it as it burrows under my skin. And then it disappears. Mercifully, I pass out.

———

I wake up screaming, slumped over the table. The first thing I do once the screams die down into moans is check my hand, and I'm shocked to discover it appears to be fine, completely healed. I hold it up to my face, stare at it – check every single patch of skin, every vein, scar and blemish. Nothing. Not a fucking thing. I'm badly rattled. I get up and stumble into the living room. Terry is sitting on the sofa.

'Terry?' I say. My voice is strangled, high.

He doesn't respond.

When I get closer, I see that he's staring blankly at the telly. There's a close-up of a roulette wheel on the screen. It's spinning.

'Terry?' I notice that there's something wrong with his eyes. They're completely white, the iris and pupils have vanished. I place my hand on his shoulder and give him a gentle shake. 'Terry? What the fuck has just happened?'

The ball spins around the wheel. It begins to slow and as it drops, Terry says, 'Nineteen, black, odd.'

'Nineteen, black, odd,' the announcer on the telly repeats.

Terry shuts his eyes, and when he opens them again, his irises and pupils have returned. He glances at me, frowns like he's trying to focus on something. He smiles.

'What's going on?' I ask, desperate.

'I've just had the weirdest fucking dream,' he says, chuckling.

'So have I,' I say.

'Well, I'm gonna have a beer,' Terry gets to his feet. 'D'yer want one?'

I'm feeling sick down to the bottom of my stomach, but I figure it must be because I'm sobering up.

'Yeah, go on then, our kid,' I say.

Terry makes his way to the kitchen, and I keep my mouth clamped shut, try and hold everything back, hoping it will pass. I go over to the telly and switch it off, because watching the wheel go round and round only increases the nausea. I slump into a chair.

'You okay?' Terry says as he comes back in, a tin of beer in each hand. 'Looking a bit peaky.'

'Just feel a bit rough,' I say as I take the beer. 'I'll be okay in a bit.'

'Why did you turn the telly off?' Terry gets himself comfortable again on the sofa.

'It was the wheel, it was doing me head in.'

He smiles, and then looks around, patting down the sofa, shoving his hand down the back of the cushions. He switches the telly back on. Mercifully, he changes the channel, and puts on a programme about police car chases.

'What's the plan?' he asks.

'What do you mean?'

'Well, it's all very nice having you round and that,' and with that he makes an exaggerated gesture of checking an imaginary watch on his wrist. 'But I'm not running a hotel.'

'Oh, come on, Terry,' I say. 'I'll have to wake the night worker if I go back this late.'

'Not my problem,' he says.

I'm pissed off, but there's no point complaining. It's a real effort, but I manage to get the beer down. I try and stand up, keep flopping back down into the chair. I can feel the liquid sloshing about in my belly, and I can feel my brains sloshing about in my head.

'I guess I'll be off then,' I say, finally succeeding in standing. I try to walk in a straight line, but the harder I try the more I wobble around, bumping into things.

Terry yawns, raises his hand and says, 'In a bit, Cuz.'

I concentrate on placing one foot in front of another until I step out of the flat. The shuffling of my feet echoes around the hallway, taking me into the crisp air of outside. It's cool and dark and quiet, and I manage to make it a few feet away from the building before the nausea wells up, the swill rising from my stomach into my throat, and I fall to my knees on the patch of grass at the corner of the street. Bathed in the glow of the streetlight, I heave my guts up. Luckily, there's no one around.

Puking, I realise that there's something wrong. In my throat, the vomit feels hard and sharp. It blocks my airways as I struggle to bring it up. When the bulky torrent finally pours out of my mouth and onto the grass, I see in the streetlight what appears to be masses of seeds. Just when I think I'm about to pass out, the last of the blockage leaves my gullet and I manage to gasp for air. I wipe the drool from my mouth, blink back tears and groan.

In my head I hear a voice, a steady, repetitive voice. It keeps saying, 'Cannot receive – / – Cannot transmit.'

I place my hand on top of the shiny white pile on the floor. They make the skin of my palm tingle, like they're generating an electrical charge. I grab a handful of the seeds and get myself up onto my feet. Under the light, I examine one closely, and realise that they're the same as the one that was placed on my hand in the dream I had back at Terry's. I drop the seeds, allow them to scatter on the pavement.

I'm petrified. I've coughed up blood before. Even shit blood once, but this is new – different. I'm gripped by fear: fear of disease, fear of dying. Fear of being alive.

On the way back to the hostel, I have another episode, finding myself doubled over and spewing up more of whatever it is that's multiplying inside me.

When I wake up the following morning, the first thing I do is vomit again. I don't bother going to the toilet. Instead, I wait until it finishes, and then I scoop up the seeds and place them in an empty coffee jar that I keep next to my bed as an ashtray. I go over to the sink and look into the mirror. I've lost a lot of weight. As I stare back at myself, I place my hand on my shrinking stomach and gently rub it. I'm changing. I know that my insides are being rearranged, refined into something new.

I hear a buzz, a low frequency, which turns into a murmur. I close my eyes, and for some reason I find myself thinking back. I'm back at school, on the field with some of my mates. We're all just hanging about laughing, and then Barry turns up with these little seeds, and we're fucking about, and I take one and pop it in my mouth. . .

. . . Soon as I swallow it, Barry starts laughing.

'What's so fucking funny?' Jamie asks.

'Sorry,' Barry says, laughing. 'I don't know what they are. I found them at the back of the field.'

I open my eyes. I'm not alone in the room anymore. There's something in here with me. I can almost see it out of the corner of my eye. It's both there and not there, somehow.

'What are you?' I whisper, my throat sore from vomiting.

'We are many things,' the voice replies. I don't hear it speak, I just *know*. That's the most terrifying thing about it. The words, they're in my head somehow.

'What's happening to me? Am I going to die?' I ask.

'You are defective,' it says. 'You cannot transmit or receive. But you are still important.'

'I don't understand what you're saying,' I say. 'Am I not good enough, or summat? Am I broken?'

I try and see this for what it is: a mad delusion or hallucination brought on by illness, but it's no good. Instead, all I can see is my life as it lays out before me in retrospect. A series of mistakes and fuck-ups surrounded by so much wasted time. Here I am, at the tail end of my thirties, washed up and living in sheltered accommodation – again. No family, no friends, no opportunities. All the self-loathing and self-obsession I feel wells to the surface. I've always tried to get on with it, just plough on, but now even the lie – the *things-will-work-out-in-the-end* bullshit has been stripped away. Poor me.

Poor, bloody me.

'I never stood a chance, did I? That's what you're saying, right? I'm fucking cursed,' I say.

'You are the vessel,' the voice says. 'You are the sacrament.'

I find myself filled with renewed purpose. I begin to gather the seeds, store them, and then I distribute them around Hull. I put them into jars and containers and leave them for people to find. Sometimes, I simply scatter them on the ground. I find that working with the seeds gives me occasional glimpses into something larger.

Producing so much material comes at a cost, unfortunately, and I quickly become even more dishevelled. The workers at the hostel are increasingly alarmed at my appearance. Angela approaches me and asks to speak to me in the office.

'I've been chatting to some of the others,' she says. 'And we think it's time you got some help. Maybe went to see a doctor.'

Leaning back in the chair, I say, 'It's not what you think, Angie. I'm not into smack or anything like that.'

'Then what is it?' she asks.

'Soon the void within you all will be filled,' I tell her. 'And then you'll understand.'

Despite not being able to transmit or receive, my proximity and relationship to the seeds grants me foresight.

I am a vessel. I am the sacrament.

It becomes clear to me that there is a complex plan, a structure that I am part of. Steve, Gaz, Chris, Gemma, Claire, Jamie and Kirk – all of us have been chosen to play a role in the Ascension.

In much the same way that I am broken, Barry is broken. He was the fuse, the link – but he burned out, became dangerous: a threat to the future. He will be removed.

I rapidly reach the end of my role. My part is nearly over, the strain on my body is too much. I'm wasting away. The answer of course, comes to me in a dream.

I leave the hostel early. Knowing what is to come, I appreciate the light of the morning in a way I never have before. Pumpkin-orange and firecracker-yellow sky. I can smell the grass, can even detect the hint of salt on the breeze from the estuary, as it hits my face.

The process that generated the seeds, the process that's killing me, has also given me a clarity I've never felt before. I feel cleaned out, renewed. I'm reborn. I realise then, what it is they're after. They want *this*. They want to be of this world, they want to experience it like we do. They're something *other*; they come from a place that is completely different to this one – a place with no sights, or smells, or feelings. They've been watching us for a long time, and they want what we have.

After wandering around for a couple of hours, waiting for the voice to guide me, I find myself on Anlaby Road. I feel so weak now that I'm brittle.

It's nearly over.

Eventually, when I get to *Pharaoh's Entertainment*, I stand on the opposite side of the road.

I watch as Steve arrives at work. Patiently, I wait for the right moment. I stand there. I wait until he comes out of the store for one of his fag-breaks.

My work is finished now, and I figure that the time is right. I take a deep breath and walk towards Steve.

'You have succeeded,' the voice says to me as I step out into the traffic. 'We will fill the void within them all.'

19

Steve

I can't sleep. I keep replaying the accident over and over in my head. The midrange screech of the brakes. The bass thud of car hitting man, the high treble of breaking glass. The percussive break of body on tarmac.

And then I see him again, his body jumbled and twisted, like all his limbs have declared independence and are trying to go in separate directions. His face is a mask of blood, snot and streaks of dirt. As I get closer, the trembling and shuddering begins to subside.

Pete. Fucking Pete.

I'm there, I'm with him as he turns from a young lad into a skinny, beardy mess. Time-lapse on Pete's life. Flick-book face turning to ruin, days spent on the bench, drinking rotgut super-strength lager. Years and years of it. All that time wasted, getting wasted.

I'm back on the field again with my mates, all those years ago, but this time I'm not me. I'm Pete. I'm easy-going Pete as he coasts along, not knowing his arse from his elbow. And then I'm Pete and I've left school, and I'm still coasting along. I spend a bit of time working here and there, but nothing really happens. I meet a girl and get a place, but it doesn't work out, so I spend more and more time alone, drinking. And then I can't get any work, so I drink more and spend even more time alone. Then I lose the flat, and I've got nowhere to go, and no-one to turn to. And that's pretty much all there is to it.

———————

I wake up sweating. Throw the covers off and head downstairs. I flick the light on. On the way past the sofa, I stub my toe, badly. I howl in agony, and then limp over to the table. I pick up the coffee jar that I put the seeds in. Unscrew the lid, put my hand in and take one out and hold it up to the light.

It's not just a seed. Examining it minutely. I notice silvery-blue veins, tiny flowing rivers that run along it, like the patterns on a microchip. Just what the hell is it?

Thinking of it as a circuit is probably one of the best ways of looking at it.

'Where are you? I know you're here, somewhere. I can't hear you, but you're in my head.'

We have a limited physical presence here. We are projections, we communicate by directly accessing the language centres in your brain. We use your consciousness to amplify the signal.

'So the seeds turn us into psychic mobile-phone towers?'

The seeds create a permanent bond to your reality. They also create a link between all those who encounter them. In time, they will allow you to become more like us. You will be able to share thoughts, feelings and memories.

'It's fucking extra-terrestrial social media, isn't it?' I say, and laugh, caught up in a moment of smug self-satisfaction, like I've just worked out something massive.

Imagine the possibilities. If you could see the world through each other's eyes, it would bring on a new age of peace and understanding. Conflict and suffering would be a thing of the past, because you would all be united, as one. The human race evolving into something more, something special.

My eyes well up. I can't help myself. I suddenly feel special. Chosen. I have this feeling in my chest that's difficult to comprehend, like how I imagine it feels to win the lottery. I feel holy, like I'm communing with God. My miserable meandering life is cast in a new light. What was once the slow-turning cogs of day-to-day drudgery becomes a singular path that leads up to this moment. And I can see the light all around me. I can feel it, thin streams of blue that connect me to everyone else, a vast, glittering highway of emotions and memories that stretch out across the entire world. And in trying to contain it, in trying to prevent it from completely overwhelming me, I realise what it is: the privilege of purpose. For the first time in my life, there is meaning.

What you have experienced so far is but a prologue. In time, you will learn mastery over matter itself, you will live forever in The Community. You will manipulate time and space to your own ends and discover that consciousness is not limited to your physical bodies. You will see your linear perception of time as the illusion it is.

'Tell me what I must do,' I say, weeping. A loose bolt of energy hits me. I feel this hum, this vibration within me, like someone's just plucked a bass string running from the top of my head, right down my spine and into my legs.

Claaaang...

I'm filled with what I can only describe as absolute certainty in who I am and what I'm doing. I have a complete surety of purpose and direction. It's like I've been plugged in.

Send. Receive.

Send/Receive.

There are others. I can feel them. Whatever this thing is, this presence has always been here. It's telling me the truth, I'm sure of it. But, despite all the preparation from years spent watching sci-fi movies and TV shows, bombarding myself with stories about space travel, aliens and robots, part of my brain resists what is happening.

It tries to use my sensations and experiences against me. Because it's easier to believe that I'm going mad, I suppose.

'How do I know that I'm not going mad?' I ask.

The sharing of our gift has an adverse effect on the mental state of the chosen. This is something you must learn to contain. The acceptance of our existence is the biggest obstacle you must overcome.

I consider what I'm being told for a moment. It's difficult. The bigger picture, that's what people say, isn't it? *I've had a glimpse of the bigger picture.* Well, that's how I feel. I've never experienced anything like this before. I'm a shit-kicker from Hull, for fuck's sake. I feel like someone has peeled back my skull, taken my brain out, stuck the fucker in a washing machine and then plonked it back in.

Got be careful now. Everything's coming to the surface, fucking rushing. Like doing fucking acid for the first time. There's all this stuff inside me – my whole fucking existence – all the actions and decisions that led me up to this point. And there's all the actions and decisions that have been made by everyone who's ever been around me. I feel them seep up through the floor.

I start to drift. I can hear the faint chatter of voices. Broken, muttering voices. I try to sort through them, understand them, but I can't. I can't because what I'm hearing is a multitude of disparate thoughts, everyone around me going about their lives, sometimes in different languages that I can somehow understand.

I manage to grasp onto snatches:

Must remember to put the lottery on. . .
I'm so worried about Mam, must pop round. . .
I fucking hate him, why did he do this to me?
Shit, I'm gonna miss the bus. . .
Thursdays are yellow, Fridays are green. . .
The spiders are not from Mars. . .
I'm losing my teeth, losing my hair. . .

Sometimes I catch images instead:

A ham salad sandwich on brown bread

A Lamborghini

A wasp behind a net curtain

A broken pocket-watch, stopped just after ten

A ferry as it heads out to sea

A pigeon hitting a windshield

I focus, gather my senses and put myself back into my own head, in my own room. I manage to barricade myself against the fierce tide that threatens to drown me.

I discover that I'm on the floor, hands pressed to the sides of my head.

'There I go again,' I say, sitting up. 'How long has this been going on? Not with me, but with you. How long have you been around on earth?'

We have always been here, around you. Just outside of your realm of perception. Preparing.

'What, Hull? Why Hull of all the fucking places?'

Not just Hull. Everywhere.

Ah, I get it now. Some version of this is happening everywhere, simultaneously.

I'm losing it, aren't I?

It's inevitable, I suppose. Seriously, what do you expect me to do?

You out there, reading this – reading me. Tell me what's next. Shall I go back to work? *Sorry, my life was interrupted by an extra-dimensional entity that seeks to use me to herald the next stage of human evolution.*

Are you listening to me?

I don't want to sound ungrateful. Being rotated through a small selection of subjectively-experienced timelines is one of the most thrilling things I've ever done. But where do I go from here? How can I possibly top the experience of merging my consciousness with the thoughts and memories of all those around me?

We're getting close to doing it ourselves with the internet and smartphones and shit, but this is a giant leap forward. It's difficult to describe.

I'm always lost for words, that's my problem.

I mean, once you're outside yourself and you start moving around... you begin to lose yourself. And when you move into someone else, you take on a part of them. But the more it happens, the more you start to lose track of which parts are yours, and which are someone else's.

I'm at my birthday party and I'm six years old, and my mam has bought me this push-bike, and she's made me this chocolate cake, and I'm dizzy with excitement. And it's time to light the cake, so she turns the lights down, strikes a match and lights a candle.

I remember closing my eyes, smelling the sulphur of the extinguished match. I remember the happy birthday song as it clumsily began. I remember opening my eyes and seeing the big steam train, with its Swiss-roll wheels and chocolate finger tracks. And I remember screaming as my sister leaps up and blows out the candles before I have chance to. Gets me every fucking time, it does.

But, do you know what's fucked up? I don't have a sister. I didn't even get a bike for my sixth birthday. I got a fucking He-Man. But I don't remember that.

What's that? Yeah, sorry, I'm drifting. Don't try putting this on me. Don't be giving me that *'it's-your-own-fault-for-not-concentrating'* shite. Fuck off.

You must reach out to those around you. All of you will become one, you will take them to where it began, and you will become the beginning.

But how am I supposed to do this? Turn up at their front doors and announce your arrival? It won't work. I'll get locked up. You're the author, you work it out. I'm just waiting to be written.

You will be able to reach out to them using your new abilities.

I can't do that, I just drift, float around like an idea without a brain to live in.

You will connect with them. You will reach out, infiltrate their dreams, their memories and imaginations. Those with children will be the easiest, so that is where you will begin.

Children, what are you talking about?

A child's mind is more potent, more present. The boundaries between their imagination and corporeal existence are less defined. They are powerful in their belief of a larger reality, a reality you are now becoming accustomed to. And the link between the child and the parent will allow you to slowly convince them of our existence. And then you will be able to alter their subjective perceptions, much as your own has been altered.

Claire Fletcher has a kid. Gaz and Gemma have got a couple of kids as well. The eldest is a teenager, though. What about him?

His sense of self, his identity is still fluid. He spends much of his time playing games in a virtual world using avatars which represent an imaginary ideal. That is how we will reach out to him. We will provide the meaning and purpose that he so desperately craves. He, and his generation, are important to us.

What about the rest of us?

There is one of you who is approaching death. He spends much of his time drifting in and out of consciousness, unable to distinguish between the two states. We are using his mind to amplify our presence and your own burgeoning abilities. His death will be the catalyst, it will bring you all together.

All together?

Your friends from childhood. All those who were there on the field when the seeds were discovered.

What exactly happened back then?

The initiation never ends. It has no beginning.

We are truly blessed.

And there is another one. One for whom the light is too bright, who has turned away from it and seeks to snuff it out. He seeks to destroy all we are building. He must be stopped.

Everything around me shifts and distorts as the true magnitude of what is happening is revealed to me. Everything shimmers, vibrates with significance and purpose, and in the glare of a fantastic blue light, I am reborn into a Higher Dimension, and I am infinite.

20

Jamie (And Kirk)

It's a couple of days before I go and see Kirk again.

Work has become a total grind, due in part to the trouble I'm having getting to sleep. My solution is to drink as much as possible when I get home so I can get to sleep earlier, but when the morning rolls around I feel like hell, so facing work is even more unbearable.

My new mantra is *'things could be a lot worse'*, so I plod on. It's Carrie I feel sorry for. Between the boozing and the general heaviness that surrounds me, I must be a nightmare to be around. She doesn't complain, though. She's good like that.

'You look like shit, bud,' Kirk says when I walk in. He's got his shirt off and Sharon sits next to him, peeling patches off his back and applying new ones. 'Morphine,' he tells me. 'Slow-release, means I don't have to take so many fucking tablets.'

I'm shocked to see he's lost even more weight. The skin of his chest is stretched across birdcage ribs. The tattoos on his arms are saggy and distorted, crinkled newspaper pictures.

243

There are streaks of grey all through the patchy beard that covers his sunken cheeks. I can't help but think of black and white photos of concentration camp survivors.

'Guess what,' he says, a mischievous smile twinkling his mouth.

'What?'

'Got the car,' he says. 'A Ford fucking Focus.'

'Really?' I say, genuinely surprised. Sharon peers at me from behind his back. The look on her face says it all.

She pats Kirk on the back. 'All done,' she says.

Kirk says, 'Cheers,' and stands up. His arms cover his torso while Sharon hands him his top. He looks away, brittle and embarrassed. Slowly, he puts his top back on.

'Can't bear to look at myself this way. That's my first priority after this chemo is finished: put some fucking weight back on. Get fighting fit.'

Sharon smiles, 'Yeah.'

'None of my stuff fucking fits,' he says. 'I've bought a couple of tops, but I don't want to buy too many new clothes. I mean, what's the point? Once I start getting back in shape, I won't have any need for them.'

'I'll make us all a cuppa,' Sharon says, standing up. She looks as though she's about to burst into tears. Kirk shoots her this look, as if to say, *don't you dare*.

All the bullshit and small talk that I had lined up has vanished. A couple of sleepless nights and crappy mornings don't seem worth mentioning. I play it safe.

'So how about this car then?' I ask.

'Fucking bargain,' he says. 'Absolute steal. Of course, everyone's panicking, thinking I'm gonna go fucking racing about and that.' He grins. 'It's an option, I suppose.'

'Yeah.'

'Actually, I wanted to nip out today, pick a few things up from the shop. Do you fancy popping out with me?'

'Yeah, sure, why not?'

Sharon comes back through with the drinks. She puts them down on the table, and Kirk turns to her.

'Me and Jamie are gonna quickly pop out for a bit.'

She looks at Kirk, and then turns to look at me. 'Where? Kirk, you've just had your meds.'

'I know,' he snaps. 'We're just going around the corner, pick up some bits and bobs.'

'If you need owt, I'll ring Lorraine or Mam, they can bring it round for you later.'

'I'm not a fucking cripple,' Kirk shouts, and it makes him clutch at his chest.

An uneasy silence falls over the room. Sharon stares straight ahead, focusing on the wall. Her eyes are round and moist, but she doesn't cry.

'I'm sorry,' Kirk says, eventually. His eyes are shut, and he lets out a little groan. He says, 'I just wanna get out of this house for a bit, do summat for mesen. I won't do owt daft, won't go too far. Jamie will be with me.'

'Okay,' Sharon says. 'Okay. Do what you need to do. I'll wait here.'

———

It's only a two-minute drive from Kirk's house to the supermarket, but I'm on the edge of my seat and hyper-vigilant for the entire journey.

When we first get in the car, Kirk puts the radio on. He fiddles about with the dial until he settles upon a station playing a familiar tune. *Set Me Free* by N-Trance.

'How mad is that?' Kirk says. 'This brings back some memories. Do you remember that time I was on leave and we drove to Withernsea? Did that mad acid.'

'Blanks? Yeah, I recall a drive out to With, but the details are fuzzy,' I say. We both laugh.

Kirk puts the key in and turns on the engine. When the engine splutters into life, a look of sheer delight spreads over his face.

At the supermarket, Kirk insists on carrying his own basket. I carry the huge sack of dry dog food for the beast. We move up and down the aisles, Kirk taking various things from the shelves and dropping them in the basket. He's on autopilot, doesn't pay attention to the stuff he's grabbing. The actual items aren't that important. It's the thin layer of normality he's looking for. He's hoping for a special offer.

'I don't know what my chances are,' he says to me in the car on the way back. 'I didn't want to know. All I know is that it's another fight. Just another fight. Happens to be the fight of my life, but there you go.'

He deteriorates rapidly over the following week. Visits from the community nurses become the daily norm. He finds it difficult to swallow the pills, so the only alternative is regular injections.

One night, I'm in bed, half-pissed as usual. Carrie is next to me, the blanket tossed to one side because of the heat. I'm staring up at the ceiling, worrying about the heartburn I've been having for the last week. I know it's just stress and cheap plonk, but a voice in the back of my head keeps saying things like *cancer* and *death.*

My phone vibrates, making me jump. Carrie moans and stirs, but she doesn't wake up. I grab the phone. Kirk's name flashes up on the screen, so I sit up, press answer.

'Hello?'

'Now then,' Kirk says. 'Sorry for ringing so late.'

'It's okay,' I say, getting out of bed. I'm wearing only my boxers and the bedroom window is open, causing me to shiver. I head towards the stairs, fumbling around in the dark.

'How's it going? Everything okay?'

'Yeah,' he replies, sighing.

He sounds strangely bright and alert, considering. Despite the late hour, I'm glad to hear his voice. It's a selfish thing, maybe, but I feel like his friend again.

When I reach the bottom of the stairs, I go into the living room and head towards the lamp.

'Trouble sleeping?' I ask as I flick on the light.

'Yeah. Spend half the night sweating, the other half shivering. I'm turning the fan on and off every two seconds. It's this fucking heat. It's fucking killing me.'

'Yeah.'

'They cancelled my chemo today.'

'Did they say why?' I go through into the kitchen, open the fridge, take out a tinny and crack it open. I really shouldn't, but I'm dry. I grab my belly, my big furry belly, and then I get an image of Kirk in my head, painfully thin, not an ounce of fat on him.

'Said I'm too ill. Can you believe that?'

'Shit.'

'That's what I said. Chemo makes you ill, that's how it works. You get worse to get better. Fucking NHS.'

I take a long, slow swig of lager.

'I'll pop round tomorrow, you can tell me all about it. Is there anyone with you now?'

'No,' he says. 'Sharon stayed over last night, Lorraine the night before, but they've got their own shit going on, y'know? Got families and kids and responsibilities and all that.'

'Have you seen anything of Jack?' Kirk told me when I first met up with him again that he was estranged from his son.

'Jack is coming to see me this weekend.' I hear the lightening in his voice. 'Sharon let his mam know I was ill and we had a quick chat on FaceTime. You'll have to pop by and see him. Fucking fifteen now, right big fucker. Don't know who he takes after.'

I laugh. Once again, I find myself in the familiar position of not knowing what to say. Anything I have to offer seems trivial and unimportant.

'How are you feeling? How are you bearing up?'

'I'm in a lot pain,' he says, quietly. 'I have patches, liquids and top-up injections, but they only do so much. And the

247

fucking shit I'm coughing up. I haven't been able to smoke a fucking jay all week.'

'Bad fucking news.'

'Tell me about it,' he says. 'I'm hoping the phlegm will start clearing up once the weather cools off a bit.'

'Yeah.'

The conversation meanders on a bit longer. Kirk tells me he hasn't had a chance to take the car out anymore, but it's good to know it's out there on the street, waiting for him to get better.

I tell him I'll see him the following evening.

———

There's a house full when I arrive.

Sharon, Lorraine and his mam are there, along with two nurses and a doctor. Everyone is crammed into the front room. Kirk is flaked out on the sofa. He looks ill. Very fucking ill.

'Hey,' I say, when I walk in, Sharon and one of the nurses moving aside to let me pass.

'Now then,' Kirk says.

'He's had a rough couple of days,' Sharon says, sinking into a chair behind me.

'Don't fucking talk about me like I'm not here,' Kirk says.

'Calm down,' his mam says.

'It's like fucking Piccadilly Circus in here,' Kirk barks, which sets off a barrage of coughs.

Everyone shuts up while Kirk hacks up a load yellowish gunk. It's a horrible sound, like cardboard boxes ripped to shreds.

I've obviously walked into a highly charged situation, and I feel like I should leave, so I start to say, 'Listen, I'll pop round later if –'

'You don't have to go anywhere,' Kirk says, cutting me off.

The doctor is young and attractive. She has short red hair. She flicks her fringe and says, 'Kirk, I appreciate that you're concerned, but we're running out of options.'

'I just need something now,' Kirk says.

'The nurse can give you an injection, but it will wear off in a couple of hours, and then you'll be back to square one.'

With great effort, Kirk grabs the sofa and uses his arms to push himself upright. He clutches at his chest, weak and tired. I glance away. When I turn back, I see the strain has left him looking as though his face has been pinned onto to his skull, loose and sagging.

'I'm going to make a cuppa,' I say. 'Anyone want one?'

The doctor says yes and asks if there's any instant coffee. Kirk's mam also says yes. Lorraine and both the nurses say no. Lorraine steps out into the front garden to ring her boyfriend, and one of the nurses gets a syringe ready.

'I'll give you a hand,' Sharon says, and she stands up, offers her chair to the doctor.

The doctor takes a seat. She's wearing a long skirt with a split in it, and when she sits, it opens and exposes her leg. I catch sight of Kirk leering. He meets my eyes, gives a little grin and a wink. *Cheeky.* And just like that we're sixteen again, and everything else is special effects – make-up and set-dressing – a nightmare vision of the future.

In the kitchen, I look out the window and into the yard. The beast is out there, walking in circles, yelping and whimpering.

'That fucking dog,' Sharon says.

I take the kettle over to the sink and fill it. 'You'll have to remind me who's drinking what,' I say.

'Three teas and a coffee,' Sharon says.

I lift the mugs from the cupboard. 'I forgot to ask if anyone wanted sugar.'

'None for me, one for Mam and however you take it,' Sharon says. 'Dunno about the doc. She strikes me as a milk-no-sugar kinda girl.'

I plug the kettle in. I wonder how it's all going to pan out – I know what's coming, but it's getting there that's got me stumped.

'They want to fit a syringe driver,' Sharon says. 'It would deliver a steady supply of morphine through the day. He doesn't want it though.'

'Still thinks he's going to pull through?'

'Yeah. He's so determined to fight that he's fighting *us* now as well as the cancer. Thinks we've all got hidden agendas, like we're trying to have him over or summat.'

'He's always been a stubborn bastard,' I say. I finish making the drinks.

Sharon takes hers and her mam's through, I take my own and the doctor's. The front room is quiet. I put the doctor's drink on the table and stand in the corner, out the way.

After a couple of excruciating minutes, Kirk says, 'I feel like yer all stood round, pressuring me to do summat I'm unsure of. I know it'll make me feel better, but it's like. . . ' He pauses for a minute, seeming to search for the right words. 'It's like I don't have any control anymore. Like I don't have a choice.'

'You've always got a choice,' the doctor says.

———————

I decide to take some time off work. Carrie's not too thrilled, because money's tight (as usual) but I can't function.

I've become so attuned to diplomatic silences that I struggle to say anything anymore. To anyone.

I spend as much time as possible with Kirk. He relents and has the syringe-driver fitted. It perks him up for a couple of days, and we spend most of that time taking turns at playing *Fall of Mankind* on the big telly and talking about various people that we used to knock around with.

And then it hits him all at once. The drugs. The pain. The lack of food. The cancer.

He refuses to go to hospital, so they take most of the furniture out of his living room and put up a hospital bed, complete with a remote-controlled adjustable frame and an inflatable mattress that moves him around the bed to stop him from developing bedsores.

I turn up one day, and when I knock on the door there's no reply. A key safe has been fitted next to the door, so I enter the number and remove the key to let myself in.

The house is quiet, and the only thing I can hear is the wheeze of the machine that pumps the air around the mattress. The first thing I do is go over to check on Kirk. He's out of it. I panic before I notice the rise and fall of his chest. *Still with us.* It's odd that the house is empty, so I call out 'Hello?' and have a quick look around. I nip upstairs, and back down and through into the kitchen, before checking the bathroom at the back. No sign of anyone. It's then that I realise the beast has gone.

I put the kettle on and re-enter the living room. Both armchairs have been removed to make way for the bed, so I sit on the sofa. Kirk is still snoozing. I'm about to go back to the kitchen when Kirk opens his eyes.

'Now then,' he says. 'It's funny, but you were in my dream.'

'Yeah? Nothing dodgy I hope.'

He smiles. 'We were back at school. We were in the field, that day after everyone had seen lights in the sky, and then Barry turned up with these seed-things.'

'I remember.'

'I've been seeing all kinds of mad shit, Jamie,' he says. 'I know a lot of it's the drugs, but there's something else going on.'

'What do you mean?'

'You know me, mate,' he says. 'I did enough mad shit when we were kids to know when I'm hallucinating and when I'm seeing straight. And there's mad shit kicking off all over this city. They're *here*, Jamie. They've always been here.'

'Who's been here, Kirk, what are you on about?'

'Make me a spliff and I'll tell yer.'

'What?' I'm caught off-guard. 'I can't do that.'

'Please,' he says. 'It's not gonna make me any worse now, is it?'

'Where's the shit?' I ask.

'Under the sofa.'

I reach under the sofa, and sure enough, the tray is there. I pick it up and place it on my lap. I take a king-size paper and set about it. I'm out of practice, so it takes me a couple of attempts to get it right. Sparking it up, I take it over to Kirk, along with an ashtray. Leaning over him I place the spliff gently on his lips. He takes a couple of deep drags. He pauses a moment, savouring the smoke in his lungs, before coughing it all out in a storm of phlegm and saliva. His eyes are red, swollen.

'They were there that day on the field back at school,' he gasps. 'And they were there that time we drove down to Withernsea.' He's croaking, trying to hold it together. 'They were there when I fucked up in the army and got discharged. And they're here now, in this room, with us, manipulating things. I can feel them rattling around in my head. They're using me.'

Kirk is illuminated by the afternoon sun pouring in from the living room window. He's pale and the light bleaches out any last remaining colour from his face. I know it's just all the drugs he's on that's making him talk like this, but it still freaks me out. I feel a judder, a little twitch up and down my spine, like there *is* something in here with us.

'Who are they? What are they?' I ask. Leaning forward again, I place the joint back between his lips.

'Aliens. Spirits. Demons. *Greys*. Fuck knows. Different people see them as different things, depending on what they believe,' he takes another weak pull on the joint. 'But they're here. Always have been.'

Kirk breathes out, a plume of smoke fills the air above his bed, mingling with the afternoon sun.

I swallow, tap the end of the joint into the ashtray.

'What do they want?'

'They want to make us like them. They want us all to be one thing, one mind. See that thing in my arm?' He nods downwards, towards the tube that runs from his arm to his syringe-driver.

'Yeah?'

The lines and wrinkles around his forehead and eyes are highlighted by shadow. He looks so old.

'They're pumping me full of this stuff, Jamie. It's their distilled essence, that's what they're putting in me. They make it out of those little white seeds. They take the seeds, and they crush them and extract the powder, and then they refine it and turn it into a liquid. And that's what's in the syringe-driver. That's why I didn't want it fitted.

'They're taking everything that's makes me. . . well, *me*. I'm being erased, Jamie. Erased and replaced.'

His voice is flat and calm, like he's reading from a script. I put the joint to his lips again. 'They've been observing us, humans I mean, ever since we started walking upright and thinking and dreaming. And now they're making their move. We're just portals to them, Jamie; a way in.'

Despite coughing, he manages to keep the joint clamped between his lips. 'They need to bond with us and use us to access this plain of existence. They're fascinated by our reality, and our relationship with it. They want our ideas, our dreams. They want to embed themselves in our minds.'

I take the joint from Kirk's mouth and have a deep drag myself. The end is wet with Kirk's spittle. *Doggy ender*. My head hurts, and it takes all my effort not to burst into tears. I gently let my hand rest on Kirk's shoulder. 'It's okay, mate. We'll figure this out.'

'It's too late, Jamie,' he says, whispering. 'It's too late for all of us.'

I get the call early the following morning. My phone wakes me, and seeing Sharon's name on the screen, I know what's happened. When I answer, I can hear her crying.

'It's Kirk,' she says. 'He's gone, Jamie.'

It's supposed to be my first day back at work, but I ring in and tell them what's happened. To my surprise, they're quite understanding.

It takes me a while to wake Carrie up and tell her. I know telling her will make it real, will set me off, so I struggle to face up to it. I don't know how long I sit there.

'I'm so sorry,' she says, rubbing her eyes, and she gives me a big hug. She feels warm, and solid, and *alive*, so I cling to her, breathing her in.

All day I feel like I should be crying, but I'm not. I feel numb, then relieved that he's out of his misery, and then guilty because I feel relieved, so I end up going back to numb again. I feel like I should be doing something, because I'm supposed to be at work, but I can't think of anything else to do, so by the time the afternoon rolls around I'm half-pissed on whisky.

Carrie is on evenings, so she leaves me to it. As soon as she's left the house I make a joint out of the stuff I put aside for this moment. I figure Kirk would rather I raise a joint than a toast, so after I light it, I hold the spliff up as a sort of tribute.

———

A couple of nights later, I'm drunk again. Carrie's out, so I allow myself to fall into a snooze on the sofa. My phone beeps to let me know I've received a message. Holding it up, I'm stunned and confused to see Kirk's name and numberdisplayed.

'What the fuck?'

It takes a moment for me to work up the bottle to read it. Opening the message, it flashes up:

– THEY WILL FILL THE VOID WITHIN US ALL.

21

Steve

This was it. The event that I had been waiting for, getting ready for: the final phase.

The Ascension.

I see all the people, my friends, leave their comments of sympathy, along with their assurances that they will be at the funeral. There's no getting away from it. It's happening just like they said it would.

A lot of shit goes through my head in the run up to the Ascension. Maybe I've lost the plot, and this is just the final symptom. Seeing patterns everywhere, within everything. But as everyone's thoughts turn to Kirk, I see the mind-web that was described to me begin to light up. There's myself, Gemma and Gaz; Jamie, Chris and Claire at the centre of it.

And now, for the first time I sense a presence – one I was warned about – hovering near. The one that wants to snuff out the great light.

It's Barry.

He was in the paper, wanted for murder. And he's still out there. I don't know where he is or what he plans to do, but he's there on the periphery, biding his time just like I am.

I get my shit together. Start meditating in preparation, projecting myself outwards. I'm still so limited in what I can do, but I reach out to the very edges of my abilities. Gemma and Claire's children make crude drawings, they try to render me as I appear in their dreams.

Lee, Gemma's eldest, is a crucial part of the process, although he doesn't realise it. I place the seeds in jars and leave them near his house. He collects them, first out of curiosity and then out of compulsion. He sows them, scatters them on street corners and parks; drops handfuls around the community. I watch him to begin with, and then leave him to his own devices.

My friends begin to experience episodes of disorientation and déjávu: Gaz sees an eerie figure at a bus stop in the dead of night; Gemma is approached by a man muttering incomprehensible phrases; an unsettling photo of Claire's house is posted through her door.

It's like the whole city is readying itself for the transformation. I feel energy bleed into its foundations, a signal so powerful I can see the waves – white lines – reverberating from my bedroom window: a great, tangled web descending from the sky.

Addicts and schizophrenics alike experience incomprehensible visions of vast structures, networks and cables. It permeates their dreams, preventing them from sleeping. All around Hull, people are compelled to draw and write as means of contextualising the images that invade their subconscious. They spray strange symbols and jumbled words onto walls and surfaces throughout Hull. And the seeds... the seeds are everywhere.

22

Jamie

The day of the funeral rolls around. I decide to walk to the crematorium, instead of getting one bus into town and then another up Chanterlands Ave. It's the last few days of summer, and the walk will do us good. Carrie agrees.

She gets ready and we walk down De La Pole Ave, onto Spring Bank West, then cross the road. We head down Brooklands towards the little footbridge that crosses the railway lines. I grip Carrie's hand tightly, drawing strength from her presence. There's a short bike track at the back of *Ideal Standard* that runs alongside a railway embankment. It leads to the back of Perth Street West. Passing the small graveyard by the social club, I'm thinking about death already.

I don't know how I feel about death anymore. Drained, certainly. The past few weeks have taken a toll on me and Carrie is getting frustrated. All she can see is the drinking and late nights. I want to talk to her, but I don't know what to say. We walk in silence.

I like Chanterlands Ave. It's busy without being oppressive. Not that far away from Anlaby Road, but as different as a whole other world. It's tidy, and there aren't as many bag-heads about. The Avenues back onto Chants, and big trees are dotted along one side of it.

I'm walking down Chants Ave in a suit and the sun is shining through the branches of the trees and onto my face, and I feel anonymous: normal. It feels good to feel anonymous and normal.

Walking briskly, it takes us about half an hour to reach the crematorium. The service is in the main chapel, so we take the winding gravel track to it from the main road. The cemetery is well-groomed and orderly. The grass is neat, and the headstones are ordered. There are little wooden benches conveniently placed here and there.

Approaching the chapel, I can see the crowd gathered outside. A big turn-out.

Steve

Some of the faces are familiar, some are not. I glance around, searching for the people I came to see. And there they are: Jamie Clements, Chris Morton, Claire Fletcher, Gemma Price...

Someone grabs my arm, and I see Gaz standing there. Fucking hell. We stare at each other for a moment, looking each other up and down, taking in all the ways in which we've changed. Then he leans forward and puts his arms around me – practically fucking crushes me.

'How the fuck are you?' he says. 'Haven't seen you for a long time, man.'

'I'm okay,' I say, feeling awkward. 'How are you?'

'I'm good,' he says. He steps back, head darting left to right, searching for someone. 'All things considered. What are you up to? Where are you living now?'

'Anlaby Road.'

'Really?' he says, looking a bit confused. 'I live down Melrose, thought I might have seen you about. I mean, it's been fucking years since we saw each other last, right?'

'Yeah, well,' I say. 'I keep a low profile.'

He gives me this look, cocks his head like he's trying to work out if I'm taking the piss or not, and then he says, 'Come over and say hello to everyone.'

'Everyone?'

'Yeah, it's like a fucking reunion!' He motions towards our former group, standing around the entrance to the chapel.

We walk over together.

'Look who I've fucking found!' Gaz says.

I smile and wave. Jamie Clements approaches me, although it takes a couple of seconds to work out that it's him, because of all the weight he's put on. 'Now then,' he says as he offers his hand. 'It's the international man of mystery.'

I grab his hand, shake it, and give him a playful slap on the belly. 'Fuck me,' I say. 'Yer looking healthy, Jamie. I assume all this is paid for?'

He looks down at himself and his cheeks turn red.

'Um, yeah,' he says, eventually.

It's a bit awkward, I realise immediately that I've hit a raw nerve. I'm about to say something else, try and defuse the atmosphere, but he smiles and then goes over to this young bird, who I recognise as Carrie Taylor. She used to knock about with one of Kirk's sisters.

Chris waddles over. He's wearing a cheap suit. His pale, sun-starved bonce is shiny and round, and he frequently reaches up and scratches his head, as though he needs to be reminded that he's losing his hair.

He gives me a big grin, shakes my hand. 'Good to see you, man,' he says.

Gemma

I'm so glad Claire is here. We stand chatting to each other, talk about the weather, work, kids. Anything to avoid talking about Kirk, really. I can tell his death has rattled Claire, and she's having to keep it together.

She keeps saying, 'I was only thinking about him last week,' over and over again, like she's struggling to find anything else to say.

'It's okay,' I say and put my hand on her arm, to try and calm her down.

I spot a big, gangly bloke, someone whose arms seem to be moving with a mind of their own, and I realise that it's Steve.

Then I spot Gary.

Gaz

Claire's looking good, real good. I know she runs that bar on the avenues, so she must be doing alright. Her hair, long and blonde, is piled up on her head. She's wearing dark make-up around her eyes and bright red lipstick. Her deep tan and fitted dress seem more suited to a night out than a funeral.

I ask her how she's bearing up and she smiles. It's a forced smile, like she's really making an effort, and I can't tell whether it's because she's upset about Kirk, or she's heard about me from Gemma, and hates me as a result.

She says, 'I'm okay. I mean, I hadn't seen Kirk for years. I found out over Facebook.'

While I'm talking to Claire, Gemma fidgets. She looks tired and distracted and keeps glancing at Claire, as if for reassurance.

Finally, the two of us exchange awkward hellos.

'I think we need to talk,' I say.

She looks at me, all weary.

'You know where I am, Gaz. You've always known.'

'I'm sorry,' I say. 'I didn't mean for it to get like this.' I shuffle my feet. 'After I didn't see them for a couple of weeks, I just figured they'd be better off without me.'

'Gary...'

260

'And then the weeks turned into months, and it got more and more difficult to find my way back. I assumed you all hated me, and I wouldn't blame you. I was broke, I didn't have any money. I was in a bad way.'

'*We've* been in a bad way. They miss you.'

'I miss *them*, they're all they think about.'

She looks drained. 'I can't talk about this now, Gary.'

She walks away, and I stand there briefly before moving closer to Chris. I grab his arm and take him to one side. I don't know what I'd do without Chris. He's always there.

'Everything okay?'

'I need to talk to you after this,' I say. 'I think I've fucked up. Big style.'

He sighs, asks: 'What now?'

I look down at the floor, choking back tears, feel my face burning with shame.

'D'yer remember that Lizzie?'

He squints as he thinks. 'Er. . . is that what's-his-name's lass?'

'Yeah, her,' I say, tugging my ear. 'Well, we had an *encounter*. She's been texting me, she thinks she's up the duff.'

Chris sighs again, looks at me in much the same way Gemma looked at me.

'Fuck me,' he says. 'You never learn, do you?'

23

Steve

We stand together, and the all the strange quirks and memories of our shared past emerge, bubbling up to the surface. There's the beginning of an electric tension, I'm sure I'm not the only one who perceives it.

The old gang is back together. A quietness has descended over our group, interrupted by Gaz who blurts out, 'Well, it's all fucked up, innit? All this, I mean.'

Chris nods his head sagely, says, 'It's been a fucking mad year, annit?'

A couple of us laugh, but it's brief, and what follows is a pause, a simultaneous moment of reflection. We're here together, but we're dislocated. Adrift in time and space. There are shared bonds, our intertwined childhoods, which should make us close, make our friendships and relationships firm as iron. But we're lost, all of us, in our own little narratives. We're all friends on social-media – theoretically, we're constantly in touch, that's how we found out about Kirk – but we haven't been together in the same room for years, and that's a shame.

We should be a community.

'Guess you all heard about Pete?' Claire asks.

There are a couple of mumbled "yeses" followed by a pause.

'I was fucking there when it happened,' I say.

'What?' Gaz says.

'I was at work. I was outside smoking a fag when he ran out into the road. Saw the whole fucking thing.'

'Jesus,' Gaz says.

'That's awful, I'm sorry,' Claire says. She reaches up and pinches the bridge of her nose, like she's holding something back, and then she comes over and gives me a hug.

We embrace, and something passes between us. She steps back, I sense her confusion, like the answer to a question has just occurred to her.

'And then there's the whole Barry Thompson thing, in't there?' Chris says.

No one speaks for a moment.

'Fuck him,' Gaz finally says. 'Fucking bag-head. It's a shame, how he turned out. But fucking murdering that poor bloke.'

The mere mention of Barry's name rattles me. I have this feeling that he's being drawn here somehow.

There is unfinished business.

Everyone shifts back into blank reflection, uncomfortable pause.

'Anyway, fuck him,' Gaz repeats. 'It's Kirk's day today.'

'I can see the hearse,' Gemma says.

———

The mourners' car pulls up, followed by the hearse, and everyone gathered around the crematorium slowly stops talking. They pull up to the chapel, and the doors on the car open and Kirk's sisters and mam step out and join us by the chapel. The pall bearers, dressed in identical black suit-jackets and grey slacks, walk over to the hearse. There's a huge wreath, in the shape of letters, 'KIRK'. They open the back of the hearse, and two of the pall bearers slide out the coffin. They're all big lads, and the coffin appears tiny on their broad shoulders.

A woman and a kid get out of the car.

'Who's that?' I ask.

'It's Kirk's ex, and his lad, Jack,' Jamie says.

Claire looks at Jamie, and then she looks back at the woman and the kid. Claire's gone pale.

'In another universe, that's me,' she says.

The service is a humanist one, short and dignified. Kirk's mam says a couple of things, before Jamie gets up and mumbles his way through a poem. And then the celebrant talks about Kirk's life.

The service finishes with *Angels* by Robbie Williams, and for the last song they play N Trance's *Set You Free*, which makes us all smile, before making us all cry. After the service concludes, we're ejected from the chapel and out into the afternoon sun.

The wake is to take place at the Humber Street Social club, on Anlaby Road, where Kirk's mam is apparently the bar manager.

Gaz offers to give me a lift in his van, so I pile in along with him and Chris. It feels strange sat between them. Like we're off on some big, daft adventure.

A trip to the beach at Withernsea, or something.

Gaz puts the radio on, and it's Shabba Ranks' *Mr Loverman*.

'Fuck me,' Gaz says, turning it up. 'Kirk used to love this fucking song.'

Chris shouts: 'SHABBA!' and when the refrain kicks in, we sing in unison: 'THEY CALL ME MISTER LOVERMAN THEY CALL ME MISTER LOVERMAN.'

At the do, the crowd breaks up into smaller groups. I gather together what remains of the old fucking gang, the

Amy Johnson crew. We find a bunch of tables at the corner of the club and congregate around them.

I've never understood the whole buffet-after-funerals tradition. Personally, I lose my appetite when forced to consider my own mortality, but it's clear that I'm alone in this, because everyone else laps it up.

Besides, there are other forces at work today.

It's hard to keep it in, I want to tell them something wonderful is about to happen.

'It's a shame that it takes summat like this to bring us all together again,' Gaz says as he busily demolishes his second piece of quiche. 'I'm serious, it's good to see you all again.'

'Yeah,' Gemma says, quietly.

Gaz exhales. I see him lean close to Gemma, cup his hand around his mouth and whisper something to her.

'Mad, innit?' Chris says. 'I mean, we all live within, what? A couple of miles of each other?'

'That's Hull for you,' Claire says, and she downs a glass of white wine. She slams the glass down on one of the little tables.

'How's business, Claire?' Gaz asks her. 'How yer been keeping?'

'Okay, business is going well,' she says. 'I've split up with Max, but shit happens and you get on with things, I suppose.'

Gaz smiles blankly. He says, 'I used to see Max quite a lot. In the casino.'

Claire smiles like she's just bitten into a lemon, and says, 'And him spending half his life in the fucking casino is the main reason we're splitting up.'

'Sorry,' Gaz says. He glances at Gemma.

Jamie, who has been in a daze since we arrived, pipes up 'Hey, Carrie was just saying about how you both work at the same place, Gemma.'

'That's right,' Gemma says. 'I ask after you all the time, Jamie, don't I, Carrie?'

'Yeah,' Carrie says. 'I don't have much to tell you though, do I? He doesn't give me much to work with.'

Jamie opens his mouth like he's about to say something, thinks twice, then closes it again, reaches up and scratches the back of his head like he's trying to remember if he locked the front door.

An almost-imperceptible flicker of anger washes Gemma's face. A raised eyebrow, a twitch of the lip. I can't tell who it's directed at.

Conversations ebb and flow. They emerge, swell, and break upon jagged rocks of emotion and association. A few of our group swap places so they can talk to each other more easily.

'Hey, did anyone ever see owt of Pete Ashworth?' Gaz asks. He looks at me. 'Before he died, like?'

'He was in a bad way,' Jamie says. 'On the plonk. In and out of hostels. A fucking mess, really.'

'Yet another fucking casualty,' Gaz says, taking a swig of his pint. 'Sometimes, it gets you wondering what the fuck is going on. I mean, we're not *that* fucking old, and we're dropping like flies. Makes you wonder how much time you've got left.'

How much time we have left. I find myself thinking about how expressions like that will cease to have meaning soon, once we all start to exist outside of linear time.

Gemma looks forlornly over at Gaz.

Gaz turns to me.

'What's the score with you then? I mean, no one's seen anything of you for ages. Bring us up to date.'

'Yeah,' Claire joins in. 'What's happening in your life?'

The innocuous question catches me off guard, but I know that it's my cue. *It's now or never.*

Time to set things into motion.

I take a deep breath, and check to make sure I have everyone's attention.

'I know you've all been experiencing some strange occurrences, things you can't explain. . . '

I feel the shiver of recognition as it moves around the table, connecting all of us.

No one knows what to say at first, but Claire is the one who breaks the silence.

She stares straight at me, her brow furrowed.

'Like what, Steve? What kind of "occurrences"?'

Gaz looks at me as if he's seeing me for the first time.

'Yeah. . . what are talking about, Steve?'

I reach up, rub the back of my head. I'm stalling because I'm nervous. This could still turn out to be entirely in my mind.

'You know. Dreams. Encounters. Stuff that seems a little. . . *off*. Creepy.'

I take advantage of the awkward to pause to quickly glance around their faces. They look at each other, like they're each waiting for someone to be the first to admit they've experienced something out of the ordinary. And the longer they wait, the clearer it is that they've seen something, heard something; *felt* something. But they're unable to comprehend it, because they've all kept their individual experiences under wraps. They don't know that I've been inside their minds.

They've all doubted everything they've seen and experienced. And now here I am, making it real.

Gemma is the first to react. Scraping her chair back, she lunges at me, her face twisted with anger. She grabs me by my collar. Her face is flushed, and I sense confusion, fear and anger emanating off her.

'What the fuck is going on with my kids? What have you done to them?'

I'm shocked by her fierce reaction. Even though she's shorter than me, she shows no sign of backing down, and keeps hold of my shirt, tightly.

'What's happening with the kids, Gemma?' Gaz stands and moves closer, placing his hands on her shoulders.

'Maybe if you made the effort to see them, you'd know,' Gemma snaps, whizzing round to confront Gaz. Gaz withdraws his hand as if he's been stung.

'Lee's in counselling,' Gemma's voice breaks. 'He has been for a couple of weeks. We had a... incident... He was hallucinating, hearing voices. He's been *taking* stuff, Gary, drugs. They've had to put him on medication while they do further tests.'

Gaz sags as though he's been hit in the stomach.

'Calm down, Gemma,' I say. 'That had nothing to do with me.'

It's a lie, kind of, but I'm trying to diffuse things. I watch Gaz, half-expecting him to launch at me, but he doesn't know what to do or say, so he hangs there, gently shaking his head.

'I saw a lot of Kirk before... y'know,' Jamie says loudly. 'He started saying things, crazy things... I thought it was just the drugs, but...'

Gemma relaxes a little, releases me. Claire looks at me with her eyes narrowed.

'What is this, Steve? Is this some kind of weird game, a prank? Now, tell us. What the fuck is going on? What's been happening to us? If you're in any way responsible for the strange shit that's been going with my daughter, I'll be teaming up with Gemma to fucking kill you.'

Gaz comes out of his strange suspension, clenches his fists as though he's getting ready to hit somebody. Me.

'I've seen a lot of mad shit lately,' he says, slowly, like he's finding it difficult to form sentences. 'Especially in a house that me and Chris were working on.'

'Turns out Barry used to live there.' Chris picks up the thread. He lifts his drink and knocks it back. 'What's the score, Steve? Have you been stalking us, or summat?'

I look around the room. Kirk's family and acquaintances continue to drink and chat, completely oblivious to our microcosm. Probably just think we're drunk, boisterous.

269

Funerals and weddings, there's always a bit of drama, someone booting off.

Our little group, our little circle, scatters.

Gemma and Claire move to a smaller table off to one side, pull up a couple of stools and sit next to each other. Claire puts her arm around Gemma. I hear her say, 'Don't worry Gemma, we'll get to the bottom of this, it'll be okay...'

But Claire's trembling, obviously trying to convince herself as much as she's trying to convince Gemma.

Gaz glares at me.

'Better start explaining,' he says. 'And if I don't like what I hear, you're not gonna like what's gonna happen.'

I put my hands up. 'I know you're all getting freaked out, but if we can all just keep it together. I promise this isn't as terrible as it sounds.'

Things are going badly. I didn't know what to expect, but I should have expected this. I feel smaller and more out of touch with each passing second. I'm losing them, and they're losing patience.

'What are you on about?' Claire says, snapping her head around, either unable or unwilling to mask the disgust in her voice. 'You need to start making sense before something kicks off. You're upsetting people, Steve. This isn't the time or place to be fucking with people. Have some respect for Kirk.'

I take another deep breath.

'We need to go back to Amy Johnson,' I blurt out. It's too soon, but I can't think what else to do. I can't explain, I don't have the words, but if I could only *show them* something...

'Amy?' Gaz says, surprised. 'It's gone, it's not there anymore.'

'The field's still there,' I tell them. 'Where we used to meet up. It's still there, at the back of the new housing development.'

Jamie laughs. It's a hollow laugh, an effort. It's the sound of someone desperately trying to break a deadlock. He turns to his girlfriend and says, 'Fucking hell. Been thinking about school a lot lately, haven't I? Dreaming about it.'

'Same here,' Chris says.

'Me too,' Claire says, and she grabs Gemma's hand, squeezes it tight.

'Do you remember that time we saw the lights?' Gaz says, absently, hands relaxing as his anger breaks and subsides. 'That's what I've been dreaming about. That, and them seeds.'

Gemma bring her hand down on the table, sharply, making a couple of empty half-pint glasses – and Claire – jump.

'Seeds?'

'Yeah, seeds,' Gaz says. 'Barry gave them to us, remember? He was fucking around, said they were pills. Pete swallowed one, so when he admitted he was joking, me and Kirk forced him to swallow the rest.'

Gemma opens her mouth as if to say something, but then seems to decide not to.

A breakthrough. I feel the relief pass through me, and I'm suddenly giddy with excitement.

They're beginning to understand.

'So, are we going, or what?' I ask.

'This is ridiculous, you can't seriously be thinking of going along with this?' Carrie has so far has kept completely silent about the whole thing, but now she's looking at Jamie, who blankly sips at his pint.

'I can't explain it, but I think we have to,' he says.

Carrie frowns, glances at each of us in turn: Gemma and Claire, sitting at the table, eyeliner smeared by tears; Gaz and Chris, the cronies, standing firm, ready for whatever; me, the clown, forehead covered in sweat, arms unable to stop jerking; and finally Jamie, who slouches, defeated, his belly hanging over his belt.

'You're all fucking mad,' Carrie says. 'You were into some seriously deranged stuff when you were kids.' She rolls her eyes at Jamie. 'I think I'm going to finish my drink and go home, if that's all right with you, darling.'

271

24

Jamie

I tell Kirk's mam and sisters that we're off on a little jolly; we're going to one of the places where we all used to knock about. We're going to have a drink, light a candle, think of Kirk, stuff like that. His mam looks bemused but concerned.

'You're not all pissed out of yer faces, are yer?' she says. 'Go steady, we've don't want to lose anyone else on a day like this.'

I've felt completely blank all day, like I'm miles away and observing everything remotely, but this is enough to set me off.

'I'm so sorry Marge,' I say. I hug her tightly, for far longer than necessary.

We file out into the car park at the back of the social. I give Carrie a kiss, hoping to reassure her that everything will be okay.

'Get a taxi home,' I tell her. 'I won't be too late.'

Gaz puts his arm around me, as we make our way to his van. He pulls my head close to his and says into my ear, 'What the fuck do *you* think's going on?'

I don't say anything, just shrug, because I'm still surprised we've all agreed to go along with Steve's mad plan. But deep down, I have this feeling that we don't really have a choice, because things are slotting into place now.

We all pile into Gaz's van. Chris and Claire sit up front with Gaz, while I sit in the back with Gemma and Steve. We're crammed in amongst Gaz's extensive collection of tools. It's cold and dark in the back, and we have to make space to sit by pushing aside various drills and gadgets, which poke at us when the van moves. No one says anything. For the entire journey, Gemma sits opposite me, staring at me like she expects me to make a run for it or something.

This entire situation has put her on edge, and I can't say I blame her. It's like she's meeting us all again for the first time. She doesn't know who to trust.

Steve

Hawthorn Avenue is only around the corner, so it doesn't take us long to get there. Although I can't see outside, I can tell by the way the van is bumping and shaking that we are travelling along the temporary road that leads from the back of the new-build houses to the last scrap of open land, which is still waiting to be developed.

The van pulls up and stops. I hear the grind of the handbrake, and the engine judders to a halt. There's a creak which reverberates around the back of the van, followed by the bump of a door being slammed shut. The side door is pulled open, and Gaz, Chris and Claire are standing there, in the lingering daylight.

'We're here,' Gaz says.

Stepping out of the van, I examine the grass beneath my feet, then look up at the sky. It's getting dark.

We trudge over uneven ground towards the grey iron fence that used to run along the back of Wheeler Street, now existing in name only since all of the houses are gone, knocked down. Claire is cursing, loudly.

'Fucking hell, my heels are sinking. This is fucking stupid.'

She hobbles around, reaching out and grabbing Gemma's arm for support.

'Fucking hell, should have brought a beat-box and mixtape,' Gaz says, out of breath. He laughs, too loudly, and no one else joins in. I catch a glimpse of his face, and he looks jubilant, a grin etched across his mouth, and for a moment he looks how he did back then, young and bright. But as his lips drop, the lines on his face return, the marks left by time and years of uncertainty and anger

They're following me across the rutted ground, but I don't know where I'm going.

Eventually, I stop moving, and so do they. It's hard to get orientated, but I can see the big patch of ground that used to be the foundations of Amy Johnson high school.

No one says anything for a while. I close my eyes, feel the breeze against my skin and hear the rattle of a train on the tracks as it cuts along the avenue on its way to the station. I sense that each of us is lost in our own recollections, and when I open my eyes, I almost expect the school to have returned, to have somehow reconstructed itself from the bricks and mortar of the houses that now occupy the site where it once stood.

It's Claire who snaps us out of it, with her usual no-nonsense approach.

'We're here, Steve. Now what?'

They all look at me. My stomach drops. Gemma starts to stride towards me, like she's going to grab me again, so I hold up my hand, reach out and. . .

. . . there's me, Pete Ashworth, Jamie Clements, Chris Morton, and the "couples": Kirk Banks and Gaz Porter have both managed to snag girlfriends, a novelty. Up until a couple

of months ago, our get-togethers on the field had been an all-male affair, dominated by football and just the talk of girls.

Kirk is seeing Claire Fletcher, which caused a bit of trouble, because everyone knows that Barry Thompson has a major thing for her. Gaz has just started going out with Gemma Price, who's in mine and Chris's class. No one would ever admit it, but we're all a little jealous.

Gemma is sitting next to Gaz, he's got his arm around her, and she laughs too loudly whenever he tries to say something funny. Moving over to them, I tap Gemma on her arm. She looks up at me and smiles.

Meeting her eyes, I say, 'Remember where we are. . .'

. . . and we're out of it and back in the present. Gemma stumbles and drops onto her arse on the hard ground. She bursts into tears. Jamie grabs his stomach, bends over like he's going to be sick. Claire is rigid and mute, hands clamped to the sides of her head. Chris's eyes widen, his jaw hangs open.

Gaz lunges at me.

'What have you done to us?'

Gemma manages to shout, 'No, don't!' as his fist connects with my cheek. It's a good punch, a strong hook, and it flips my head to one side. I'm losing my footing, swaying, trying to stay upright. I can taste blood in my mouth, and my face feels raw. Gaz stands in front of me, like he's sizing me up for a second swing. I wince and hold my hands up. Hesitating slightly, he feints like he's trying to catch me off guard, and I totally fall for it. He swings another punch, one I'd have no chance of stopping, but stops short of hitting me. He keeps his fist in the air, a couple of inches from my nose. Even though I'm taller than Gaz, he's solid, a lot wider than I am, always has been. I don't stand a chance. I cower, covering my face. He lets his hand fall, breaks away and goes to Gemma, crouches beside her and places his hand on her shoulder.

'Are you okay?' he says. 'What just happened?'

Chris, Jamie and Claire seem to have been rooted to the spot, but they slowly start to move and look around. They drift towards Gemma. I rub my cheek. No one bothers to ask if I'm okay.

'Gemma, talk to us,' I hear Claire say, crouching down to get a better look at Gemma's face.

Gemma wipes her eyes with the back of her hand and clears her throat.

'I was young again,' she says. 'We all were.'

I steady myself. They huddle over Gemma, tending to her, but Chris straightens up and walks towards me. Gaz has kicked off, and now it's Chris's turn to step in and be the diplomat, defuse the situation. Just like how it used to work at school.

'We're all really freaked out, Steve. What's going on?'

I find myself flinching, expecting to be hit again. I can feel that my cheek is already beginning to swell.

And I'm shaking violently, partly because I'm cold, partly because I'm scared. *It's really happening.*

'This is all going to sound nuts,' I say, my whole body tensing with anticipation. 'But you need to let me speak, and when I do, you need to let me finish what I have to say.'

Gaz is crouching next to Gemma, stroking her hair. He flashes me a look before speaking quietly to her.

'I'm sorry,' I hear him say 'I don't know what's happening, but when this is over I'll set things right, I promise.'

He helps her to her feet. She nods at him, her lip trembling.

'Let's get this over with, Steve,' Gaz says to me.

'Twenty years ago,' I blurt out. 'We were... *chosen* by something. This entity, this presence, has been around us – humans, I mean – trying to communicate with us. This has been going on for hundreds, maybe thousands, of years. It wants to link with us – share its abilities with us.'

No one says anything at first, which is understandable. Gaz shakes his head. Claire rubs her eyes, like she's waking up. They look like an audience waiting impatiently for the comedian's punchline. I can't say I blame them – just hearing myself saying it out loud is enough to stretch my own belief to breaking point.

'Are we talking about fucking aliens here?' Jamie asks.

'In a way, yes,' I reply.

Energy surges through me, adrenalin and electricity charge through my limbs. I take a deep breath, because I don't want to rant or talk too fast, it's important that they understand me.

'But they're not "little green men" or anything like that. The only way I can describe it is as a vast, extra-dimensional intelligence. They don't have bodies, not like we do anyway. They exist outside of time and space, and if we join with them, we'll be able to communicate with each other without talking. *Imagine that.*' Their faces are blank. But I continue, feeling awkward. 'We'll be able to exchange our memories and our feelings. We'll be able to move through time and space freely, like they do. We'll be united. *The whole fucking human race.* And us, those of us here today – we'll be at the *forefront* of it. We'll be the first.'

My breath shudders as the energy surges through me once more. I realise my eyes have been squeezed shut, and I open them to see the group staring at me.

'Well, you were right about one thing,' Claire says, unfolding her arms. 'Sounds fucking nuts to me.'

I close my eyes again, raise my hand. I'm about to reach out and try and establish a link with the presence, when I hear Jamie's voice.

'Who the fuck is that?'

Opening my eyes again, I move my body so I can see where he's pointing. Two figures are making their way towards us. Because of the failing light, I can't make out their features, only their outlines, silhouetted against the murky sky. It's a man and a woman, I think.

As they get closer, Chris shouts out to them.

'Hello? Who is it?'

The man is a slight, scruffy bloke. There's something familiar about him. The woman is little and thin, and she stands behind him, just out of view. Gemma moves forward slightly, to get a better look.

'It's Barry Thompson,' she says, quietly.

Fuck, it is *actually happening*. I'm trembling, because now I understand: It's Barry, Barry is the dark force I was warned about. Everything is coming full circle.

Gaz, always so eager to throw his weight around, marches towards Barry as he looms closer.

'What the fuck do *you* want, yer fucking bag-head?'

He stops when Barry takes a knife from inside his jacket. Barry waves the knife about.

'Nice to see you, too, Gaz. Looking well, mate.'

Gemma shouts, 'Gaz, stop, don't do anything!'

'Listen to your lass,' Barry says.

Gaz looks at me, as if hoping for further instructions, but I feel frozen. He steps back and puts his arm around Gemma.

'What the fuck are you doing here?' Chris asks. 'I mean, how did you know we were even here?'

I come to.

'Don't listen to him,' I say, pointing at Barry. 'He's the fallen. They warned me about him. He's evil, he wants to prevent all this.'

Barry laughs.

'Evil? What a load of bollocks... but you're right, I'm here to stop what you're about to do, any way I can.'

'But why, Barry?' Gemma asks, pleading. 'I've experienced it. Steve's not making it up. It's beautiful. We can all be a part of it.'

Barry shakes his head, looking at her.

'You've bought into it already? That's a shame. A big, fucking shame. All of you here have been terrorised by this thing for the past few weeks, and now you're ready to give yourselves over to it? Just because *Steve* says so. Are you all fucking mental?'

'I can only see one nutter here, mate,' Gaz says.

Barry lets out a loud breath. He reaches an arm backwards.

'Time to meet my friends, darling,' he says in a soft voice. The woman that has been standing behind him steps forward. Her eyes are wide open. Her arms dangle from her shoulders like loose strands of cotton.

'What have you *done* to her?' Gemma asks.

'Me? *ME?* I've done fuck all to her, it was *them.* This is the glorious future that awaits the human race. This is what's waiting for you, and all the fuckers like you who go through with this. Look at her, she's a fucking zombie.'

Gemma screams *stop*, as Chris, Jamie and Gaz rush forward and tackle Barry.

Chris and Jamie flank him, grabbing his arms. Gaz forces him down to the ground and punches him. Gemma lurches forward and grabs Gaz's shoulders, while Claire seems rooted to the spot, her hands covering her eyes. Barry's companion stands mute and still, doing nothing at all.

It's all going wrong. This wasn't supposed to happen. I should have known that Barry would be drawn here. I feel helpless, and for the first time since the presence reached out to me, I feel alone, cut off from everything. Have I caused this?

I see Jamie and Chris step back, and that's when Chris says, 'Oh, bloody hell.'

He places his hands on his stomach, looking down. Blood gushes from the wound that must be underneath his fingers. He walks sideways, weaving like a boxer trying to stay on his feet. But he can't keep going, so he falls to his knees before flopping forward onto his face.

Gaz scrambles to his feet, leaving Barry on the floor. Gaz's hands are covered in blood, and he holds them out wide as he rushes over to Chris.

'Fucking hell mate. Oh, fucking hell mate,' Gaz mutters. He crouches next to Chris, grabs his shoulders and rolls him over onto his back. Blood gushes from the wound in Chris's gut. Gaz desperately grabs at it, trying to stem the flow. But it's not working.

I curl my hands up into fists, jab them into my eyes. *What have I done?*

Barry pushes himself up into a sitting position. His face is covered in blood and dirt. He screams at all of us.

'*Don't you understand?* Why do you think they use seeds? They *plant* themselves in our minds. In our fucking *minds!* They grow in our dreams, take over our memories and our imaginations. They consume them until all that's left is *that*.' He points at his girlfriend. 'She used to be Natalie, now she's just a fucking husk.'

Through the thickness of the dusk, I move closer to Chris, close enough to see his eyes flicker. He's starting to lose consciousness. Jamie kneels at the other side of him, opposite Gaz. He lightly slaps Chris's cheek.

'Chris,' he says. 'Hold on mate, hold on.'

Gemma is also on her knees, rocking back and forth, crying hysterically.

'We're the leaf and they're the caterpillar,' Barry continues, howling now. 'This isn't a *new dawn*, or *the future of the human race* or any of that shite. This is a *fucking invasion!*'

Gaz slowly gets to his feet. He bends over, reaches down, and rummages through the grass until he finds the knife. Calmly, he strides over to Barry.

'Shut up,' he says. Slowly, deliberately, he pushes the knife into Barry's abdomen.

Breathing hoarsely, Claire turns to face me. She grabs my arm. Her eyes are bulging, wild with fear. There's a small fleck of blood on her cheek.

'What's happening? What happens now?'

The low-frequency hum fills our ears, our heads. We're frightened.

A shaft of brilliant light fills the sky, bathing us all in in its vivid, electric-blue glow.

It's too late to change anything now, of course.

They're here, whoever they are.

Everything I can see, everything I can hear; everything I can feel – the world – shatters. Nothing but white is left in its place.

It comes into my consciousness that this is how it feels to be born.

Wrenched from time and space, our reality crumbles. My head – what was my head – floods with memories, with a multitude of sensations.

We are all fused together.

Our minds have converged into a unified consciousness. I am no longer an individual.

We are no longer human.

The last, singular, thought that runs through me – through us – is this:

What have I done?

THE BEGINNING

Acknowledgements

Thanks to Russel D McLean, without whom this book would have never developed beyond its first draft. And thanks to Nick Quantrill for making that connection.

Thanks to Wayne Leeming for his editorial input.

Thanks to Ray French, Peter Calder, Ben Edmunds and Jonathan Squirrell, and the rest of the University of Hull Creative Writing department for their feedback and notes.

Thanks to Leanne and Jude for their love, support and patience.

And thanks to Phil and Tracey Scott-Townsend and Wild Pressed Books for believing in this book, and for all the hard work they've put in to make it a reality.

And thank you to Mike Covell, Hull historian, for uncovering what is possibly the world's first UFO sighting, which was spotted over the Humber in 1801. The story made the national press in mid-2015, during one of my major rewrites of the text, so I took it as a sign and referenced it in the book.

About the Author

Joe Hakim lives and works in Hull.

This is his first novel.

CPSIA information can be obtained
at www.ICGtesting.com
Printed in the USA
LVHW111729300819
629529LV00003B/422/P